VIXEN OUTLAWS

Rolf Semprebon

2026, TWB Press
https://www.twbpress.com

Vixen Outlaws

Edited by Terry Wright

Cover Art by Terry Wright

ISBN: 978-1-967888-24-5

ACKNOWLEDGEMENTS

Though writing is a solitary act, this trilogy would not have been possible without the help and encouragement of many people. My thanks to KBOO FM, community radio station in Portland where I did radio theater for fifteen years and where the germ to this project originated. A big thanks to my writing critique groups, Portland Writers Workshop and The Critiquery, who had to endure earlier drafts of these books and who helped me refine my vision on it. Thanks to encouragement from writer friends: Patricia Horvath, Greg Donley, and Willy Vlautin and the writers at the various Shut Up & Write and Write More sessions in Portland. Greg was also a beta reader, so gets another big thanks, along with my other beta readers, EB Bruce, Tim Samsonite, and my brother, Jeff.

PART I: ESCAPE FROM PORTLAND

Chapter 1

Summer, 1880, Portland, Oregon

On the small stage, Rosa tunes out the yells and hoots of the drunken men. She knows they are out there, in the dark room, at the tables and the bar, with hungry eyes, but she's only aware of Varla Vixen on the stage next to her, and the plink of the upright piano beyond the cigar smoke as Tony caresses a playful vamp from the keys.

Why do I put up with this charade, she thinks, copying Varla's movements, swaying hips and torso while she unbuttons her blouse. I'm stripping for you, Varla, not these uncouth hicks and rubes, the dregs of Portland's North End. Let them look with eyes popping out of their heads and gaped drooling lips; they mean nothing to me, I am all yours, Varla Vixen. Even her stage name makes Rosa hot.

The North End, also known as White Chapel, is a sinkhole of crime and corruption, where every vice can be purchased for a price. It draws in farmer's sons, loggers, trappers, sailors, miners, thieves, and social misfits with the lure of lust and adventure on their minds. Every night some of them slink to the Final Frontier Saloon, to catch the nightly show, the Amazon Trio, the Big Bouncy Women.

At the far side of the stage, Blondie, the other member of the trio, giggles with enthusiasm as she jiggles her body ecstatically, egged on by the yells and whistles. Does her degradation arouse Varla? Blondie, born Loretta Blossom, a farmer's daughter in her mid-twenties, is a decade younger than Rosa or Varla.

The stage creaks and moans as the three women move to the music. Tony at the piano segues into a swanky grind, hitting the ivories with enough gusto to make the piano strings bleed. Varla shimmies and jiggles and the crowd goes wild. Rosa has her top off, and she swings it around in her hand, looking past the stage with contempt. She pretends she has a pair of rocks in the breast girdle prepared to launch them into the audience.

A man climbs to the stage, smug grin on his young face, encouraged by his drunk friends. An entitled asshole, spawn of the local elite. He reaches for Varla's breast. Her hand is quick as a bear's paw. A loud smack sends the young man flying off the stage. Rosa smiles at the commotion of his friends pulling him off the floor, and a bouncer hustles them out the door.

Varla acts like it's nothing and continues to dance. Tony plinks a swaggering shuffle from the upright. The sands in the large timer on top of the piano move down into the lower glass chamber. Thirty-five-minute topless show is all the audience gets. The sands move too slowly for Rosa, and perhaps too rapidly for Blondie, enjoying herself at the far end of the stage.

"Is this worth it?" Rosa asks, in the changing room behind the stage. "To pocket with these grab-paws?"

"Wish I smacked him harder," Varla replies. "Didn't even break his jaw."

"Putting up with these deadbeats and *gilipollas*," Rosa scowls. "We should vamoose from here."

"Come on," Blondie pipes up. "They're just out for a hoot. Why not enjoy it? Not like I have the assets of you and Varla. But they still throw money at me."

A knock on the door, and a moment later it creaks open and the tavern owner, Helios Turk, steps into the room. A big man with a sweaty face, he aims his eyes at the partially dressed Blondie before she turns her back on him.

Varla looks up from counting the bills. "You got the rest of our spondulix, Turk?"

Turk smiles, averting his eyes from Varla. "You ladies want to do a late show? Had a pair of dancers blow out. Make some extra cash?"

"Forget it, Turk." Varla shakes her head. "Not worth the time, and your bouncer needs to do a better job."

"That was regrettable but you handled it fine."

"Not our job to handle hand-grabby *pulpos*," Rosa snaps.

"I'm sorry. Some stupid kid. Won't happen again." A hurt look crosses his face. "Sure you won't do another show? I'll throw in an extra half-eagle from the till."

"Just pay what you owe," Varla replies.

"A half eagle for each of you? One more floor show?"

"Five dollars each?" Blondie whistles. "Whoo, you're desperate, Mr. He-loser Turkey."

"Worth more to see you squirm with desperation," Varla says. "The answer is no."

Rosa breathes a sigh of relief. Helios Turk shrugs and attempts another smile as he pulls some bills from his pocket. Varla grabs them from his hand. He turns, swaggers back into the noisy saloon, and shuts the door behind him.

"I can't believe you didn't take up his offer," Blondie says.

"Fuck him." Varla pulls on her black leather vest. "Had enough of his bullshit. He's got a full tavern out there because of us, and we scrape for the bills and coins thrown at us? Not like he needs money. His uncle Jim owns half the boarding houses in the North End. Makes a lot of money crimping and shanghai-ing."

It's true. Helios's uncle Jim runs several boarding houses. When drifters come to town, he lets them stay on credit and to pay off their debt, he sells them to whatever captain needs a crew. And ships always need a new crew in Portland. Soon as they dock, a runner from Jim Turk's boarding house arrives and convinces the crew of another ship with better pay. And the crew doesn't find out they've been had until they're back up the river.

The three women step out the back door and through an alleyway to the street. Varla is in black leather pants and black leather vest, unzipped halfway down in a V to reveal much of her chest, and she wears a boss-of-the-plains hat. Blondie is in a yellow skirt up to her knees, a blue blouse, and a flatter-topped gambler hat. Rosa wears brown breaches and a yellow blouse, unlike the others, buttoned to her neck, not revealing cleavage. Her hat is a cattleman style. All three wear black leather boots almost to their knees.

The sky is clear, the stars helping the feeble flicker of the street lamps to push away some of the darkness. A man kneels at the corner, puking into the gutter. Another urinates on a tree stump cut at chest height half a block farther. Laughter and yelling, drunk male voices waft from the nearby saloons and taverns.

"We should *vamos*," Rosa says.

"And what? find a different club?" Blondie asks. "Closer to downtown?"

"No. Out this *mierda* city." Rosa points to a small ditch that runs the length of the street, part of the intricate open-sewer system of Portland. "Where you don't smell shit and piss when you step outside."

"At least downtown they have boardwalks so you don't see it," Blondie remarks. "And the clubs have a better clientele, I bet."

"Still, it's us shaking our *culos* while some *bastardo* like Turk makes the real *dinero*, selling overpriced *chinguirito*," Rosa replies. "We should open our own saloon."

"No," Blondie says. "Too much responsibility."

"You'd want that?" Varla asks Rosa. "Be stuck like

that?"

"With you. Yes. Open it together. You and me, Varla. We are not getting younger."

"We'd need Blondie too."

"Why? If she doesn't want the responsibility?"

Blondie pipes in, "I didn't say I wouldn't help out,"

"You and I, Rosa, we can't own property in this damn state," Varla says. "White men only. It's enshrined in the Constitution. That's why we need her."

"Fine! She can be the front," Rosa grumbles.

Blondie smiles. "So you got to learn to like me, Rosa."

"It's something to think about," Varla says. "I'd rather try our luck on the road."

Rosa shakes her head. "Nothing out there. Bunch of hateful people." *Especially if you're a dark Mexican or half Asian*, Rosa thinks. She pulls out her favorite harmonica and begins to play as they walk. The harmonica takes her mind off things, and she even likes it when Blondie hums softly along.

They reach the edge of the North End, where the taverns and flop houses and opium dens give way to a swamp at one side and a desolate field of tree stumps at the other. The upper sails of a ship can be seen in the distance past the brush as it glides down the Willamette River to the docks in Portland or Albina, the city north on the east bank of the river.

"What about you, Blondie?" Varla asks. "You want to travel?"

"I don't know, Varla. I'll give it a thought."

"Think? That something you know how to do?" Rosa quips.

"At least I know what I want," Blondie says. "You don't know if you want to stay or go, Rosa. I think you like complaining for the sake of complaining."

To her chagrin, Rosa can't come up with a response, so she starts to play the harmonica again.

Chapter 2

The next morning, Varla and Rosa drink coffee at a table in front of a weathered shed. The tin coffee cups are attached to the wooden table by thin rusted chains, three feet in length. The old man comes out of the shed to refill their cups from the kettle. When Varla and Rosa are done, the cups will be washed in a bucket and set back on the table for the next customer.

"I have a lead," Varla says. "Might be good money."

"What kind of lead?" Rosa asks.

"Easy pickings. Waiting for the right person." Varla sips her coffee, her gaze intense on Rosa.

"That's what you said about the bank job."

"No banks. It's not even robbery, just money misplaced, waiting to be found."

"Really?" Rosa sips her coffee. "No one leaves *plata* lying around."

"Ramona and Lizzie told me about it."

"Ramona and Lizzie?" Rosa takes a deep breath to suppress a tear. Ramona and Lizzie died almost two years ago when the four of them attempted to rob a bank in Sante Fe; she and Varla barely escaped with their lives and no money. "I miss Ramona and Lizzie. They were real, not like that blond *churro*."

"Would've been our next job, Rosa. Ranch east of here. Old man lost his legs in a train accident. Won a big settlement from the railroad, but never spent any of the money. Ranch is still run down."

"An old *cojo*?"

"That's right." Varla smiles. "Old cripple. He's got two sons. One'll be gone, in college, and the younger son is a mental case. Couldn't be easier."

"Easy *dinero* like that, Varla, how you know someone hasn't nabbed it?"

"We don't until we try. Very few people know about it."

"How did Lizzie and Ramona find out?" Rosa finishes her coffee.

"That, I don't know."

"How you know it's not a whole lot of horse shit? *Espurio Mierda?*" Rosa asks.

Varla shrugs. "What we got to lose?"

"Where is this ranch?"

"Not quite sure. Ramona had said it's east of here."

"East of here?" Rosa laughs. "Whole *maldito* country east of here."

"Not that far. Oregon. Washington territory."

"Still a lot of places. A sliver in a haystack."

"The ranch is near an outpost, so that narrows it," Varla says.

"I don't like it, Varla."

"It might be quick money. You want to open a saloon? Or else we keep scrimping for money, showing our bodies to men for another year."

"*Si.* Bad as people are in this place, they are no better there in the wilderness. If I could go back to Guadalajara..." Rosa sighs. The only thing stopping her is an arrest warrant for the murder of a Generalissimo high up in the Mexican army. She fled the country ten years earlier, dyed her hair red, and renamed herself Rosa Rouge.

"With the three of us, it'd be a cinch," Varla says.

"Three of us? You mean Blondie?" Rosa spits out the name. "She part of the gang?"

"Why not? She's smarter and tougher than you think."

"Pah! We don't need her."

"She has her assets, Rosa."

"Assets." Rosa snorts derisively. "Eye candy, what she is. A *buena torta.*"

"Since when did you not cotton to attractive women, Rosa?"

"Eye-balling is one thing, but..." Rosa pauses.

Varla leans closer, her hand on Rosa's on the table, her face inches away. "What is it, Rosa? You liked her at first."

Rosa realizes her eyes are about to shed tears. Varla's hand comforts her. Looking into Varla's eyes, she feels something in her head; she doesn't want to lose Varla to the blonde whore. She senses herself slipping into Varla's eyes, the image of herself reflected in the retina, and for a moment she thinks she's Varla looking back out at herself.

Varla puts her lips to Rosa's ear. "Don't be jealous, Rosa. She may be pretty but she'll never equal you. You'll always be my favorite."

Rosa nods and lets herself be pulled to her feet and into a kiss. Varla's strong arms around her, pushing her into Varla's curvy body. She clings to Varla, not wanting to let go, even as she realizes the danger of the two of them showing their passion in public, even for a moment.

"Let's go," Varla says, pushing Rosa away. Varla walks to the shed. The man looks down at his percolator, nervously avoiding eye contact or even staring at her breasts like he did earlier when filling their cups. She drops a coin on the shelf of the shed. He nods a thanks.

As they step out in the street, a trio of men slowly walk past, staring at the two women, giving them the up-and-down.

"Mongrel trash," one mutters as they continue up the street.

"What was that?" Varla snaps and spins to face them.

"Varla, just let it be," Rosa hisses. "Not worth it, for these *fresa*."

"Fuck that." Varla starts toward the three men. They are young, barely past their teen years, with clean clothes and expensive boots and Stetsons and smug shaven faces. These aren't sailors or farm boys.

"Hey, you!" Varla calls out. "Big man in the middle. You wanna tell me that to my face?"

A couple of the men turn.

Varla stands at the center of the street with her hands on her hips and her legs spread apart.

"Go back where you came from." The one in the middle is the alpha, with a slightly larger hat and a larger brass belt buckle. Etched in the buckle is an image of an eagle with a rifle in one talon and a laurel in the other. He's slightly shorter and stockier than the other two, with short blond hair and blue eyes. "We don't talk to prostitutes."

"Because they laugh at your lame little dick?"

"I don't have to take that from your shit mouth, mongrel whore." The man steps forward, fists clenched.

"Bobby, maybe we shouldn't..." says another, with frizzy brown hair and a hint of facial fuzz.

"Shut up, Derry," the third man says, pulling on his dark goatee.

"No one says that about me," grumbles the front man. "'Specially not that..." He spits out a racial epithet and points at Varla.

"That's right," the man with the goatee says. "Can't let her get away with that, Bobby."

"Varla, what the hell?" Rosa says quietly so the men can't hear.

"I said it about you, you little piece of shit," Varla says to the one named Bobby, a smile on her face. "What you going to do about it, big boy?"

"She's crazy," the man with brown curly hair says. "Maybe escaped from the lunatic asylum across the river."

"She's asking for it, Bobby," the third man says. "She can't talk to us that way."

"You want to apologize, mongrel whore?" Bobby pulls out a knife.

Varla holds her ground. "I don't apologize to pathetic little turds like you."

"Let's just leave, Bobby."

"No. Don't listen to Derry. Teach her a lesson. Wipe that smart mouth off her face."

"Yeah? You snot-nosed spoiled little assholes think you can teach me anything?" Varla stands in the center of the road.

Two of the men advance.

The one named Derry shakes in panic. "I best get help." He begins to run up the road. Run away in fear.

Smart kid, smarter than his friends. Rosa smirks.

"Get the street cleaners to swab up her remains," Bobby says.

"Damn it, Varla! Let it go!" Rosa knows it's too late. The two men are ten feet away from Varla. The one named Bobby advances on her with the knife and the other moves around to the side of her. Beneath the tight black leather, the muscles in Varla's arms and thighs ripple with tension. Rosa turns and takes several steps away, glancing around. No one is watching. The sounds of a scuffle, booted feet clatter on dirt, Varla's grunt and a male groan, a whack as a rigid hand hits flesh, the sound of the knife sinking into wetness, and an agonized scream cut off to a gurgle by another slash to the neck. A second later a body thumps to the ground.

Silence, broken by: "Oh my god! You killed him!"

"You're the one holding the knife," Varla taunts.

A name comes into Rosa's head. Bobby Lappeus. She remembers his picture from the newspapers. The son of the police chief. Rosa turns to look. Varla faces one of the men, two abstract shapes in the shadows; the morning sun obscured by some tall firs at the side of the road. In between them, the other man is on the ground with blood spurting up from his neck. For twenty seconds they stand and stare at each other. The man has a knife, but he's frozen.

"You just stabbed your buddy," Varla says. "You see that?"

The man drops the knife, mumbles unintelligibly, and

stumbles backward a dozen steps. He turns and flees.

"Varla!" Rosa steps closer. "Let's *vamos*."

"Just need to roll him," Varla replies.

Rosa glances around. A man in a ragged poncho on a donkey comes up the side street.

"Varla, hurry!"

Varla stands up with a wallet in her paw, which she drops into her cleavage as she rushes to Rosa. Together they walk rapidly away from the body on the ground. The old man on the donkey doesn't seem to notice them. They are half a block farther when a shout arises behind them. Another half block and they reach B Street, where bar owners have begun to open their taverns and arrivals stagger up the street from the docks.

"You've done it now, Varla. You know who that was?"

"He's nobody now. Just a corpse." Varla laughs.

"That kid? The police chief's son."

"Which one?" Varla asks. "The one I killed?"

"I don't know and we can't go back to check."

"What can I say, Rosa? Asshole had it coming." They continue to walk quickly while behind they hear distant shouts and a police whistle. "Maybe I should have killed the other one too."

"Yes. Kill them all. The one that ran away. You're *loco,* do shit like that. Will the other one talk or did you...?"

"He shouldn't talk. I got into his head," Varla says.

"That fast?" Rosa asks.

"The shock of the stabbing made it easy."

Rosa shakes her head. She has no idea how Varla does it, the ability to stare past the eyes and into the mind, where she can cloud it, twist memories into pretzels, simply by staring into someone's eyes. It was a skill akin to hypnotism or mesmerism that Varla's father had taught her when she was young, a skill her father brought from Japan, called *kanpa-maindo*.

"Couldn't help yourself, could you?" Rosa asks. "We

can't stay here."

Varla grins. "Looks like that kid made the decision for us. We hotfoot out of town for a week or two until this blows over."

"Two weeks? His dad was boss cop. Who knows who the other one's dad is. This won't blow over in two weeks."

"Two weeks? Two years? We'll tell Blondie we're headed out." Varla says this casually as they reach the back alley off of B Street to a rickety wooden staircase up to the rooms where they are staying.

Chapter 3

In the room, "What do you think, Blondie?" Varla asks.

"Where're we going?" Blondie reclines in an armchair. She's wearing a thin cotton shift. "San Francisco or back east? Not many choices unless'n we want to live in the boondocks, and I don't cotton leaving town for the boondocks."

"Come on, Blondie." Varla crosses the room to face her. "You'll like the guys in the wilderness. Rugged men, not the shit that gets dredged up here every night."

"Who cares, you come or not?" Rosa says. "We split it two ways if you don't." Behind the haze of ganja smoke, Rosa leans over to pass the cigarette to Blondie. "We score big, instead of night after night, earning a pittance dancing for *varos*."

Blondie takes a hit of the cannabis. "What is this big money scheme?"

"We'll tell you when we're out of town. Stay, we won't tell you at all."

"We ride in an hour," Varla adds. "Gone a few days, maybe a week. Then we return, much richer."

"Really?" Blondie likes performing, showing her stuff off to the men; at the same time she wants to be with her two friends. She looks up at Varla standing over her. Like the toxins in the cat's claws that turn folks into its slaves, Varla has that same power with her eyes, the skill of *kanpa-maindo*, which she told them in Japanese means penetration-mind, where one's mind slips out of the boundaries of one's head and into another. She knows Varla is using it on her and she doesn't resist.

Of course she'll go with them, just for the thrill of the ride. Even if Varla's money scheme is a rumor or a hoax, a boondoggle or a mystery long-since solved or a situation exaggerated beyond comprehension. It will be fun, and she likes the feel of her horse, Chillins, between her legs.

"Count me in, even if it's just to piss off Rosa." Blondie hurries to pack her saddle bags.

An hour later the three women head to the docks, Varla on her black steed Storm, Rosa on a roan named Rusty, and Blondie on Chillins, her light-dapple mare. Men's heads twist as the trio trots past. The ferry at Stark Street to East Portland has begun to board as the hooves clatter and clop onto the dock.

The fare collector is a small greasy man in a bowler and yellowish shirt. He stares at them as they reach the gangplank.

"Three." Varla holds up three fingers.

The fare collector glances over at the sign posted at the rail near the gangplank:

Foot passengers: 12 cents.
Man on horseback or mule: 25 cents.
Wagon and one horse: 37 cents.
Wagon and two horses 50 cents.
Hogs and sheep: 3 cents a piece.

"That'll be forty cents each," he says.

"Forty cents!" Varla points to the sign. "It says two bits, you hornswoggler."

"Rules are rules. Two bits is a man on horseback. Don't say nothing about women on horseback."

"Then you should let us ride for nothing."

"Six bits all we're paying you, *hombrecito*," Rosa adds. "Unless you want trouble."

"Bet you don't treat high society dames this way," Blondie remarks.

"Let 'em on!" yells a laborer from the rail. "Let 'em on!" a couple of other men join in.

"Out of the way and let us on." Varla throws some coins at the fare collector's feet. "You're holding up everything."

Flustered, the man scrabbles for the coins while the three women on their horses trot the gangway to board. Even the few women on the ferry, a wife with her husband and a couple of nurses in white uniforms, stare at them. Blondie surveys the passengers, smiling to a couple of the men with ripped muscles beneath ragged shirts.

"I'll be glad when they finally build a bridge across this river," Varla says, loud enough for the glowering ferryman to hear. "No longer get harassed, and it'll put these clowns out of business."

"You have to cause a scene," Rosa whispers to Varla. "Everyone is staring at us."

"They'd notice anyway, most of them," Blondie says. Unlike Rosa, she doesn't mind the leers of the laborers and farmers, the way their mouths gape open, drool falling off a lip, another rubbing his tongue along his teeth, while others look down at the deck, afraid to even look. Unlike Rosa, Blondie feels power over these men, their desire, a tool to be flirted with and used. Let them look. If she'd been alone, a few would have whistled, one or two would have sauntered up to spark a conversation, but the three of them on horseback intimidate the men.

"They wouldn't stare if you learned how to dress," Rosa says to Blondie.

"You should loosen up, Rosa. Undo the top few buttons. Show a little of that nice cleavage."

"Never," Rosa scoffs. "*Nunca.*"

"You don't have to. They'll stare anyway."

"And you like it?" Rosa asks.

"Fine with me," Blondie replies. "It's a free country."

"It's demeaning."

"Varla doesn't mind. She's showing more cleavage than me. She's got more to show."

Rosa frowns, unable to come up with a comeback.

"Blondie is right," Varla says, looking out from the

shadow of her black leather "Boss of the Plains" hat. "Let them stare. All they'll remember is this." She pats her ample bosom. "Not our faces. Not even the color of our hair."

"You think so?" Glancing around, Rosa notices the men looking up, but not as high as their necks. "I still don't like it."

The ferry arrives in East Portland, at the L Street dock. As soon as the three women disembark, they urge their horses into a canter, hooves pounding loudly in a trio of triple beats against the wooden planking of the street over the swampland into downtown East Portland. The horses kick up dust on the street. At the laughter of the three women, faces look up, men freeze mid-motion while loading sacks into wagons, others on the street stop in their tracks to stare as the women on horseback stride by. Soon the houses become scarce, and they slow to a trot, riding past croplands and forests. Rosa pulls out her harmonica and begins a tune, playing off the sounds of birds and the clip-clop of their horses' hooves. Even though they've slowed their pace, the excitement pulses through Blondie, following the other two into an unknown adventure.

Chapter 4

Lindy Sue Hawthorne and Tommy Mitchell are on the swing on the porch of her father's house in East Portland.

"I wish I could go, Tommy," Lindy Sue says.

"I want you to come with me," Tommy responds.

They hold hands as the afternoon sun flashes through the foliage. Tommy has plans to leave for a few days. His father wants him to check out a recently acquired ranch in eastern Clackamas County.

"Since I was three, I've never been farther than Salem." Her heart races as she thinks about the wild country beyond the city. "Will it be safe?"

"With me protecting you, it sure will." He flexes his fist to show off his firm muscle. "Good to get away from the swamps. East Portland is all swamp and your dad's nut house."

At the mention of her father, Lindy Sue's enthusiasm flags. "I don't know if my dad'll let me go."

"You're nineteen. Old enough to make your own choices. I'll talk to your dad. And your mom."

"She's not my mother. I don't care what she thinks." Lindy Sue's mother died when she was born, her father remarried, and she now has two much-younger stepsisters. The idea of riding out of town, away from them on an adventure with Tommy, even for a couple days, seems a fantasy. Tommy, tall and muscular, with handsome round face and large blue eyes, was easy to imagine as a prince in a fairy tale, and every day she thinks she's more in love with him. But she doesn't know if she can go.

Two days later, her father leaves a note to her and wants her to come to his office to talk to him during his lunch. She looks at the note in the parlor as EC, her stepmother, stands in the doorway.

Trim and glamorous, but with a scowl etched on her face whenever she looks at Lindy Sue, EC mutters, “You’re in some kind of trouble, Lindy Sue.”

Her father, Doctor JC Hawthorne, works long hours at the asylum he owns, the Oregon Hospital for the Insane. One of the few insane asylums on the West Coast, it is also one of the best in the country. The hospital is on Twelfth Street, only a dozen blocks from where they live. An unfamiliar trepidation creeps into Lindy Sue as she enters the gates.

The admittance attendant waves her in. “Howdy, Lindy Sue.”

Behind a large wooden desk, Dr. JC Hawthorne glances up at the sound of her footsteps on the tile floor. His inner office is the size of a small dining room, with several padded armchairs and walls of shelves filled with thick reference volumes. At one corner, a restraining chair with arm and leg straps. Lindy Sue and her best friend Maggie used to love to sit in it when they were seven or eight.

“Lindy Sue, sit down.” JC Hawthorne pushes papers into a binder and looks at her, one hand pulling on his beard. “I’m glad you’re here.”

Lindy Sue pulls the chair closer to his desk before she sits. “What is it, Daddy?”

The room is silent. They look at each other. The cords in his neck move, as if he’s trying to think of how to get out the words he wants to tell her.

“Did I do something wrong?”

“No. Not at all.”

“Is this about Tommy?”

“Tommy Mitchell. Yes.” He gives her a faint smile. “The lad came to see me yesterday late afternoon.”

“He wants me to travel with him.”

“Yes. That’s why he came to talk to me.”

“I suppose you don’t want me to go.”

"You're no longer a child. I had a nice conversation with Tommy. A serious lad, which surprised me, given his father. And quite charming. You like this boy?"

"Very much." She nods.

"You're now a young woman...with urges and needs. There's some evidence that suppression of natural urges leads to a deformed psychosis. Have you been having..." he looks down at the folder in front of him, "sexual urges?"

"Daddy." She giggles nervously and feels her face get hot.

"This boy I think would make a good husband. His family has status, even if his dad was recently embroiled in scandal. Do you want to go with him on this trip?"

"If you don't think it's a good idea, I don't—"

"That's not what I asked. Do you want to go?"

She looks at him. "Yes."

"You like this boy?"

"Very much."

"I think you should go. It'd be good for you."

"You're letting me go?" She shakes with a tremor of joy and surprise.

"But I want precautions. No accidents unless he intends to wed. That may very well be his intention."

"You think so?" She has thought so too.

"That's why I want you to have these." He opens the top desk drawer, slides away some cards and pencils, pulls out a small yellow tin, and slides it across the desk to her. "You won't believe how hard it is to get these, even for a doctor like me, because of that Comstock fool."

She picks up the tin, confused. Opens it and closes it again, not sure what she's looking at, pieces of brown rubber shaped like deflated fingers, and notices the wording on the side of the tin: "Three fine fit prophylactics."

"Instructions inside," he says. "I want you to have a good time, Lindy Sue. But I don't want any unintentional consequences."

She suppresses a nervous giggle and pushes the tin deep into her purse. Walking out of the asylum, past patients and doctors, she thinks about her father's words, that Tommy might propose marriage, and how she had hoped for that very thing. Her best friend Maggie, who is also Tommy's younger sister, is getting married to Tommy's best friend Handy Doyle. Ever since receiving an engagement ring from Handy, Maggie liked to parade it in front of Lindy Sue's eyes, a gold band embedded with three small diamonds. If anything, Tommy proposing to her would take away the jealousy she harbored for Maggie. Maggie and Handy planned to wed in the early autumn, and she thinks, maybe she and Tommy can wed the same day, a joint wedding.

Chapter 5

Lindy Sue wakes up anxiously and early on the morning of the journey. Her stepsisters, Louise and Catharine, are still asleep, and her father is finishing his coffee and preparing to depart for work, like every morning, leaving at sunrise and coming home after the dinner hour.

She pours herself a cup of coffee from the silver decanter and stirs in some cream. Her father mumbles a "morning, Lindy Sue," no mention of Tommy or the trip, but his mind, as usual, is preoccupied with hospital business, whether it's patients or administration. He puts on his topcoat and hat and hurries out the door.

Lindy Sue has her saddlebags, packed for three days, out on the front porch. She puts on a red and blue silk bonnet, walks out with her coffee cup, and sits in a wicker chair.

Her stepmother, EC, steps out on the porch. "So you're riding out with the Mitchell boy this morning?"

"Uh-huh."

"I suppose that's a good thing. At nineteen, you aren't getting any younger, and prospects will be fewer and fewer. And he's the son of a United States Senator, though a disgraced one at that. Reckon it's the best chance you have, Lindy Sue, so don't mess it up."

EC Hawthorne walks back into the house. Lindy Sue thinks her stepmother will be all too glad to be rid of her as if she's detritus from her father's previous marriage.

Tommy rides in through the gate and up to the porch. "You ready?"

She points to his horse, much larger than the one he usually rode. "That's not Oatsy."

"No. Dad's letting me take Dagger instead. He's an

Appaloosa. Isn't he magnificent?"

"He's a big horse."

"Big and fast. I want to get used to him so I can run him at the rodeo games in two weeks."

"But what about Oatsy? Oatsy will feel rejected."

"Horses're dumb brutes, Lindy Sue. Oatsy won't care, and with Dagger, I've a chance to win the barrel run."

"Horses have feelings too." She grabs the saddle bags and walks over to where her mare, Annabelle, is hitched.

They ride out of town along a hilly trail south and east, along the edges of the mountain and down into a valley through a lush forest. When the sun is high, the foliage overhead keeps them and the horses cool.

"So why'd you break up with Jennifer Durham?" Lindy Sue asks.

"She broke up with me. She was being stupid."

"What do you mean?"

"When the paper ran that stuff about my dad. I guess her parents don't like him."

"Is it true your dad deserted a wife and three young children in Pennsylvania?"

"Don't want to talk about my dad," he mutters.

They ride for a minute. She breathes in the bracing aroma of cedar. "My dad said it's human nature, Tommy. He doesn't hold it against your dad."

"Your dad, I don't know how he does it. All day with crazy people."

"He doesn't like calling them that."

"Call 'em what you want. That don't change what they are."

"He's like any other doctor, Tommy. Trying to cure sickness."

"I don't know. I think hanging out with loonies would make one loony, too."

"I don't want to talk about that, Tommy." Ahead the trail thins as it winds through the woods and they can no longer ride side by side, which ends the conversation, while various birds twitter and coo from the branches above them.

Tommy's father, John Mitchell, was a US Senator before the Oregonian newspaper revealed he was a polygamist, with another wife in Pennsylvania. Tommy had told her it was all crazy things his dad did when he was too young to know better, and the paper made most of it up, but she wants to be careful, to make sure she and Tommy don't do crazy things while they're too young to know better.

Chapter 6

Tommy calls out, "You hungry?"

"Yes," Lindy Sue replies. They've ridden five hours along hilly trails through woods, and are now in a dry open range of scrubby bushes and smaller trees and fields of sagebrush and fescue, south and east of Mount Hood. She's tired and hungry and parched.

"Gruber's Outpost is up ahead." He points. "We'll eat, then another hour to go."

"We're not staying in Grubers?"

"No. The ranch."

As they round a hilltop, the outpost falls into view below them, a large two-floor L-shaped structure with the entrance at the crotch, and a few cabins visible on the wooded hill overlooking. Tommy hitches the horses and leads her into the main room, a large open area with a fifteen-foot-long wooden table at the center, several smaller wooden tables arranged at the edges, and a bar. Past the bar is an open kitchen. Behind the center of the bar, posted on a horizontal slab of wood are the red-painted words:

No Cussing
No Yelling
No Fighting
No Immorality
No Music
3 Drink Max Per Customer

A few men with thick beards drink ale or liquor at the bar. Tommy orders two bowls of chili from the old woman at the counter and, glancing around, takes Lindy Sue's hand and guides her to the end of the long table across from where another young couple is seated.

"Mind we sit here?" Tommy asks.

"Not at all," the man says with a friendly smile. He's clean-shaven, in a starch-white button shirt and tie. The woman has a lacy white dress and a colorful bonnet on her head. The couple introduces themselves as Wilfred and Althea.

"You two headed to Portland?" Wilfred asks.

"No. We stay near here for a couple nights. Then back to East Portland where we live."

"You're eloping?" Althea asks with a mischievous smile. She looks at them with the bluest eyes Lindy Sue has ever seen.

"No." Lindy Sue, blushing, glances at Tommy and back at the couple. "Nothing like that."

Wilfred laughs. "We don't make judgments. We live south of here, in New Era Valley."

"New Era? Part of that church?" Tommy asks.

"Yes. You heard of us?"

"Uh huh," Tommy murmurs, his lips tight.

"I heard of that church, but I know nothing about it," Lindy Sue says.

"We welcome visitors and new members to our community," Wilfred replies. "If you two are starting out in life, you might check us out."

"We're a spiritual community," Althea adds. "We live a wholesome, fulfilled life, where everyone helps everyone. We follow the teachings of Jesus, not the dictates of the Pope or a Baptist minister. We're not bound by the rules of the Christian church. We seek answers from all faiths."

"But you believe in Jesus?" Lindy Sue asks, confused. "You read the Bible?"

Althea smiles warmly. "The teachings of Jesus, yes. But we don't limit ourselves to one doctrine. We believe everyone has their own path to enlightenment. Our farming community is only an hour-half ride south of here."

"Huh? Sounds interesting." Lindy Sue doesn't know what to make of it, these spiritualists, but the couple seem confident and happy, two things she feels she lacks. She looks over at Tommy. "Should we go there?"

"We already have a place to go," Tommy says. Two bowls of chili and a plate of bread are set down in front of Tommy and Lindy Sue.

"A place is not always a destination," Wilfred replies. "But maybe later, next time you're out this way?"

"I think not." Tommy abruptly stands, grabbing his bowl of chili and the plate of bread. "Lindy Sue, let's eat at the other end of the table."

"I'm sorry, Wilfred, Althea." Lindy Sue rises slowly from the table. "It was nice meeting you, and New Era Valley sounds like an Eden."

"A bit like that," Althea says. "A place where men and women are equal. Men don't boss women around."

"Lindy Sue!" Tommy barks from a dozen feet away.

Reluctantly, Lindy Sue picks up her bowl of chili and glass of water and follows him to the far end of the table. She's seen what Tommy is like when he gets mad, seen him almost get in fights with people he deemed inferior, and she doesn't want him to create a scene.

"Tommy? Why were you so rude to them?"

"My dad told me all about them. It's a cult. Nudists, socialists, anti-capitalists."

"But they seem like good people."

"My dad says they're dangerous. To be avoided. Not real Christians. They corrupt their faith with paganism."

She shrugs. They finish their meal in silence and get back on their horses.

On the trail to the ranch, a pair of men on horseback head toward them. One is middle-aged, in a black wide-brimmed fedora, a vest, and bow tie over his white shirt, and he has guns holstered at both hips and a rifle barrel poking upward behind his head. His companion is much younger, perhaps the same age as Lindy Sue, in a similar white button shirt and fedora. He has a peach fuzz beard and frizzy brown hair that flows out the sides of his fedora, and he also has a holstered gun. They both have metal badges on their chests.

"Tommy?" she whispers nervously.

"I think it's okay," he says. "Some kind of law, I reckon." They stop and wait for the men to approach. As the men near, Lindy Sue makes out the badges: Pinkerton National Detective Agency.

"Whoa, there!" The older man holds up his hand from ten yards away. Beneath his blond beard, his face is ravaged by the elements, wrinkled and red. His eyes are sharp as he looks from Tommy to Lindy Sue and then focuses back on Tommy, his mouth in a tight, emotionless sneer.

The younger man, a few feet behind the other and to his left, looks toward Lindy Sue until he catches her eye, and then he flinches down at the ground. He slowly looks again at Lindy Sue. He has a round face and sweet, kind of hurt eyes. He's as tall as Tommy but slender. His gaze is steady on her; she feels herself get hot inside, as she tells herself to look away. He is blushing, she realizes, same as her.

He probably notices she doesn't have a ring. He'd probably lose to Tommy in a fight, a funny thought that pops into her mind while she...ogles him.

She isn't sure what is up with Tommy and this trip, would he propose to her or dump her? A final farewell tour or where their hearts get sealed? Perhaps Tommy doesn't know either. This is their test. And maybe this young man is part of the test, as she smiles and he smiles back and even dips his head to acknowledge her. He glances at her feet and back up to her face to slowly meet her eyes, and she feels guilty she's doing it behind Tommy's back, literally behind his back while he talks to the older Pinkerton.

"You the owner of yonder ranch?" the older Pinkerton asks with a southern drawl.

"My father is," Tommy replies. "There a problem, sir?"

“We’re talking to people in these parts. Looking for a missing girl.” The Pinkerton pulls a piece of yellowed paper out of his vest pocket and unfolds it to show them a drawing of a young woman’s face, bisected by the fold creases. “Name is Bethany Tremain. Wondering if you seen her.”

“No, not hide nor hair,” Tommy replies. “We just arrived.”

The Pinkerton nods and glances toward Lindy Sue for a second before looking back at Tommy. “You be careful. She same age as that one. Frail and wispy too.”

“We’re only staying a couple nights, sir. I do hope you find her, sir.”

“Don’t know if we will. Been missing near four months. Last seen at Gruber’s Outpost.”

“We just came from there, sir.”

“Very well then. What are your names?”

“Mine is Tommy Mitchell and that there is Lindy Sue Hawthorne.”

“You two have a good afternoon.”

“You, too. And good luck, sir.”

The older Pinkerton turns to the younger. “Let’s go, Derry.”

Derry. Lindy Sue repeats that name in her head. She glances over her back to see him vanish down the trail while she follows Tommy. She begins to worry about what the older Pinkerton said as they continue to the ranch.

“Maybe we shouldn’t stay here, Tommy. We could ride home.”

“Too late for that,” Tommy says. “Wouldn’t get back until after dark.”

“Or stay at the Outpost.” After she says it, she regrets it. No, that’s the last place they saw the missing girl.

“Don’t busy your head with that stuff, Lindy Sue. It happened four months ago. The guilty are long gone.”

“I guess you’re right, Tommy.” She shudders. “Who’d do such an awful thing?”

"Injuns. Bandits. Or Mormons. They kidnap young girls to add to their wives. Who knows, girl like that."

"Girl like what?" The Pinkerton said the girl was the same age as her.

"Maybe the girl ran off, eloped with some guy."

"Like you and me?"

"No. Anything we do'll be proper. We don't get that freedom, with our fathers and their reputations. We have to uphold standards that mean nothing to others."

As if Tommy's father still has a reputation, now that he'd lost his US Senate seat, exposed as a bigamist.

"But that girl," Lindy Sue says. "Her parents are probably important people too."

"Why you say that?" Tommy asks.

"Someone's paying the Pinkertons. They don't work for free."

Chapter 7

Back on the trail with the Pinkertons: "What ta yawl make of that pair, Flanders?" Willard Stark asks in his gravelly drawl as they ride their horses at a leisurely trot away from the young couple they've just questioned.

Derry Flanders looks over his shoulder. Lindy Sue and the man on their horses are no longer in sight. "I don't know, sir. The girl...she looked cute."

"Sue Hawthorne?" A small smile breaks on Willard's weathered face.

"Lindy Sue Hawthorne, what they said, sir."

"Lindy Sue Hawthorne. And Thomas Mitchell. Said his dad owned the ranch."

"I think his dad's the senator, sir. The one in all the papers."

"Yeah," Willard replies. "Reckon you're right. A thorough scoundrel, that one. And the son philandering with the good doctor's daughter."

"You think the son might be..." Derry has an idea in his head that Thomas Mitchell is the perpetrator, having kidnapped the missing girl, Bethany Tremain, and now luring Lindy Sue Hawthorne to a remote place to rape and murder her, too. Derry imagines himself riding to the rescue, shooting the fiend and saving Lindy Sue, and the two of them trotting into a beautiful sunset like in one of the magazine serials he reads.

"Thomas Mitchell, a scoundrel?" Willard muses. "Reckon so. A thorough one at that, just like his dad."

"But we let him get away. What if he harms Lindy Sue?"

"A scoundrel, yes. But not a killer. Only thing he'll

murder is that girl's maidenhood." Willard chortles, the sound of a crow coughing. "Reckon we'll check on who was living in that ranch four months ago before Mitchell got his talons on it."

"You think they might've done it?" Derry asks.

"Prob'ly not. That's what distinguishes the Agency from local law. Due diligence. Follow every lead. You got to learn that, Derry, if you want a career with the Pinkertons."

"Yes, sir." Derry sees the main road through the trees up ahead. They ride in silence for a minute and turn toward Gruber's Outpost.

Willard clears his throat. "You never told me what happened when that kid got stabbed. Friend of yours, was he?"

"Jimmy Montgomery," Derry replies. "Yes."

"What's the story?"

"Not sure."

"But you were there."

"Bobby and Jimmy were talking to a woman," Derry says. "I wanted nothing to do with it. Next thing Jimmy's dead, stabbed in the gut and the throat."

"The Lappeus kid did it, didn't he?" Willard says.

Derry shakes his head. "Bobby? Why would Bobby?"

"Rumor they were fighting over the girl. Not that Police Chief Lappeus would arrest his own kin."

"Bobby said it was a gang. Too many of them, he had to run."

"And strangely his knife ended up in the other boy's gut?" Willard guffaws loudly. "Don't take Pinkerton experience to figure out what happened."

"Bobby had no reason to stab Jimmy. We're all good friends."

"A mess of trouble," Willard muses. "You lucky you're out here, not in Portland. A cesspool, what it is."

"I guess so. I miss Portland but..." Derry thinks of

Jimmy Montgomery, slain several days earlier. He still can't believe Jimmy is dead, or understand how it happened. One moment Jimmy and Bobby were arguing with that woman, the next Jimmy was on the ground with blood gushing from his belly and his neck, and Bobby and the woman faced off with each other.

Derry watched from a window in a tall thin telegraph tower, where he'd run to when the woman advanced on Bobby and Jimmy. But all he saw was Bobby and the woman facing off, Jimmy on the ground between them. Bobby dropped the knife and dashed away. The woman stooped over Jimmy and then hurried to where her companion stood a block farther. Meanwhile, Bobby was headed down the street near the tower, and Derry raced down the steps to confront him.

"Bobby, what happened?"

"I don't know. She stabbed Jimmy." Bobby shook his head. The incident had drained Bobby of his cocky confidence and smugness. He seemed broken inside.

"But how'd she get your knife?" Derry asked, though realizing he never saw the woman hold the knife.

"The others, with her. Jimmy and I were outnumbered when you ran away."

"Others? That other woman?"

"No, Sailors. Mongrels, I think, like the women."

"I didn't see them, Bobby."

"Listen, Derry. We can't say anything about this to anyone. Can't make it look like we were cowards."

"But what really happened? How'd she stab Jimmy?"

"I can't talk about it," Bobby snaps. "We got to get our stories straight. You ran away. You saw nothing. I ran too. Neither of us saw what happened. We got to tell them that."

Derry didn't know what to think. How could the woman grab Bobby's knife? Or perhaps there's another story, perhaps Bobby killed Jimmy fighting over the woman. He had seen them fight over a woman before, but not when

Bobby was holding a knife. And the story with the gang, from the tower Derry saw nothing like this, but Bobby insisted it was true and got angry at him for not trusting Bobby.

A bunch of bad stories rattled Derry's head, and he is still wrenched with guilt because he ran away before it happened. Maybe things would've gone different if he stayed, maybe he'd know what happened, maybe he'd help stop it, diffuse the anger between Bobby and Jimmy.

The police chief, Bobby's father, disliked Derry ever since Derry joined the Pinkerton Agency, or so Derry heard from Bobby. "Damn Pinkers elbowing into our business," Bobby said, imitating his father's gruff voice. Jimmy's uncle, a wealthy railroad baron, wanted answers from the police chief, and was suspicious of both Bobby and Derry, since he knew Jimmy had been with them in the North End.

Derry's father thought it best Derry not stay in Portland, given the situation, and he knew Derry was suffering from his friend's death. To get Derry out of Portland, strings were pulled with the Pinkertons to get Derry assigned out of town. That's how Derry came to be riding alongside Willard Stark, in the thankless search for the missing girl, Bethany Tremain.

Chapter 8

An hour later, Derry and Willard are back in the main room of Gruber's Outpost, at one of the small tables near a wall. The dinner hour hasn't set in yet, and the room is mostly empty. Willard has a map spread out across the entire table.

"Only a few more places to check out," Willard says, making a couple marks on the map.

"You think we'll find her?" Derry asks.

"Most likely not, unless she's down here, joined the cult." Willard points to an area of the map marked "New Era." "She might not be meant to be found. Might be buried in an unmarked grave out in the unknown. We do what we can, write up a report, get paid."

"Whether she's found or not?"

"Far more pay if we find her alive." Willard takes a sip of his beer. "But gone for four months, that's doubtful."

No one knew Bethany Tremain was missing until the Grubers finally opened her room because they needed it for the summer season and all her stuff was still there, including personal effects. No one knew where she went. The Grubers contacted her family, and now Willard and Derry are on the case.

Since beginning the investigation a few days ago, they've learned another girl, eighteen-year-old Abby Appleby, had been missing a year before Bethany but since Abby's parents are poor farmers, Abby is a footnote to the case.

"Tomorrow we'll check this ranch over here by itself." Willard points to the map. "And we'll go down here the days after."

"New Era Valley?"

"Yeah." Willard grits his teeth. "Those freaks. Don't trust them at all."

Derry glances up to see a short fat man amble toward them. "Here comes Elber Gruber," he whispers. Elber, though in his forties, resembles a large adolescent with his huge round head and big smile. Whereas Elber's parents, who own the outpost, are tight-lipped and circumspect, Elber is garrulous.

"How goes the search for the little girl?" Elber asks.

"Almost done in these parts, I reckon," Willard replies. "Just got to check out New Era Valley and one more homestead." He looks down at the map. "The Pitts ranch. Sixteen miles east-northeast of here."

"I know them," Elber says excitedly. "They come every Sunday to pick up supplies."

"What you know about them?"

Elber leans over the table, voice quiet and a hand over his mouth. "Old man Pitts, he's in a wheelchair. Ornery old guy. Don't have much to do with other people."

"He's a cripple?" Willard asks.

"Yes. Lives there with his retard son." Elber glances over at his mother working behind the bar.

Willard nods. "I suppose we don't need to bother him yet. A poor cripple like that, probably don't get out much to see anything."

Elber leans in closer to the two seated men. "Want to know how he became cripple? It was a train accident. Train cut off his legs."

"Elber?" The mother's voice pierces the room.

"Train accident, you say?" Willard's eyes narrow on Elber.

"I hope you find her," Elber says. "I best get back to work." Elber waddles toward his mother.

Willard stares at the map silently, deep in thought. Derry listens to Elber's footsteps on the floor.

"Elber!" The mother sounds cross. "How many times

we tell you not to be spreading stories that shouldn't be told."

"I wasn't telling anything, mommy. Honest I wasn't."

The door clatters open and some men come in talking loudly, drowning the voices of Elber and his mother.

Derry glances around, to see that Elber is at the far side of the room, at the bar filling a glass with draft beer. "You know what I think, sir?"

"What's that, Derry?" Willard asks, still looking over at Elber and distracted in thought.

"The person who kidnapped Bethany Tremain." Derry leans closer. "How we know it wasn't Elber Gruber?"

Thirty minutes later, Derry and Willard are back in their cabin on the hill overlooking the outpost. At the desk, Willard composes a letter while Derry lies on one of the beds, reading a dime-novel western. Willard drops the pen and seals up the blue sheet of paper.

"Coach come yet?" Willard asks.

Derry looks out the window. "Pulling up now."

"Good. Just in time." Willard pulls some coins out of his pocket. "Give them this message to send by telegraph. This should cover it."

Derry takes the envelope and money and runs out to flag down the stagecoach before it takes off for Portland. The coachman reins the horses and takes letter from Derry's hand. The message has a man's name, George Emmett, and an address in Tacoma. Derry returns to the cabin.

"What's all that about?" Derry asks.

"Friend of mine," Willard says. "Fought with me in the Dixie Rangers."

"So why you in a hurry to get a message to him?"

"Something came up, kid. A side job. Tell you more later. Tomorrow we'll go to New Era. After that, we wait for a couple of my friends to arrive."

Chapter 9

Tommy points down the hill. "Look! There it is." Lindy Sue rides up next to him. At the bottom is the ranch at the edge of a flat area of treeless land with bits of brush. The clapboard house is a two-story box, with a porch and hitching post out front, while beyond looms a barn and stable area, surrounded by a rudimentary post and rail fence that runs far into the back.

Several crows greet them from the roof of the barn. Lindy Sue dismounts. Tommy hitches the horses in front, pulls out a key, and unlocks the door to the ranch.

"Where're the owners?" she asks, following him.

"My dad owns it now. And he says I can use it. Too far from town for him is what he said."

The interior is hot, with a stale smell. She looks around the kitchen, with all the pots and pans, and even a bag of flour and some root vegetables beginning to rot. "He bought it from them? Why'd they leave all their stuff?"

"Foreclosed on them. They're at the poor farm, working off their debt."

"But...it feels kind of spooky." She remembers Tommy saying his dad didn't like the New Era people, and now she wonders if it's because John Mitchell can't swindle them out of their property, the way he did the poor rancher whose house they now intruded on. As a tight-knit group, the New Era people have a better chance of standing up to bankers and lawyers of John Mitchell's ilk. She keeps this opinion to herself while she and Tommy examine the house's interior.

"We'll be fine, Lindy Sue. Don't be scared. I'm with you. Anyone tries to abduct you, and I'll smack them back where they came from."

"I believe you could," she says as she gazes at his

muscular arms. Tommy has recently graduated from Willamette University where he also played on the football team.

"And don't forget I've got this." He taps the six-shooter holstered to his side.

They step out the back porch and look across at the flat, fenced-in pasture beyond. "This is perfect," Tommy says.

"I need to clean the dust from my face." Lindy Sue sets about to find the well, and she pumps some water into a small wooden tub to wash her face and hands. She glances over to see Tommy roll a five-foot barrel toward the pasture. She brings her saddlebags to the porch, sits in the wicker chair, and pulls out a novel, A Beautiful Fiend or Through the Fire, by Mrs. Southworth. She begins to read.

Ten minutes later, pacing across the porch to the side of the house where the pasture is in view, she notices Tommy at the edge of the pasture, in quarter profile, looking away. After a moment he extracts an object from his waistcoat, what looks like a silk bag, and he pulls open the top to peer into it and then tucks it back into his pocket and begins to turn. She ducks behind the edge of the house before he sees her.

She sits in the wicker chair and picks up her book. Not that she can continue to read, in her excitement. He has a ring. From the corner of her eye, she sees him walking toward her determinedly. An engagement ring. Rolling the barrels out in the pasture, he was building up his courage to propose marriage. He's brought her out here to ask for her hand. The words of Mrs. Southworth's novel in front of her are unreadable in her trembling hands. Despite her ambivalence toward Tommy, she realizes how thrilled she is. Once a boy puts a ring on a girl's finger with a promise to marry, a girl is closer to becoming a woman and is saved from a life of old spinster-hood.

Of course she'll say yes. Her friend Maggie, Tommy's sister, is already engaged to Handy Doyle. How excited

Maggie was two months ago when she showed off her ring while Lindy Sue burned with envy. He'll put the ring on her finger, and then what? They'll spend the night together. This brings on a new rash of nervousness. Lindy Sue has read about sex, but she's never actually done it. Will Tommy want to tonight? Will she let him?

She thinks of her father's words, that one is not always compatible with one's spouse, and some men have problems in that way, a compulsion to find other sexual partners, looking for something better. He claimed it's better for couples to sleep together before marriage, see if they were compatible in bed. Not that he told her this, but she heard him say it to the other doctors at the asylum, while they shifted in their chairs and a few chuckled nervously.

Anticipation races through her as she pretends to read. Tommy's boots clatter loudly on the wooden porch.

"Lindy Sue!"

She looks up from the book. Feign innocence, don't spoil the moment. "Tommy?"

He steps up to her. "I want to show you something." With a slight flourish, he pulls the silk bag out of his pocket and opens the drawstrings on the top to reach inside. The sun flashes on the surfaces as an object far bigger than a ring emerges from the mouth of the bag. "Isn't she a beaut?" Tommy gushes as he holds it in front of her face.

"What is it?"

"A timer watch. My dad brought it from back east."

"It looks....pretty."

"Be careful when you hold it." He places it in her hand. "It's a Vacheron, made in Switzerland. A certified chronometer. I want you to time me."

"Time you?"

"Yes. I've set up the barrels. I want to practice for the barrel race next weekend."

"The barrel race?"

"Yes. I'm good, but I got to be better than Johnny

Snotgrass. He won it last two years, but man, I really need to take that away from him. With Dagger and a few trial runs, I can do it."

"Oh," she says and follows him out to the pasture.

Chapter 10

Night, the house cooled down, Lindy Sue and Tommy are at the table, drinking tea by flickering candlelight. She has changed into her nightgown, and he into a nightshirt. Beyond the house, the continuous chatter of crickets is the only sound.

"I reckon it's time for bed," Tommy says.

"I reckon so. I'll follow you."

He picks up the candle. She follows him down a short hallway into the master bedroom. The bed is made of burlap stuffed with straw, on a simple, unpainted frame. The sheets are not as soft as what she has at home. She walks around to the far side and climbs in. Tommy snuffs the candle, plunging the room into darkness. A moment later the bed creeks as he climbs in on the other side.

"Thank you for timing me," he says.

"You did really good, Tommy."

"Reckon I'll do several more runs tomorrow. Dagger'll be fresh so I can run him a half a dozen times, at least."

"Tommy?"

"What is it?"

"Do you love me?"

"Of course I love you, Lindy Sue."

"I love you too."

"You like it out here?"

"I don't know. It's very quiet." It feels strange, to be lying in a strange bed next to a man. She closes her eyes, but her mind races. Tommy shifts positions. Somewhere in the house, a creak of wood settling. Lindy Sue turns on her side, and after more time, shifts back to her back. She sighs.

"You still awake?" he asks quietly.

"Don't think I can sleep."

"Me neither." He rolls on his side toward her. "Maybe that's what it is. People can't sleep when they're together in bed. Can't sleep unless..."

"Unless what?"

"The other thing."

"What thing?"

"That people do in bed."

"Oh." A memory comes into her head. "I think I read that. They have sex and then it's easier to fall asleep."

"Yes. Maybe it's that. You read the craziest things, Lindy Sue."

It's odd, she thinks, that they are talking in hushed voices when there's no one around for miles.

"Do you think it's true?" Tommy asks.

"What's true?"

"That it makes you sleepy afterward?"

"That what can?"

"You know. What a man and a woman do in bed."

"I wouldn't know."

"Me neither."

She turns to face him, a shadow in the darkness. "You never did it with Jennifer Durham?"

"No. I mean, we didn't spend the whole night together. It was just a thing."

"So you know what to do?"

"Not much to know," he says. "One just does it. I even brought my condom."

She doesn't mention that her dad made her bring some too. "Why did she break up with you?"

"Like I told you, her damn father." Tommy scowls. "And that terrible thing the papers wrote about my dad."

"Maybe she didn't really love you."

"Not enough, I suppose. But you love me, don't you, Lindy Sue?"

"Yes."

"You want to do it?"

"Do what?"

"You know." He reaches out his hand and caresses her face. "Otherwise we might not ever get to sleep."

"I don't know if I'm ready."

"If you think that way, you'll never be. It's one of those things."

If he had put a ring on my finger, she thinks, *I would not have questioned having sex with him.*

"No one who's done it ever wants to not do it," he says. "You're too old to be virgin."

"But once gone, it's something I'll never get back."

"You think too much. You can't just read about stuff in books."

She relents. He kisses her. His nightshirt is open, and he fumbles with the buttons of her gown, and pushes it open at her thighs.

"We'd best use this," he says. So maybe he hasn't decided completely until this test. He opens the tin and pulls out a sagging bit of rubber.

"My dad gave me some too," she says.

"I haven't used this one yet. This part I hate, getting it on, and you don't want to lose the drive." He fiddles with himself as he kneels above her in the bed. She lies back with her legs wide open.

He pushes her down on her back and climbs on top of her, jabs his hips to hers. *He's like a cage over me,* she thinks, his arms and legs around her, his large body above her. He enters her. She gasps. It hurts. She bites her lip. He begins to thrust and groan.

He pushes away from her and lies back spent. She feels a wetness on her inner thighs. "That was good, Lindy Sue," he says. He stands up and walks toward the window. The condom slurps as he peels it off. It thunks wetly on the table by the window, and his footsteps pad back to the bed. "Reckon I'll clean it in the morning so we can use it tomorrow night too." After a few minutes, he begins to snore.

She still can't sleep. That was it? This thing she'd read about, what her father and the other doctors talked about? It was over so quickly. She can generate more pleasure with her hand, which she does, biting her lip to keep herself from making noise, not that she could wake Tommy over his sawing and hawing. Finally she drifts to sleep.

Chapter 11

The next morning they are back in the pasture so Tommy can do several more trial runs. Lindy Sue clutches the pocket timer carefully, in her sleepy state more nervous than the evening before about dropping it, knowing it's expensive. The timepiece catches the sun as she holds it up and watches the large gold hand race around the dial, while the smaller gold hand nudges forward.

The barrels are set in a triangle, and when Tommy races past the post she sets the timer going while he swerves Dagger in a clover pattern around them, a feat where he must constantly pull Dagger in 360-degree turns around the barrels before running back past the starting post. Dagger's hooves kick up a cloud of dust. She pushes stop as Tommy and Dagger race past the post.

"How'd I do?" Tommy asks half a minute later, still on Dagger, leaning down to take the pocket watch.

"Faster than yesterday."

He smiles and carefully hands back the watch. "Good. I'm getting comfortable with Dagger." He pats the steed on the side of the head.

Lindy Sue notices movement on the craggy hill beyond the pasture. Three horsemen ride down quickly, kicking up dirt as they head toward the ranch.

"Tommy?" She points.

He turns to look. "Guess we got company."

She thinks again about the Pinkertons and the missing girl. She steps closer to Tommy and Dagger. "You don't think..."

"Don't worry, Lindy Sue. I'll handle it." Tommy pats the gun holstered at his right hip. "Probably the boys from the club. Dang. I was hoping they wouldn't catch me out here."

The three on horseback reach the bottom of the hill, and start to veer around the fenced-in area. As they emerge from the haze kicked up by their horses, Lindy Sue realizes the front rider is a woman. The other two as well.

"Look, Tommy!"

Tommy laughs. "Nothing to worry about. Just three dames. Fooled me at first with those hats. What the hell they doin' out here by themselves without a man? Probably got lost from the rest of their party."

Lindy Sue feels herself relax. "What do you think they want?"

"I reckon we'll soon find out."

PART II: THE MITCHELL RANCH

Chapter 12

Varla and Rosa drink coffee and read a three-day-old newspaper at a wooden table beneath a tarp of animal furs, in front of a couple of large enclosed wagons. The wagons are arranged at an angle with a bar counter set in front of them to form a wide "A." Behind the bar is a wood-burning stove with a coffee percolator and a large iron griddle pan. Straddling the tops of the wagons, a large wooden sign painted black with red letters reads:

GET THEE TO A NUNNERY!

NANCY'S

NUNNERY

"Breakfast almost done," Eliza Boggs yells to be heard over the sizzle of ham-hock grease on the griddle. Twenty-four-year-old Eliza is cherubic, softer version of her shrewd mother, Nancy. Nancy Boggs ran a side-by-side whiskey house and seamstress shop in downtown Portland, and if her seamstress girls wanted to make extra money at night, the whiskey bar had some small bedrooms in back. The nunnery is an idea Nancy and Eliza cooked up, a mobile bordello that Eliza ran the last two summers, traveling out to the stagecoach routes with a couple of girls, where they'd stay at one location for a few days or a month, depending on the local law. One wagon has a couple of small bedrooms where the two girls worked, and the other a small office and a lounge area where Eliza might entertain the right man for the right price.

"We have to move," Eliza says with a small frown. "The Grubers."

"Why would they mind?" Varla asks. "Not like they offer what you do."

"They think we take away drink sales." Eliza tops off the coffee cups in front of Varla and Rosa. "And the morality. Comstock prudes is what they are. Must have sickened their souls to conceive that horrible kid of theirs."

All three women laugh at the image.

"When?" Varla asks.

"Next week, when the sheriff drags himself out here."

Rosa tunes out the conversation as an item in the newspaper leaps at her. Railroad magnate's nephew stabbed to death in the North End. Her pulse quickens as she reads more, ignoring the plate of eggs, stove cakes, and smoked-hock toast that clatters on the table in front of her.

Varla flirts with Eliza as she eats. "Thanks for everything, Eliza."

Rosa thinks to herself: *Thanks?* To sleep on the ground on some sheep skins? Where they could hear the creak of the wagon during the nightly business of the *putas*.

"Isn't this coffee delicious, Rosa?" Varla says.

"Coffee *esta bein,*" Rosa mumbles, taking in the article. The murder victim is James Montgomery, nephew of railroad magnate James Boyce Montgomery, and not Bobby Lappeus, the police chief's son. Evidence leads to a gang of Filipino sailors, believed to have shipped out afterwards. Bobby Lappeus and a third kid, Derry Flanders, are not mentioned until near the end, as the last ones known to see their friend alive. An inability to locate one or two foreign women, also wanted for questioning. Varla not implicated, only wanted for questioning.

When Eliza walks over to check on the stove, Rosa

speaks quietly, her mouth pointed to Varla's ear as Varla eyes Eliza.

"You got off easy this time, Varla. *Afortunada.*"

"Really?" Varla smiles at her. "I feel like I didn't even do it. It's a nice memory, but the memory is nothing to the thrill it gave me. You say I got off easy?" Varla grabs the paper and scans the columns as she downs more coffee. Her eyes squint when she finds the article, and her lips move, just slightly, as she reads the words.

"A big nothing," Varla laughs. "No one gives a shit about a nephew of some shady railroad man. Unless there's something they're not saying."

"You should be more careful. Was it worth the few *dinero* you got off him?"

"You saw how they insulted us. What was I supposed to do?"

"Not escalate *el problema.*"

"Takes two to tango, Rosa. They asked for it."

At that moment at the periphery of her vision, Rosa notices Blondie at the corner of the wagon. Sleepy-eyed, she saunters slowly up to the makeshift bar and flops on the stool to the far side of Varla. "I need coffee before I go back to dreamland!"

"That's all she likes," Rosa quips. "Things done in bed."

"Glad you're up," Varla says to Blondie. "We head out in half an hour. Before the John Thomases show up."

"Unless you want to stay here and make money on your back," Rosa remarks.

"I'm not a whore. I only fuck who I want to fuck," Blondie snaps back.

"Any man between fifteen and sixty?" Rosa replies.

"Listen to her impugn my character, Varla." Blondie takes a sip of coffee. "So what were you two finding so interesting in the news?" She reaches for the paper on the counter in front of Varla.

"Nothing much," Varla says. "Catching up on what's happening in Portland."

"This page is mostly ads for bridal dresses and concentrated cocoa extract, Varla, and I know you're not into that." Blondie glances down the page. Her eyes light up as she stops two-thirds of the way, on the article. *It's like Blondie has a homing device*, Rosa thinks, like when a dog heads to the one dangerous thing in the yard you don't want it to be near.

"We head back in a few days," Varla says.

Blondie's eyes go wide. "Look at this. This boy stabbed to death three blocks from our place in the North End."

"People get murdered in Portland every other day," Varla counters. "It's nothing."

"It happened the morning we left." Blondie looks up and aims her gaze at Varla. "There something you're not telling me?"

Varla shrugs. "No."

"These two foreign women they're looking for. You and Rosa?"

"*Yo no!*" Rosa shakes her head. "Not us."

Varla puts down her coffee cup. "We walked past them. Three drunk angry boys. Waving their money around, and they were fighting over some girl. Some frail little rich bitch with golden hair. Looked like trouble so we walked the other way."

"Is that you, Varla?" Blondie giggles. "Running away from trouble?"

"Mess with rich kids with important fathers?" Varla says. "No way! That police chief controls the North End."

"The one kid went *loco*, stabbed the other kid, fighting over a girl," Rosa says. "The other is covering up. And they blame it on people with darker skin, the *racistas*."

"The police chief won't investigate, when his son's who did it," Varla adds.

Blondie scans the article. "Bobby Lappeus. He only

gets a mention as an acquaintance of the deceased. Bobby Lappeus and Derry Flanders."

"Here comes Eliza with more stove cakes," Varla says. "Eat up, finish the coffee so we can go."

"Unless you want to stay here, Blondie," Rosa adds. "Maybe Eliza can use another *puta*."

"I told you, I don't sleep with just anybody, Rosa."

"Could've fooled me."

"Knock it off you two," Varla snaps.

Chapter 13

The sun rises above the hills, throwing long shadows behind the three women on horseback. They ride three abreast with Varla at the center, through the open scrub-lands. The air is still cool and the morning birds still give song.

"So you haven't told me what it is," Blondie says. "This big money opportunity. So far, riding around for nothing."

"We're looking for a rundown ranch," Varla tells her.

"Shouldn't be hard around here."

"This one has a cripple," Varla says. "Old man with no legs. Got a lot of money he doesn't know how to spend, so he might give us some of it."

"Just like that?" Blondie shakes her head. "Sounds like a load of flummadiddle."

"It is what it is," Varla says.

"Doesn't sound like fun," Blondie says. "A crippled old man. How depressing."

"Having our mitts around some of his money won't be depressing," Varla replies.

"If I'd known this caper centered around a crippled old man, I might've stayed in the North End. And we might never find it."

"We'll look a few more days. Who knows?" Varla lets out a deep breath. "I've a good feeling about today."

Sure Varla has a good feeling, finding out a necktie party *ejecución* isn't waiting for her in Portland. "This whole thing's *un busto*," Rosa says. "A dance of nonsense."

"For once I have to agree with her, Varla," Blondie adds. "I'm tired of sleeping on the ground. Riding all day. We're better off at the Final Frontier."

"Maybe we call it quits, Varla," Rosa says.

"Let's take a vote," Blondie rattles on. "Go back to Portland or keep riding around to nowhere."

Varla gallops ahead of the others and quickly spins her horse to face them, her hand out flat. Rosa and Blondie reign their horses to a halt.

Expressionless, Varla looks from Rosa to Blondie. "Is that what you want, a vote?"

Blondie's horse, Chillins, whinnies. "I... I guess so," Blondie says, a quaver in her voice.

"How about you, Rosa. Think we should go back to Portland?"

"Of course you do, Rosa," Blondie says.

Rosa glances at Blondie and back to Varla. "No. Nada. *Aun no*."

"Not yet? Why not?" Blondie asks.

"In a day or two, we don't find anything," Rosa says. "We can't give up so soon."

"Good. That's settled." Varla turns her horse around and continues on the trail to the top of a hillside, and the other two follow.

"I'm tired of sleeping on the ground," Blondie tells Rosa.

"Farm girl, pretending to be *una princesa*." Rosa scoffs.

"At least on the farm one slept in a proper bed."

"A bed at an inn costs *dinero*. We're low as it is."

"Shush! Both of you!" Ahead Varla abruptly stops her horse. She leans down to pull a small spyglass out of her saddle bag as the others reach her.

"What is it?" Rosa asks.

"Something down there. Maybe nothing." Varla unfolds the spyglass and scans the valley in front of them.

In the valley below, in the distance is a ranch house, a barn, and a large pasture fenced in by wood posts. Rosa sees a flash from the pasture, a glint of a shiny object catching sunlight.

A smile curls on Varla's lips.

"The cripple?" Blondie asks.

"Check it out, Rosa." Varla hands over the spyglass.

Rosa puts the eyepiece to her face and aims where the flash of light came from. In moments, she sees a young woman in a pink dress, holding the shiny object that reflected the sun. The woman stares out at the pasture. Rosa follows her gaze with the spyglass and spots a man on a steed galloping fast around a bunch of barrels, kicking up dust. Rosa turns the spyglass back to the young woman.

"That *reloj de bolsillo* she's got. She's not some farm girl," Rosa remarks.

"No, she isn't"

"What's he doing down there? Barrel racing?" Rosa hands the spyglass to Blondie.

"What it looks like," Varla says.

"Barrel racing?" Blondie looks through the spyglass. "That's for rodeo sissies, guys afraid to dirty up their expensive duds."

"Guy's no ranch hand," Varla says. "Let's go down and meet the catalog cowboy. But first, deep-six the six shooters so they know we're friends." She reaches down and pulls off her holsters from her hips and stashes them into one of her saddle bags. The other two follow suit.

"So what's the plan?" Blondie asks.

"We honeyfuggle them out of the watch and some money. Have a bit of fun." Varla starts down the hill. Rosa follows.

"I have first dibs on seducing him!" Blondie shouts behind her.

"He's yours!" Rosa yells back. "Just don't muck things up!"

They reach the pasture, jumping over where the upper piece of the fence has fallen off, and bring the horses to a trot. Ahead the man and the woman are at the far side near the ranch. He's large and husky, the athletic type, a bit pompous as he sits on his horse, his hands out at his sides, and standing eight feet away, a frilly frail little *princesa*, golden-haired and baby-fat face.

Fifty yards away Varla reigns her steed and calls out. "Howdy, friends!"

Chapter 14

Lindy Sue watches the three riders slow their horses as they approach.

"Nothing to be afraid of." Tommy, still on his horse Dagger, cracks a grin. "A bunch of dames."

"How curious. I wonder who they are."

"I reckon we'll soon find out."

The horses come to a halt. The woman in front wears a black leather vest and breaches, and a black boss-of-the-plains hat. She calls out: "Howdy friends! Can we rest our horses a spell? Been riding since sun up."

"I reckon so," Tommy yells back.

The three women climb off their horses and stride toward Lindy Sue and Tommy while the horses watch placidly. The woman in black has shoulder-length jet-black hair and large exotic eyes that gleam like dark gems beneath the shade of her hat brim. She's almost as tall as Tommy, Lindy Sue realizes when they get closer. The other two are near as tall. One has a dark complexion and short, bright red hair beneath the wide brim of her tan cattleman hat, and wears a yellow blouse and light brown breaches. The third has a mane of blond hair beneath an off-white brick hat and wears a light blue blouse and a skirt that exposes her knees.

They might be a race of Amazons. Lindy Sue thinks for a moment, if they all weren't so different in other ways. Lindy Sue is both awed and slightly fearful, though the women seem friendly and, as Tommy notes with a whisper, they appear unarmed. There is something brazen and dangerous about them that excites Lindy Sue as if she is in one of her melodramatic novels.

Lindy Sue realizes she still has Tommy's pocket watch in her hand. She puts her hands behind her to hide the timepiece.

"You girls need directions?" Tommy asks. "Separated from the rest of your party?"

"You said party?" The blonde has a big smile on her face. "I wouldn't mind finding a party."

"No party here." Tommy peers up at the hill from where they came. "Where're your menfolk, anyway?"

"Nowhere near here," the one in black says.

The blonde steps up to Lindy Sue. "What's your name, cute Buttercup?"

"Lindy Sue."

"Lindy Sue. I'm Blondie, and this is Varla and Rosa." The blond points to the other two.

"I'm Tommy," Tommy says from his horse. "You girls from New Era?"

"The Valley?" Varla puts her hands out to her sides. "Does that matter?"

"You should be careful traveling alone," Tommy says. "Dangerous out here."

"Is Blondie your real name?" Lindy Sue asks, staring at Blondie who looks back at her from a few feet away with wide blue eyes.

"Loretta Blossom. But friends call me Blondie."

"You like racing around by yourself?" Rosa asks. "Barrel racing? *No cojones.*"

"That's right." Tommy puffs up his chest. "Big tournament in two weeks in Albina."

"You think you'll win with that nag?" Varla jokes. "Ready for the glue factory, you ask me."

"Come on, Varla," Blondie chides. "That horse give Storm a run for the money."

"Wouldn't be close." Tommy smirks as he runs his fingers through Dagger's dark mane.

"You think so?" Varla asks. She strides toward Tommy and Dagger.

"Why don't you two race to find out?" Blondie

suggests. "More exciting than running around barrels by yourself."

"Maybe the *pejero* likes beating off instead of real action," Rosa remarks so casually Lindy Sue is unsure Tommy hears it.

Tommy shakes his head. "Wouldn't be fair. Race against a woman."

"What are you? *Pendejo?*" Rosa jeers.

Tommy turns to Lindy Sue. She shrugs. *Maybe he should race the women,* she thinks. Put them in their place. Dagger is faster than any of their steeds.

"A friendly race..." In front of Tommy, Varla has her hands on her hips. Tommy lingers his gaze low, and Lindy Sue wonders the view he has, looking down from the horse at Varla's ample cleavage.

Varla's horse, a black stallion, walks up to her side. A fine horse, but not as large and powerful as Dagger. Varla points to the way they came. "Through the gap in the fence and around that big rock over there."

Lindy Sue peers to where the finger points. A large block of dark rock she hadn't noticed before, about a quarter mile away where the valley begins to dip up to the hills.

"Are you kidding?" Tommy scoffs, squinting across the pasture. "That quarter-breed against Dagger?"

"Show us your *cojones*, big boy," Rosa says.

"You can do it, Tommy!" Lindy Sue cries out. Those women are embarrassing themselves. She knows Tommy will win easy.

Varla, so full of herself, has a leer on her face as she looks Lindy Sue in the eyes, her own eyes hooded by the shadow from the brim of the boss-of-the-plains. "Let's get it on. Show your filly over there what you got."

"Dagger is purebred appaloosa," Lindy Sue says. "Won't be close."

"Did you call Dragger a pure appa-loser?" Blondie giggles.

"Afraid to lose in front of his *princesa*, that's why he won't race."

"You really want to race?" Tommy glares at the women.

"A friendly race." Varla slings herself onto her horse. "See who's faster. You or me?"

"Tommy, you can do it!" Lindy Sue cheers.

"You're on," Tommy says.

"Finally, excitement." Blondie puts her hand on Lindy Sue's shoulder. "You think he can beat Varla?"

"Yes, he will. Why are you standing so close to me?"

"I like you, Lindy Sue. You're adorably cute. That Tommy's one lucky buck to have a sweet filly as lovely as you. He needs to ring you before someone else grabs you."

The race begins. Tommy soon has twenty feet on the woman as they gallop through the pasture.

Lindy Sue turns to Blondie. "No way Tommy loses. He'll make her eat dust."

"*Neta*?" Rosa chuckles. "*No manches.* He doesn't have a chance."

"You women have so little respect for others. Tommy knows boxing and he's a halfback."

"Does he bareback?" Blondie asks with a giggle.

"No. Halfback of the football team at Willamette University."

"So what?" Rosa says. "He throws a deflated ball to a bunch of knuckleheads so they can slap each others butts and pile up on each other. An all-boy *Orgia.*"

"You have no class. Tommy's dad was in the Senate."

"How many bankers he *sopladota* for that?" Rosa shapes her lips in an "O" and jabs her index finger between them.

"Pay no mind to her, Lindy Sue." Blondie has her hand around Lindy Sue's shoulder and nudges her away from Rosa. "She's egging you on."

"I don't think she likes me," Lindy Sue says quietly,

out of Rosa's earshot.

"Who cares about her? I like you." Blondie stands in front of her and puts both hands on Lindy Sue's arms. "I'm curious what you have in your hand."

"In my hand?" Lindy Sue remembers the watch, still held behind her back.

"What is it? You don't want to show me?"

"Tommy's timepiece. His dad gave it to him." Lindy Sue glances at Rosa, who is thirty feet away, leaning on the fence and watching the race. Tommy is almost to the rock, Varla several paces back.

Lindy Sue reluctantly brings her hand up in front of her, fingers open to show Blondie the watch.

"It's beautiful. What a nice gift for him to give you." Blondie brings her fingers closer to Lindy Sue's hand. "Can I?"

"I don't know. It's not...mine," Lindy Sue stammers.

Rosa has not moved from the fence. Blondie reaches for the watch. Lindy Sue feints back a step. She and Blondie eye each other, as if in a duel, and yet the blonde smiles at her and steps closer, now towering above Lindy Sue.

"Why are your friends so mean?" Lindy Sue asks.

"They can be nice, too," Blondie purrs as her fingers curl around Lindy Sue's hand with the watch. Her face so close Lindy Sue is reminded when she and Maggie Mitchell stood close together, looking into each other's eyes and then kissing and making out on the floor of her room when her family was out, and afraid of her father coming home from the asylum. Lindy Sue blushes as she has these thoughts while looking into Blondie's eyes.

Blondie's hand caresses hers. Lindy Sue lets her take the watch. "Be careful," she whispers.

Blondie holds the watch to her face.

Lindy Sue holds out her hand. "Give it here before Tommy gets back. He wouldn't want other people to hold it." Lindy Sue glances over, too much dust to see the race, but Tommy will return in a minute or two.

"This must be worth a lot of money," Blondie says.

"It's from Europe." Lindy Sue reaches out her hand. "Can you give it back?"

"Here! Let me see!" Rosa holds up her hand and takes a few steps toward them.

Lindy Sue shakes her head. "I can't show it to everyone. Wait for Tommy. Now give it here."

"How much you think his rich daddy paid?" Blondie asks.

"I don't know. Tommy didn't tell me."

"Rosa might know. Hey, Rosa."

"No," Lindy Sue whispers. "Don't let her see it."

"Why not? Don't you trust us?"

"Please! Give it back!" She grabs for the watch.

"Let Rosa have a look. She'll know its worth." Blondie pulls the watch away from Lindy Sue's grasp and flings it in a high arc. With horror, Lindy Sue spins as the watch sails over her head and into the waiting hand of the Mexican.

Rosa smiles as she dangles the watch on the thin gold chain in front of her eyes. "This one, *muy valioso.* Valuable."

"Please, give it back, Rosa." Lindy Sue's voice quavers as she steps toward her.

"I give back. To Blondie." With a flip of Rosa's wrist, the watch arcs over Lindy Sue's head to Blondie. Giggling, Blondie catches it and baubles it in the air.

Lindy Sue rushes at her. "Give it back!"

"I don't have it. Rosa does." Blondie flings it back to Rosa.

Lindy Sue turns to Rosa. "You! Give it back! Tommy'll be furious!"

"Tommy's lost the race," Rosa says.

"Lost the race!" Lindy Sue stares out. Two horses head back toward them but only one has a rider. And beyond she sees a distant figure, walking at a furious pace toward them.

Chapter 15

A race is exciting: a spark of competitive angst missing from the timed barrel runs. Tommy can easily beat this black-leather prostitute, his appaloosa against her half-breed stallion. Her steed is powerful, but not as big and muscled as his.

They get on the start-line. The Mexican, Rosa, stands at the side with a make-shift flag. The horses snort with anticipation.

Tommy plans it out in his head. He'll ease during the run to the rock, let her think she's keeping up, and then he'll speed full-bore around the rock and back to the corral to leave her in the dust. The stupid woman, she even forgets to remove her saddlebags.

They take off and he holds his distance ahead of her, keeping her at a pace by the sound of the hooves behind him.

He risks a glance over his shoulder. She's a dozen yards back, leaning down low on the horse. The dark boulder, twenty feet high and two dozen wide, looms ahead like a tooth of a giant.

He races around the rock with ease compared to the tight corners of the barrel run. He's almost around and she rushes at him, a lasso twirling at her side. She hurtles toward him, hand and rope raised. The rope whips around his head and he grasps to pull it off but is thrown backward off his horse. It happens so quickly. He hits the ground with his hands pushing free the lasso.

Dazed and furious, he staggers to his feet. The woman cheated! He whistles for Dagger, now following the other horse back to the corral.

Hands bowling his mouth, he yells: "Dagger!" The appaloosa continues moving away. Tommy'll have to walk back. A jab of pain hits his ankle with each limped step, fueling his anger at the woman and her friends, these New Era whores or whoever they are. He's had enough of their sass.

As he enters the far end of the pasture, his heart sickens. The women circle Lindy Sue, playing keep away with his dad's timepiece. Why did she show it to them? Is she playing along or is she... No, her face is pale, in panic. He quickens his pace as he stomps through the pasture.

"Give it to me! Now!" he orders, thirty yards away.

Chapter 16

Lindy Sue can't believe it. Tommy was so far ahead. "But how?"

"Wiped out on the turn," Rosa says. "*Chocar*."

"The turn?" How could he? He'd practiced sharper turns with Dagger all morning. And Dagger would've downed, not be trotting beside the woman's stallion. Tommy can't possibly lose, but here rides the woman toward them while Tommy's at the far end of the field beyond the pasture.

"She cheated!" Lindy Sue cries out. "No way Tommy lost. You'll be sorry when he gets back. You don't know who you're dealing with."

"So sure you'd win." Rosa laughs. "But you lose. *Pierdes*. Victor claims spoils. Toss it over, Blondie."

The watch arcs into Rosa's hand. Instead of heading toward Rosa, Lindy Sue steps closer to Blondie. "Please, make her give it back."

"Not yours and not ours," Blondie says. "Let Varla and Tommy decide."

"Tommy will tell you all to leave us alone."

"You're no fun." Rosa waves around the watch. "Come and get it, you *chiflado*."

"His dad'll buy him a new one," Blondie says.

"That was fun!" Varla shouts as she leaps off the horse and rushes toward them.

"Varla wins!" Rosa holds up the pocket watch. "*Victoria!* A bet is a bet, *princesa*."

"She cheated!" Lindy Sue clenches her fist. "You don't want to make Tommy mad! He'll teach you all a lesson."

"You think so?" Varla says. "Can he teach anything besides how to lose?"

"Tommy won't put up with this, not at all."

"Oh, oh, Varla," Blondie says, as Tommy reaches the fence. "He's more pissed than a tomcat thrown in a tub of water."

"Throw it here, Rosa." Varla holds up her hand. "Me and Tommy'll work this out."

"Maybe we should cut out," Blondie says. "He looks dangerous."

Varla steps away from the others, to face Tommy. With a slight limp he storms across the pasture, face livid red.

They're in for it now, Lindy Sue thinks. Tommy will put them in their place. He won't take this insolent behavior. She has seen how he can get with insubordination from inferiors.

"You want me to give it to you?" Varla says. "Come and get it, big boy. Let's get it on."

"She's asking for it, isn't she?" Blondie says. "Completely off her chump. Hope he doesn't hurt her too bad."

"But she deserves it!" Lindy Sue doesn't want to watch, though she does yell out, "Go, Tommy!" She hears noises behind Blondie. A couple yells, almost like what one thinks of a man and woman grunting in sex, and a thump on the ground and a scream and a crack of something breaking, cutting off the scream to a gurgle. Lindy Sue looks past Blondie to see how badly Tommy has hurt Varla.

Chapter 17

Seething with anger, Tommy approaches the woman. "Give it back!"

"I've got it here." Stepping forward, Varla holds up the watch, dangling it from her fingers with a flourish.

"What a sore loser! And now he make excuses!" The Mexican taunts him.

The blonde giggles. "He wiped out making the turn!"

"Tommy?" Lindy Sue gasps.

"I said give it!" Tommy approaches Varla.

"Give it to him, Varla. Give it to him with a bunch of fives."

"Tommy!" Lindy Sue's strident voice cuts through, from behind Varla, who stands in front of him with the watch.

"I've had enough!" Tommy glares at Varla, eye to eye. Varla is seven feet away from him. He'll daze her with a clip and slap her around, smack her to the ground, and pry free the watch even if he has to break fingers. "One last chance. Hate to hit a lady but a mongrel can't be no lady."

"You done beating off?" Varla laughs, one hand on her hip, the other holding out the watch, as she leans back slightly.

"To be treated this way by a..." Tommy holds back a derogatory word, crouches into a boxing stance, and advances. He pretends to grab for the watch as he cocks his other hand back. He glares at her. With a demonic grin, she stares back, enjoying his anguish, enjoying the suffering of Lindy Sue.

He lunges at her and swings.

His right fist misses impact as Varla slides under it. He lets go with the roundhouse from his left. Suddenly he's off-balance stumbling. Her hand a blur slams hard into his neck as he falls. He reels forward and hits the ground with her on his back. A loud crack shatters through his body. A burst of pain in his throat and he's looking up at her face framed by the shimmering blue sky.

He can't move. He doesn't even know if he's alive. Everything is quiet for a moment. From a long way off comes a whimper.

"Tommy? What did you do to Tommy?"

I'm right here, Lindy Sue! Nothing comes out of his mouth, and the words stay in his head. Voices far away. Are they going to help him? He no longer feels the heat of the sun or the hard clay of the ground. The pocket watch, he'll never again see the glint as it plays with sunlight. Never see Lindy Sue's pretty face. Never play football, and never run the Barrel to show up Snodgrass and the guy who stole Jennifer Durham from him, but maybe it's okay because he's riding an invisible horse off into a strange unknown that we all must face.

Chapter 18

Lindy Sue's blood curdles. Varla walks toward them with a slight smile and beyond, Tommy lies in the dirt.

"Tommy? Tommy? What did you do to Tommy?" Lindy Sue runs over to Tommy. He stares up at the sky, eyes open, mouth agape, his crushed throat bleeding.

"Tommy?" The image burns into Lindy Sue's brain. Tommy murdered. She's surrounded by murderers. The black-haired one, Varla, killed him. In rage, Lindy Sue lunges at her with her fists. "What did you do to Tommy?"

The big hand comes fast. A flash of light bursts through Lindy Sue's brain, and then all goes black as the dirt at her feet flies up in front of her.

Chapter 19

The smack drops Lindy Sue to the ground a dozen feet from Tommy. Out cold. Varla picks her hat off the ground and places it on her head. She has a big catlike grin on her face. “That was fun.”

“You done it now, Varla,” Rosa says. “You shouldn’t’ve killed him. *Arroyo de Mierda.*”

“Out here in the middle of nowhere?” Varla shrugs.

“His dad... big shot Senator back in Washington DC.”

“Too late to rewind the wax cylinder now.” Varla winces. “Besides it was an accident.”

Mouth agape, Blondie looks pale as she stares at Varla. “What did you do to him?”

“He attacked me, Blondie. It was an accident.”

“Is he..?”

“You saw it, Blondie. He attacked me. I didn’t mean for this to happen.”

“But you provoked him,” Blondie says.

Varla shrugs. “Didn’t mean to kill him. I was afraid to hit the girl too hard, but a tough guy like that? Didn’t think he’d be the fragile one.”

“Are you sure?” Blondie narrows her eyes.

“Get a hold of yourself.” Varla strides toward her. “Things’ll be fine. He shouldn’t have died. It was an accident. We need to stay calm.”

“An accident?”

“Maybe after he fell off the horse, and then falling again when I hit him.” Varla shakes her head. “I thought he’d get up. We’re all a bit shook up.”

“You didn’t try to kill him, Varla?” Blondie asks.

“Of course not. How could I? Strong man like that. I was defending myself. He falls and dies. Freak accident.”

She stares Blondie in the eyes. Afraid, Blondie tries to look away.

"We might be thieves, but no one wants to hang for murder," Varla says.

"The law might see different," Rosa says.

"The law's meant for some people, not for us."

"I was afraid he'd kill you," Blondie says.

"He would have, too, he was so pissed off."

"What about *princesa*?" Rosa jerks a thumb at Lindy Sue.

"Can't leave her here," Blondie says.

"Why not?" Rosa replies. "Let her feed buzzards with her *papacito*."

"I can't believe you'd say that, Rosa. The kid didn't mean no harm."

"She comes with us," Varla says. "Blondie, go get her horse." Varla points toward the ranch house, where a mare is tethered near the porch.

"I don't like it," Rosa grumbles when Blondie is out of earshot. "Alive she's a witness. Dead she's..."

Varla shakes her head. "Alive she's worth money. And a dead rich girl? No end to those troubles. Even worse than the senator's dead boy."

"So we ride her back to Portland? That's *loco,* Varla."

"We dope her up, anyone asks, she fled the big crazy house in East Portland, and we're rescuing her. Now roll him, see what he's got."

Rosa shakes her head with a scoff and bends over Tommy's corpse to pat it down. She brings out several coins and a wallet stuffed with bills. She flings the empty wallet into the pasture.

"Here's the plan, Rosa," Varla says. "You head over to Gruber's. Rent a cabin, one far in back. Then you ride to the apothecary in New Era Village. We'll need more opium and some sleep powder, and some ganja. When you return, we take her and her mare under cover of darkness."

"What about Blondie?" Rosa asks.

"She stays here with me," Varla whispers. "She can help sweet talk the girl, maybe get her to calm down."

"Like that kid'll calm when you murder her boyfriend."

"You're an accomplice, and you know they'll be just as happy to hang you as me, so don't do anything stupid."

"What're you two talking about?" Blondie asks as she returns with the mare.

"Nothing," Varla says. "Rosa's getting us a cabin for tonight." Varla bends down to scoop up Lindy Sue and flops her over her shoulder.

"What're you going to do to Lindy Sue?" Blondie asks.

"Take her inside. Make her comfortable. She's had a terrible day, Blondie. We need to convince her we're taking her home."

Chapter 20

In the Outpost dining area, Mrs. Gruber's small eyes squint at Rosa across the bar counter. Rosa does her best attempt at a friendly smile, but the old biddy seems to try to squeeze her pointy eyes into the interior of Rosa's mind, and Rosa wonders if Mrs. Gruber has the same powers as Varla.

The husband, equally as withered, hobbles about the store to the right of the entrance, restocking shelves from the barn out back, grunting as he carries a heavy burlap sack of sugar over his shoulder. Their kid, Elber, in the corner of the dining area, sweeps the floor and sneaks looks at Rosa.

"A cabin?" Mrs. Gruber frowns.

"That's right. Number seven. Doesn't look taken." Rosa points to the wooden key rack on the wall behind the bar, surrounded by bottles of booze.

"Number seven?" The old woman narrows her eyes more. "That one is farthest from the facilities."

"*Si*. The one we want."

"We don't cotton to misbehaving. And we don't let to unmarried couples."

"I comprehend." Rosa nods.

"That's a big cabin. Will you be alone?"

"Me and my two sisters." Rosa holds up two fingers.

"And how long?"

"Few days."

The withered woman's desire for money outweighs her suspicions of Rosa, or so Rosa supposes as she watches Mrs. Gruber walk to retrieve the key on peg seven. It can't be easy running an outpost in a remote area like this when more travelers take the north route along the Columbia, and it will even be worse when the train tracks connect Portland to

Minneapolis and the East Coast. One can almost feel sorry for the Grubers, spending their whole life on a business that will probably fail.

"Payment in advance. Any immorality and you're out, no refund."

"That enough?" Rosa drops a couple bills on the counter with a smile.

"More than enough." Mrs. Gruber mutters, not smiling back and not quite disguising her suspicions and disgust as she grabs the currency in her talon and pockets it in her vest. She pulls some coins out of another pocket and smacks them on the counter without counting them. A penny rolls to the edge of the counter and Rosa slaps it down before it falls on the floor.

Rosa glances up. Elber Gruber is much closer to the open front door with his sweeping. He leers as she approaches. She scowls back as she strides quickly past.

The cabin is a larger one, a twelve-by-twelve shack with small dirty windows, two beds, a desk, two wood chairs, an armchair, and a couple lanterns hang from the ceiling on chains. She places her saddle bags near the door and shuts the curtains over the windows. The closet is deep enough to lie in, especially after she struggles the dresser out into the main room.

She lies down on one of the beds for a moment. One never misses the pleasures of a real bed, and this one is nice. She takes deep breaths as she lays and empties her mind of thoughts. Then she arises. Time to head to New Era Valley.

She slides on her boots and opens the door. Elber Gruber is a dozen feet away, loping forward like a not-so-great ape up the path. He freezes in his tracks.

"What you want?" Rosa snaps.

"Didn't... didn't mean to startle you, ma'am." He trembles.

"You're the one startled. Even though you sneak on me." Rosa steps closer to him and lowers her voice. "Maybe

I tell your *mama* you are *miron?* Window peeper?"

"No!" He shakes his big head vigorously. "I wanted to tell you...if you need anything, let me know. My name is Elber."

"I don't need a thing, and you told me your stupid name last time I was here."

His eyes do the up and down, as blatantly as a North End drunk. A hoarse voice calls his name.

"*Vamos*. Papa calling you, little boy."

"Elber," his voice rasps out. "Come help with these feedbags!"

Rosa watches Elber scurry away as she strolls down casually to the hitching post near the front door. Rusty throws his head back and whinnies. Rosa pats his head and releases his tethers. She climbs up and sets off to New Era Valley.

Chapter 21

The curtains of sleep curdle away, and Lindy Sue awakens in an armchair and remembers the three women. She hopes it was a bad nightmare. “Where am I?”

“She’s waking, Varla.”

Fear fills Lindy Sue as she realizes she can’t move her arms. Her hands are tied behind her back and her ankles are tied to the front feet of the armchair, leaving her legs spread. They are in the ranch house, and Blondie sits on the couch in front of her.

“Untie me! You can’t treat me this way.”

“Don’t want you to hurt yourself,” Blondie tells her.

“Help!” Lindy Sue screams at the top of her lungs. “Help me! Help!”

“Yell until you puke, Cupcake. There’s no one for miles around, nobody to hear you.” Varla is out of view behind Lindy Sue, but she knows it’s her.

“We won’t hurt you, Lindy Sue,” Blondie says. “It was all a bad accident. We want to get you home.”

“It wasn’t an accident. She killed Tommy!”

Varla appears in front of her. “It was an accident.” Varla has a pipe in her hand. She drops the match on the floor and sucks on the pipe. An odd smell, sweet and pungent, not tobacco.

“You killed him! You...”

Varla grabs Lindy Sue’s lower face in her hand as she continues to draw from the pipe. Lindy Sue tries to scream again as she struggles against the hand. Varla leans into Lindy Sue. The hand is too strong on her, then fingers squeeze on her cheeks to force her lips open. Varla puts her lips to Lindy Sue’s.

She blows smoke into Lindy Sue, so much smoke until Lindy Sue feels herself convulse, and her lungs twist inside her from the smoke. Varla releases her. Lindy Sue coughs out the smoke, gasping for air.

"Are you trying to kill me?"

Blondie shakes her head, but her mouth is shut as she mumbles something and leans her face down to Lindy Sue. Lindy Sue opens her mouth to speak, but Blondie puts her mouth over Lindy Sue's mouth. More smoke, less than before, but Lindy Sue coughs again.

"We won't hurt you, Lindy Sue," Blondie says. "Don't you feel a bit better?"

"No!" Lindy Sue squirms in the chair to get free. Her head becomes dizzy, and the room begins to swim and swirl around her, the objects unfamiliar, the face of Blondie in front of her distorted. "My head. What are you..." Even words seem weird as they fall from her mouth. All at once a word pops into her head. Opium. She's heard her father and his peers talk about it, the uses and misuses, how it distorts the perception of reality.

Lindy Sue's reflection in Blondie's blue eyes looks back out at her, and Lindy Sue imagines she's become tiny, trapped in an eye and looking out at an expanding world. She shuts her eyes to stop the dizziness. She starts to float in the room, even as the bindings tug at her wrists and ankles.

"Feels nice, doesn't it, Lindy Sue?" a voice whispers in her ear.

She can't say the feeling is all that unpleasant, almost enough to lull the fear. She realizes how exposed she is, with her hands behind her back and her ankles lashed to the legs of the chair. A shadow falls over her. She opens her eyes. Varla's face fills her vision.

"Look at me," Varla says. Legs straddling the chair, Varla crouches over Lindy Sue.

"No!" Lindy Sue twists her head to the side. Blondie watches from the corner of the room a dozen feet away. A hand clasps at Lindy Sue's head and twists her to face Varla.

Why is she staring at me like that? Varla's eyes are two dark points that pierce into her, throbbing into her own eyes. In spite of her fear, and maybe because of the weirdness in her head from the smoke, Lindy Sue is reminded of when she and Maggie Mitchell would look into each other's eyes, heads close together, though this woman's eyes, nothing like Maggie's, are large and almond-shaped, with tiny wrinkles at the inner corners.

Lindy Sue shuts her eyes, but the eyes linger in front of her in the swirl of darkness and colors. She opens her eyes. The hands are no longer on her face, and though she can turn away, she stares at her captor.

Lindy Sue becomes aware again of the leather straps on her ankles and wrists, a minor shock that she has forgotten for a moment where she is. "Untie me!"

Varla straightens up and steps away. Lindy Sue turns to Blondie, still at the edge of the small parlor. "Please, untie me."

"Why should we?" Varla says. "We don't want you to run off and hurt yourself."

Blondie steps closer. "We won't hurt you, Buttercup. We're taking you back to your family. Isn't that right, Varla?"

"Of course," Varla replies.

"You need to trust us," Blondie says.

"Then why are you drugging me?"

"For your own good. Calm you down. Don't you feel better?"

"I don't know," Lindy Sue replies, though she realizes she doesn't have the same terror and angst as before. "Was it opium?"

"What's a nice girl like you know about that?" Blondie smiles and steps closer.

"I know about it. It can make people addicts... make them crazy. My dad's treated several of them."

"Your dad's a doctor?" Blondie pulls up a stool and sits down in front of Lindy Sue.

"That's right. My dad runs the Oregon Hospital for the Insane."

"The one in East Portland?"

"Uh-huh." Lindy Sue nods. "My dad is JC Hawthorne."

"Well isn't that something. You hear that, Varla?"

"So you're a kid of the famous doctor Hawthorne," Varla says.

"That's right," Lindy Sue replies. "If anything happens to me..."

"Nothing'll happen to you, Cupcake. We'll get you home safe." Blondie reaches out and brushes Lindy Sue's hair out of her eyes, the fingers caressing her cheek. Lindy Sue still feels the touch after the hand is withdrawn.

Blondie strides to Varla, in the doorway to the bedroom, where they stand close together and talk in low voices beyond Lindy Sue's hearing. After a few minutes, they vanish beyond the doorway into the small bedroom. Minutes later, Lindy Sue hears the scuffle of clothing, some other faint noises, and soon a rhythmic creaking and some panting and low moans, a loud gasp followed by several seconds of silence, broken by a burst of giggles from Blondie.

Her eyes close, her face hot, her breath quickening in her lungs, Lindy Sue suddenly feels weak to emotions she hasn't felt before. The opium is doing strange things to her head, and she doesn't know what to think of it as she listens to the faint whir of whispers from the other room.

Chapter 22

Blondie lies in Varla's arms on the bed while the bright sun shines through the smudgy window to warm their naked bodies.

"You serious, Varla? You won't hurt her?"

"Course not. Why'd you think that?"

"I don't know. What about Tommy Mitchell?"

"Who?"

"The dead boy out in the pasture. The senator's kid."

"What about him, Blondie?"

"She's a witness. But I suppose you'll use your mind mumbo-jumbo on her too. Make her forget all about it."

"Nothing to forget. It was an accident, Blondie."

"Was it?"

"You saw it. I defended myself. Didn't hit him that hard."

"You sure, Varla?"

"I'd never want to hurt anyone, let alone kill them."

Yeah, right, Blondie thinks with a roll of her eyes. "She doesn't think so."

"She's upset. That's all."

"Yeah, and you'll get inside her head and convince her everything is good."

"Everything will be. Once we get her back to her dad. Hawthorne, that guy is raking it in with that nuthouse. Think of what a guy like that will pay to have his daughter back."

Blondie nods. "At least there's that. So far this trip's been a bust."

"Listen, Blondie. The girl, I think she's cottoned to you. Keep talking to her. Find out more who she is. Her father. Her family."

"But can't you get that out of her?"

“I can. But better you get it from her willingly.”

“So you do have an ounce of kindness in you, Varla.” Blondie grins.

“Don’t push it,” Varla replies. “Kindness is for suckers.”

Chapter 23

Words she can't understand whisper into Lindy Sue's head. The words are soothing, seductive, lulling. She opens her eyes, confused where she is. Tied to an armchair at the ranch house. Varla's face is in front of her. Varla's eyes stare at her with an intensity as if penetrating into her head. Varla continues to utter words in a low tone, unintelligible sounds barely heard.

"Are you trying to hypnotize me?" Lindy Sue asks.

"Hypnotize you? Why do you think that?"

"You are, aren't you?" Lindy Sue glares at Varla.

"You learn about that from the famous doctor?"

"Yes. Are you?"

"No." Varla smiles. "Nothing of the sort."

"You are, aren't you? It won't work. It only works if the subject allows it to work. It won't if the subject refuses to comply."

"The famous doctor teach you that?" Varla asks.

"I heard him say it a couple times."

"Not true. Not that it matters. I'm not trying to hypnotize you."

"Then why were you whispering things in my ear? Why are you staring at me like that?"

"No reason. Make sure you're okay."

"Okay? How can I when you murdered Tommy."

"We told you, it was an accident."

"I don't believe it."

"Doesn't matter what you believe. It's the truth."

"Where is the other one? Blondie?"

"I'm right here, Cupcake," says a voice behind Lindy Sue.

Chapter 24

Later, someone puts a canteen to Lindy Sue's lips, cold water that soothes away the dusty dryness in her mouth, and fingers feed her bits of food, small pieces of meat and bread, which she chews and swallows, while the next piece hovers patiently in front of her, from Blondie's un-gloved hand.

Then they are outside, in the dark. She's lying on the porch of the ranch house. Several horses are beyond the steps, barely visible in the light of the half-moon.

"Ready to ride," Varla says. "We'll bring her mare too."

"What about the appaloosa?" Blondie asks. "I'd love to try that big guy."

"Rare horse like that, too many questions. We leave him here."

Hands grab at Lindy Sue. She's pushed atop a horse, a bigger one than Annabelle, and her hands are around the chest of the rider in front of her, her wrists bound together. A piece of sour cloth is stuck in her mouth so she can't scream. The side of her face slaps lightly against the leather collar of the vest with the horse's movement. Another rider is to her side, the Mexican, Rosa.

The night is cool. Despite her discomfort, Lindy Sue drifts in and out of sleep. An hour or two passes before the horses stop.

"Here we are," Rosa says.

"Now to get this one inside. Blondie, you stable the horses."

A yank at Lindy Sue's arms and the rope comes off her wrists, but as quickly, she's yanked off the large horse, and her hands are bound behind her again. She's pushed forward, almost stumbling but kept upright by the strong arms of the person behind her. A cabin in front of her, she thinks it might be one at Gruber's Outpost. Rosa unlocks the door and enters.

Lindy Sue is manhandled through the cabin door, across the floor, and into one of the beds.

PART III: GRUBER'S OUTPOST

Chapter 25

New Era Valley, a two-hour ride southwest of Gruber's Outpost, is a smattering of small wood houses and a few tents on a hillside in a half circle around a large yellow-painted grange. As Willard Stark and Derry Flanders on horseback enter the town, a dozen men and women stand in the path, alerted to their arrival.

A tall spry man with a thick white beard strides out in front of the others and holds up a hand. "Whoa, there!" he calls when Willard and Derry are a few horse-lengths away.

The Pinkertons rein their mounts.

The old man takes another step closer. Derry glances around at the faces looking at him, men and women of various ages in breeches and cotton shirts.

"What brings the Pinkerton Detective Agency to our community?" the old man asks.

"We're looking for a missing girl," Willard replies. "We'd like to ask around, if anyone of y'all has seen her."

"I'm the Elder here. You can ask me."

Willard pulls the drawing from his vest pocket, unfolds it, and holds it out for the old man and the others. "Her name is Bethany Tremain. Last seen at Grubers."

The Elder steps closer and leans forward, squinting at the image. "She's not been here. How long missing?"

"Since late March," Willard replies. "Perhaps we can ask the others?"

In unison, the other town folk approach. Willard's horse gives a nervous whinny, and Derry feels a moment of dread, but the villagers merely fan around the old man, their eyes on the drawing of Bethany Tremain.

"Have any seen this woman?" the old man asks.

A chorus of "No," and shaking heads.

"She's not been here. Good luck in your search."

"What about the other two settlements, south of here?"

The old man shakes his head. "They're part of our community. We'd know if this woman had shown up. We can save you unnecessary travel."

Continuing to hold up the drawing, Willard scans the crowd. Derry does too, pausing at the face of one young woman, and another, but none resemble Bethany Tremain.

"Anyone?" Willard asks again.

"If we learn anything new, we know where to find you, Pinkerton man." The old man and the others continue to block the pathway.

With a sigh, Willard folds up the drawing and tucks it back into his vest pocket. He lowers his voice. "No more to do here, Derry. Let's get." He reins his horse around and starts toward the outpost at a trot.

Derry follows.

"Glad to be away from there," Willard mutters as they ride side by side. "Can't trust a word of that old dodder. Keep your eyes peeled, the field ahead for our girl."

The trail passes a cropland where several men and women work in the fields. As they near, Derry hears singing, a harmony of voices rise and fall in layers. The sound is mesmerizing and uplifting. He's thankful that Willard slows the pace as they pass. Willard scowls as he scans the workers, then gets his horse moving at a quicker trot. The singing fades behind them, replaced by birdsong and insect drone.

"Didn't think we'd get anything out of that cult," Willard remarks. "And that horrible racket they were making back there. Worse than the slaves back in the good old days."

Chapter 26

As Derry and Willard leave the farmlands behind, a rider appears on the road in front of them, riding toward them at a good clip, horse hooves kicking up dust. Derry moves behind Willard to leave space for the rider to pass. At first he thinks it's a man with the brimmed hat, but past Willard's shoulder, as the rider gets closer, he realizes his mistake, a dark-skinned, dark-eyed woman. In a flash, she's past them and heading toward New Era Valley, but the brief glimpse of her face sparks Derry's memory.

"Mexican whore," Willard mutters.

"Think I seen her before," Derry says. He's abreast with Willard again. "In the North End. The morning Jimmy was stabbed."

"How would you know?" Willard grunts. "They all look alike. You're imagining things, kid. Need to get over what happened to your friend. You could use a good war, to make a man out of you. Stop acting like a kid."

Maybe Willard is right. He only caught a glimpse of the woman as she rode by. Still, he can't shake it from his head.

Many hours later, returned from New Era Valley, they eat large bowls of beef stew and drink beers at Gruber's Outpost. Darkness falls and the chirruping of night insects rises.

Willard yawns and pushes his mug and plate away. "I'm tuckered. About time for bed, I reckon."

Derry pulls out a stunted carrot from his vest pocket. "Reckon I'll check on Sir Galahad."

"That horse?" Willard rolls his eyes. "Don't know why you call it that silly name. A horse is a horse. A dumb brute."

"I've had him since he was a colt."

"But the name." Willard shakes his head.

"It's from King Arthur."

"I know that." Willard scoffs. "But why paste that name to a horse?"

Derry shrugs. He can't tell Willard how, as a youth, he and Sir Galahad pretended to be knights, riding around on adventures. Those memories, riding a horse and also pretending the horse was another knight, seem silly now.

Derry steps outside. The night is clear. The stars and a sliver of moon create enough light to navigate the trail to the stables. An owl calls out in the distance, and a cool breeze rustles past him.

As he reaches the stable doorway, he almost bumps into someone leaving. He steps back. "Excuse me, sir."

"I'm no sir." She steps out into the starlight, a shapely woman in a gambler hat, almost as tall as Derry.

"Sorry about that, ma'am."

"You don't have to ma'am me neither." She brings up a hand. "The name's Blondie." A large smile on her face, she looks directly into his eyes.

Derry reaches up his hand, realizes he still has the carrot in it, and grabs the carrot with the other hand before shaking. "Yes, ma'am, I mean, Blondie." Her hand is firm in his. "I'm Derry. Derry Flanders."

"Nice to meet you, Dairy Philanderer. Why they call you that? You like squeezing cow udders with those nice hands?"

"Flanders," he says, unsure if she's insulting him, not that he cares. His heart is pounding faster, and the heat rises up through his body as he takes her in.

"You going for a late-night ride?" she asks.

"No. Just feeding my horse a treat." He holds up the carrot.

"What a sweet boy you are." The woman steps back and gives Derry the up-and-down with her eyes. "Maybe I'll see you around, Derry Philanderer." She reaches out and pinches his arm below the sleeve of his shirt as she strolls past.

Derry turns. The woman's hips sway provocatively as she saunters away. He rubs his hands over his eyes, to make sure he hasn't imagined her, but her silhouette is there, an alluring shadow on the path before she vanishes around the corner of the outpost building, and he can still feel where her fingers pinched.

Derry scurries into the stable. Wait until I tell Sir Galahad about this. He replays her words in his head: "Maybe I'll see you around, Derry Flanders."

Chapter 27

Derry Flanders? The name rings familiar to Blondie as she heads back to cabin seven, but she can't think of where. A nice-looking lad, this Derry Flanders, and like any man or woman she finds attractive, Blondie imagines holding him in her arms, pulling off his clothes to have her way with him. He looks like the type that would let her lead.

She says nothing of the encounter to Rosa or Varla. Rosa plays a tune on the mouth harp while Varla takes a few puffs of ganja. Lindy Sue is asleep on one of the beds. When the candles are snuffed, Varla settles into the bed with the girl while Blondie shares the other with Rosa. Lying in bed, thinking about Derry Flanders, she still puzzles over where she heard that name.

Next morning, awakening to sunlight poking through the top of the curtains, the name comes to her. The newspaper article about the murdered boy in the North End. Derry Flanders, one of the boys mentioned in the article who last saw their friend before he was murdered.

Chapter 28

Varla and Rosa drink their morning coffee at a table in the corner of the outpost's dining area. The room is mostly empty, a group of cowboys at one table, a family of six at another, muted murmurs of half-awake conversation muffled by the thick odor and sizzle of frying bacon.

"What's eating you?" Varla asks.

Rosa shakes her head. "Nothing's eating me. Why the girl give you so much trouble?"

Varla lowers her voice. "I don't know. Maybe her dad, the big psychiatrist, did something to her. I just need more time."

"I don't like this. Safer we leave her at the ranch. Now she our problem. Better if we..." Rosa indicates a finger across her throat.

Varla scoffs. "Dead, she's worthless."

"Every day we have her, one more day to be caught."

"One more day. That's all. We go back tomorrow. By then I'll be in her head."

"I hope so." Rosa's not so sure. *Maybe Varla's losing her touch*, she thinks, unsure if Varla can read her, as Varla gazes into her eyes. Varla looks up and waves to someone in the doorway. Althea, from New Era Valley waves back as she walks to the counter. She sits with them to catch up on news.

"I need more coffee." Varla abruptly stands and walks to the counter with her cup.

Behind the counter, Ma Gruber grabs the cup and paces to the pot of coffee grounds boiling on the stove. Varla hears footsteps coming down the stairs. The man at the bottom of the steps stares at her. He's in his late forties, a mean face, pinched at the corners of the mouth and eyes. A small round pin on his lapel has the letters "CS." Not taking her eyes off him, Varla reaches behind her, feeling for the coffee cup that she's heard land on the counter.

He frowns. "Stop staring at me."

She snorts contemptuously and walks to her table. Glaring at her, Rosa, and Althea, the man shakes his head and steps to the counter to order breakfast.

"Who your *amigo*, Varla?" Rosa asks quietly.

"Racist piece of shit. I see it in his eyes."

"And that pin on his shirt. One of those." Rosa makes a face.

"Lost the war but won't admit it," Althea adds.

"Long time before this country is rid of that scum," Varla says. "Maybe it will never be."

The man glares at them again as he takes his breakfast tray and walks to the stairs up to the rooms.

"That's the Pinkerton I told you about," Althea says. "I didn't like him yesterday, and even less today."

Varla and Rosa finish their meals. They go up to the counter to order two more breakfasts. "We're checking on our horses, and we'll be back in ten minutes to pick them up," Varla tells Ma Gruber before she and Rosa saunter out of the outpost and head to the stables.

Chapter 29

In the cabin, Blondie watches Lindy Sue awaken. The girl is slightly less anxious than the night before, her head is still cloudy from the dope, but the fear remains. Hands bound behind her back, she struggles to sit up and face Blondie seated on the other bed.

"Morning, Buttercup. You sleep okay?" Blondie asks.

"My wrists. They hurt. Can you untie them?" Lindy Sue's eyes are teary.

Blondie shakes her head. "Not yet."

"Are they really taking me home?" Lindy Sue asks.

"Of course we are. You mustn't worry, Cupcake."

"But she killed Tommy. She's a monster."

"It was an accident."

"An accident? No." Lindy Sue shakes her head.

"You're confused," Blondie says.

Lindy Sue pinches up her face. "I don't think so."

Blondie rises and walks to the dresser. She pulls from a small round tin one of the joints Rosa rolled earlier, and snatches the matches off the dresser top.

She turns. Lindy Sue stares at her, lips quivering.

"Are we going back today?"

Blondie shakes her head. "Don't think so, Buttercup. Tomorrow."

"Why not today?"

"You need to ask Varla."

Lindy Sue shakes her head.

"She didn't mean to hurt him," Blondie says. "And we won't hurt you."

"Are you sure?"

"Yes." Blondie lights the reef, crossing the room to Lindy Sue.

"What are you..." Lindy Sue begins to shake. "Is that opium?"

Blondie shakes her head, breathing out a wisp of smoke. "Nope. Ganja. Cannabis." She takes another draw from the stick.

"You don't have to drug me, Blondie," Lindy Sue pleads. "I'll behave."

Blondie exhales the smoke into the girl's face. "It'll make you feel good."

"I don't want to feel good. I want to go home."

"It's not as strong as dope," Blondie says. "I bet your smart dad knows facts like that. He's probably experimented with both dope and ganja. It won't hurt you."

Lindy Sue leans closer, voice just above a whisper. "Listen, Blondie. Why don't you untie me and take me home. Leave the others behind. That way you won't have to split the reward my dad will pay for my return."

Blondie blows out another puff of smoke between them. When Lindy Sue's face reemerges, Blondie leans closer. "That's cute, Buttercup. But I can't cut on my friends."

"Why not? You really trust them?"

"Of course. Know them better than you do." Blondie puts her hand on Lindy Sue's shoulder. "This will clear your head from the other."

Alarmed, mouth agape, Lindy Sue stares at her. Blondie brings the lit joint between them, takes another hit, and crouches in front of Lindy Sue, her hand at the back of Lindy Sue's head as she holds the thin reefer in the other hand. Lindy Sue barely struggles, for which Blondie is thankful, while Blondie hovers over her mouth and blows smoke into it.

Lindy Sue coughs out the smoke. "Are they making you do this?"

"No. For your own good. Trust me, Cupcake."

Blondie takes another drag, their faces inches apart.

This time Lindy Sue doesn't cough as much. Blondie tamps out the cannabis cigarette on the small table near the bed.

"Don't you feel better?" Blondie pulls a wooden chair to the bed to face Lindy Sue.

Lindy Sue shrugs. "I don't know. I want to get home."

"Tomorrow."

"Can I tell you something?" Lindy Sue asks.

"Uh-huh."

"And you won't tell the others?"

Blondie smiles. "A secret. Of course you can, Lindy Sue."

"What if my dad doesn't pay?"

"Of course he'll pay. Why wouldn't he?"

"But what if he doesn't?" Worry crosses Lindy Sue's face.

"Don't be silly." Blondie brushes her fingers through the girl's hair. "Your parents love you, don't they?"

"My dad does. My stepmother..." Lindy Sue's voice cracks.

"Stepmother?"

"My mother died when I was born."

"You poor child." Blondie leans over, puts her arms around Lindy Sue, and hugs her. "I lost my mother when I was five."

"My stepmother, she handles the money," Lindy Sue says. "What if she...what if she won't..."

"They'll give us some sort of reward, won't they?" Blondie straightens in the chair. Lindy Sue has tears on her cheeks.

"I don't know," Lindy Sue chokes out. "She said if I got into trouble, don't come back to them. She hates me."

"Don't worry, Cupcake. Everything'll be fine."

"Your friends... They won't get mad and...and hurt me?"

"No. No one wants to hurt you. I'll make sure you get home safely."

"You will?"

"Yes."

"You promise?"

"Yes, Buttercup." Blondie plucks a yellow hanky from the breast pocket of her nightgown. "Now let's dry those eyes." She lightly brushes the cloth across Lindy Sue's face, one cheek and the other. Lindy Sue's father will pay them good money for the girl's return. But what if he doesn't? Varla and Rosa will be pissed. No telling what...

Blondie doesn't want to think about that. She relights the cannabis cigarette. She breathes the smoke into her lungs, and waits a moment, relishing the high, before leaning toward Lindy Sue.

This time they touch lips and the girl trembles, but yields to Blondie blowing smoke deep into her throat.

The girl arches her head up to press her lips into Blondie's. Something fleshy slides into Blondie's mouth and brushes against her tongue. Blondie freezes and pulls away.

"Whoa, Lindy Sue! What was that?"

Lindy Sue's face is red, her eyes wide. "Will you untie my hands? Please? We can leave before they return?"

"No, Lindy Sue." Blondie shakes her head.

The dropped reefer is on the floor, flame dead. She considers giving Lindy Sue another dose, but the thought of Lindy Sue's tongue lingers in her mouth and her head. Was Lindy Sue trying to tongue kiss her? Where did she get that from? Had Varla tongued her during the night, quietly, while Blondie and Rosa slept?

Blondie picks up the remains of the joint and strolls to the dresser to put it in the tin. She turns to Lindy Sue. Brief as it was, Blondie can't get the kiss out of her head.

Chapter 30

Her head jumbled from the drugs, Lindy Sue stares at Blondie in front of the dresser across the room. The sun through the top of the shades hits the wall behind Blondie in the shape of a scimitar. Blondie moves to glance out the top of the window. She turns and strides toward Lindy Sue and sits on the bed facing her. She nudges Lindy Sue's foot.

"You mustn't do that again, Lindy Sue."

"Do what again?" Lindy Sue asks, looking at her feet.

Blondie grabs her chin and pulls her face up so they are eye to eye. "You tried to kiss me, Buttercup."

Lindy Sue hadn't known what came over her, to do it. She feels shame as if she had given away something, exposed something secret inside her. She wants to blame it on the drugs, waking up still dizzy from the dope. She hadn't meant to do it, not until the last second, when she dared herself, remembering those few times with Maggie.

"You were kissing me, Blondie."

"Not like that!" Blondie has a look of mock horror on her face.

"You didn't like it?" Lindy Sue blurts out, confused.

"That's not the point, Buttercup. It's wrong."

"At the cabin, you kissed the other one, Varla."

Blondie leans closer. "What of it? Did she kiss you?"

"Me?" Lindy Sue trembles at the memory of Varla's leering face looming above hers. "Of course not. Not like that! I hate her!" But can she be sure in her drug-induced state? The thought sends tremors of fear and revulsion through her body. She instinctively reaches to wipe off her mouth, forgetting her hands are tied behind her back. "Can you untie me? Please." She presses her foot into Blondie's.

Blondie shakes her head. “You’re a smart girl, Buttercup. Maybe too smart for your own gander. You kiss other girls, Buttercup?”

Lindy Sue vigorously shakes her head. “No.” Even to herself, this sounds feeble.

“You can tell me, Cupcake,” Blondie says, nestling her foot on Lindy Sue’s smaller one. “Who’ve you kissed like that?”

“Tommy,” Lindy Sue offers. Speaking his name, memory floods into her head. Tommy. Tommy lying in the dirt at the ranch. It hits her out of nowhere. She’s shocked she forgot about him, after the other one, Varla... She can’t believe he’s dead. Maybe he was merely knocked out. They didn’t know, none of them are doctors. If she and Blondie can find a doctor...

“What if Tommy’s still alive?” Lindy Sue looks at Blondie pleadingly. “Let’s go to him. Untie me and we’ll go together, Blondie.”

Blondie shakes her head.

Hopelessness overwhelms Lindy Sue. She sobs.

“Don’t cry.” Blondie leans over to put her hands on Lindy Sue’s cheeks to rub the tears off with her fingers. Lindy Sue gazes at the marvel of Blondie’s chest, barely concealed beyond the diaphanous nightwear.

“Why were you kissing her?” Lindy Sue asks.

“Who? Varla?”

“Is she your girlfriend?”

Blondie shrugs. “It’s complicated.”

“I don’t know if I can stand another minute with them. Varla and Rosa. I hate both of them.”

“Listen, Cupcake. You’ll be home soon. All this will be sockdolager to tell your friends.”

“I hope so.”

They hear yells from the direction of the Outpost and loud female laughter. Blondie rises and peers through the crack above the curtain before returning to Lindy Sue.

"Behave, Cupcake. Everything'll be a hunk of dory. I like you. I'll miss you after we get you home."

"I like you too, Blondie."

"Now hush!"

The door bursts open. Varla and Rosa pile in, Varla with a coffee pot and two cups and Rosa with two plates of eggs, griddlecakes, and bacon. They both glance at Lindy Sue, and she glares daggers back at them. Rosa strides toward her with one of the plates.

"Look at the crybaby. Poor little spoiled *princesa*, crying her eyes out. Here's your food, *princesita*."

"I don't want it!" Lindy Sue head-butts the plate with a lurch forward, her cheek hits an edge, knocking it from Rosa's hand. The plate clatters upside down on the floor.

"Look what she did," Rosa says. "Now she eat off the floor like dog." A huge smirk erupts on Rosa's face.

"No she doesn't! Don't be mean, Rosa," Blondie snaps.

Varla laughs. "Rosa's just rattling you, Goldilocks. Blondie'll go down and get you another plate of food, won't you, Blondie?"

Blondie nods, about to take a forkful of griddlecake. "As soon as I eat."

Lindy Sue sucks on her upper lip, trying to push back the fear, watching Blondie devour the food and knowing Blondie will soon leave her alone with the other two.

Chapter 31

One week earlier, Elber Gruber was cleaning the storehouse behind the outpost, pulling cans and boxes with faded labels off shelves. A yellowed piece of newspaper fell on the dirt floor. Picking it up, his eye caught an article. “Man wins...” a big word, “...from a train accident.”

Elber put the paper to his face and read as much as he’s able. “Look at this, Pa,” he called out to his father, at the other end of the storeroom, rearranging large jars.

“Back to work, Elber.”

“I think this is about Old Man Pitts.” Elber shuffled closer to his dad.

Elber’s pa looked up. “What’s that you got?”

“Did old man Pitts get a bunch of money for that train accident? When he lost his legs?”

“That was years ago, Elber. Best not think of it. We keeps our noses out of the affairs of others.”

“Don’t make no sense. All that money and him living that way.”

“Hush, Elber.” The older man yanked the yellowed newspaper from Elber’s fingers, crumpled it into a ball, and stuffed it into his apron pocket. “Put those things out of your head before you make trouble, Elber Gruber.”

But Elber can’t put it out of his head. Old Man Pitts, condemned to a wheelchair, and his monstrous brute of a son Butch, alone on a rundown ranch. The tragedies that surrounded that family, his wife dying giving birth, the huge son a mental handicap, and then the train accident years later that left Old Man Pitts crippled. Every Sunday Old Man Pitts and his son rode into the Outpost to pick up supplies.

Elber learned of the train accident, several years ago,

but not about any money from the railroad to make it right. But where was the money? Pitts's ranch was run down.

A memory came back into Elber's head from many years ago. He and his pa in front of the Pitts house, delivering some bags of feed. Pitts in his wheelchair, talking to Pa while Elber unloaded the heavy sacks from the Outpost wagon and brought them to the porch.

Suddenly Old Man Pitts's voice rose in anger. "Damn savings and loans! Don't tell me about the damn banks, Horace! Don't trust those crooks as far as I can piss."

Riding back to the Outpost with Pa, Elber had wondered about the outburst. Why would his pa tell the dirt-poor Pitts about savings and loans? Even Elber knew about cold hard cash. He didn't ask Pa, and Pa offered nothing, his mouth buttoned tight, the wrinkles around the lips that are now, seven years later, more permanently etched in pa's face, even at those rare moments when he tries to smile.

As he walks from the stables, Elber wonders about the money again. It takes his mind off the harsh tongue-lashing he received from the two women from Cabin Seven as they carried plates of food back to the cabin. He only offered to help, and they had taken it the wrong way. He can't even remember what they said, just the mean laughter and humiliation.

The money must be out there on that ranch, buried somewhere. He cannot get it out of his head. He knows he mustn't say anything about it. He almost blabbed it to the Pinkertons last night as they looked over their maps when they mentioned the Pitts ranch.

Elber looks into the dining area. A woman at the bar talks to Pa. She's tall and shapely, like the other two from earlier, but she has waves of blond hair flowing out beneath the wide brim of her cowboy hat.

Elber steps away, out of view of his pa. A peek through a window reveals the woman still at the counter. She hasn't sat down, which means she'll soon come back through the door, or so Elber figures.

Another glance through the window, his father at the bar hands the woman something. As she emerges through the door, Elber calls out. "Howdy, there."

"Howdy." She glances at him. "You must be El-burp Goober."

"I am." Giving her his most charming smile, he takes a bow. "Elber Gruber at your service. If you need anything—"

"I don't need anything. I heard what a pest you are."

"Your friends?" He starts to follow her toward the cabins. "Are you with those two women? Cabin Seven?"

She pirouettes. He freezes in his tracks. He can't help himself, ogling the curves of her body, the swell of her breasts beneath the buttoned-to-the-neck blouse, and her hips in a dress that reveals her knees.

"Are you following me, El-barf Goober?"

"How many of you up there?" He takes a step and points at the plate of food. "Other two ate and already brought food up. Two more plates."

"Maybe we got a big guy up there with us. Big guy with a big appetite, and he wouldn't cotton me talking to a jimber-jawed pokey like you, Elbert Goof-off." A look of utter contempt crosses her face.

"Big guy? It's not Butch Pitts, is it?"

"Who's that?"

"Butch Pitts. Comes here every Sunday with his pa."

"No. This guy is bigger than Botch Piss, so stay away from Cabin Seven for the next few days, Elbert Boober."

"Bigger than Butch Pitts?" Elber doesn't think it's possible.

"Now shoo. Mommy's calling you, little boy." She turns and sways up the path. Watching her, Elber wants to follow, but his pa is in fact yelling for him. He takes one last leer, slapping his tongue on his lips and rubbing his groin before slinking back to the dining area.

Chapter 32

Waiting at the bar for breakfast, Derry Flanders glances around the dark interior of the dining area of Gruber's Outpost. A woman sits at a table, and drinks coffee by herself. Her hair is tucked into her bonnet, only a few wisps frame her freckled face. She is reading a newspaper. He recognizes her from New Era Valley.

He takes his plate and sits next table over. She glances up. *She's only a few years older than me*, he thinks.

"Hello, there, Pinkerton."

"Name's Derry Flanders, ma'am."

"You can call me Althea. Mind if I sit with you?"

He shakes his head. "Not at all, ma'am."

"Call me Althea, Derry." With coffee and her newspaper, she settles into a seat across from him, studying him.

He glances around the mostly empty room. Old Lady Gruber is behind the bar, wiping some glasses with a rag, ignoring them.

"You're from New Era Valley," he says.

"Yeah?" She smirks. "Saw you yesterday with your friend."

"Willard? He's my boss."

"So what's his intentions?" Althea asks. "Is he satisfied New Era has nothing more to do with his affairs?"

Derry thinks for a moment. "I reckon so."

"It's not like we have anything to hide, Derry, but sometimes outsiders get wrong impressions, start spreading vicious rumors."

"That's not good." He takes a bite of the griddle cake, chewing as he talks. "And that's not our intention, not in the least."

"How long you been a Pinker?" she asks.

"Only a couple months. I'm still training."

"You know, Derry, if you've nothing to do, come back down. Alone, not as a Pinky."

"Huh?"

"I'm headed back this morning. Come with me, just a day. See if you like it there."

"Don't know about that. I thought you didn't like visitors."

"Not ones who question our ways. But I don't feel that way about you."

"I don't know. Willard thinks—"

"Who cares what Willard thinks, Derry. Think for yourself. What do you want?"

Gazing at her, Derry remembers the people harmonizing and laughing as they worked in the field and Willard's harsh assessment of them. At the sound of boots clattering on the stairs, Derry turns. Willard reaches the bottom step and pauses to look over the room. He paces quickly toward Derry.

"Maybe I should leave?" Althea begins to rise.

"You don't have to go." Derry enjoys her pretty face and talking to her.

As she stands, Willard looms over the table. "What the hell! You!" Willard grabs Althea by the shoulders and shoves her hard. Althea propelled backward knocks over a couple chairs and falls on the floor. "I ought to break your jaw!" Willard growls.

"Hey! You! No fighting!" The cock of a rifle. Mrs. Gruber has pulled a long gun out from under the bar and has it pointed at Willard Stark. She gestures her head at the sign above the bar. "We run a peaceful establishment."

Willard opens his hands, puts them out to his sides. "Right you are, ma'am. Didn't mean to get so angry, but you understand. Young impressionable lad around these cultists. You would not let your son cavort with them, except to conduct business."

"I'm not your son," Derry says to Willard.

"No, but I'm responsible for you. We'll eat breakfast in our room."

"That's a good idea." The old woman still has the rifle, though no longer aimed at Willard. "You two get upstairs, and you, young lady," she turns to Althea, getting off the floor, "I believe you've finished breakfast and were on your way out the door."

Reluctantly Derry grabs his plate and follows Willard upstairs, and down the narrow corridor to their room. Willard takes the one armchair and Derry sits on the edge of his bed.

"Told you yesterday, Derry, stay away from those socialist heathens."

"You didn't tell me."

"Telling you now," Willard says between bites of griddle cake, crumbs dribbling down his scraggly beard. "Can't trust them as far as you can spit."

Derry bites a piece of egg off his fork. "So what're the plans today? The Pitts ranch?"

"Another couple days for that," Willard says. "We sit tight, that's all."

"What we waiting for?"

"Couple of friends of mine. Emmett and Crawford. Fought with me in the war. They're now bounty hunters. They'll be here day after tomorrow."

"I don't know why we need them, Willard."

"For this side thing, got to have some real men...know how to handle a tough situation, like Emmett and Crawford."

"To help us find Bethany Tremain?"

"No. A thing on the side I been hinting at."

"At Pitts Ranch."

"That's right, Derry."

"I wish you'd tell me the whole thing."

"I'll tell you when we're ready. For now—"

They both hear a loud voice from outside, followed by laughter. Curious, Derry leans over to the window. He barely sees the people below, beyond the edge of the eaves, Elber talking to a pair of men, no, women wearing men's cowboy hats. They walk away from Elber, beyond the view from the window, their faces caught in profile a split second, enough to jar Derry's memory. The voice, the laughter, the black leather vest and pants, the way she strode calmly away, the woman's face... could it be the same woman who argued with Bobby and Jimmy before Jimmy was stabbed?

And the other one with her, the same woman that rode past them outside New Era Valley the day before, who was also there that morning of the stabbing.

Willard glances out another window, and chortles to himself. "That pathetic Elber Gruber. Forty-five years of age and never got his dick wet. You done?"

"Almost." Derry lifts his plate to scrape the last scraps of food into his mouth and sets the plate next to him on the bed.

"Let's head to Nancy's." Willard sits on the bed across from Derry's and begins to yank on his vest.

"I don't feel like it," Derry says. "Reckon I'd stay here, do some reading." He indicates the three books he borrowed from the shelves at one side of the dining room.

"Something on your mind, son?"

Derry shakes his head.

"If you're thinking of talking up that New Era wench, or those other ones, forget it. Stay away from those people."

"Not at all." Derry shakes his head. "I was thinking about Jimmy."

"Your dead friend?"

Derry nods.

"Forget about it." Willard scoffs. "Don't dwell on it."

"Those woman...outside. I think they were there...when it happened."

"When what happened?" Willard stands. "Not making

sense, boy."

"When Jimmy was stabbed. I think they were there."

Willard shakes his head. "Don't be silly, Derry. The mind plays tricks. It happens to me too. The friends I lost in the war. Sometimes I think I see them again. Move on and forget. Come to Nancy's with me. That'll take your mind off it."

Derry glances at the window and back at Willard. "Think I'll stay here, just the same."

Willard stares at him for a moment. "Suit yourself. Be careful, Derry. You're too young to know what's what." Willard clomps out of the room, his boot-steps fading down the hallway. Derry opens the shade and looks out the window. A couple minutes later he sees Willard ride off toward Nancy's Nunnery, the bordello that has set up a few miles away.

Derry opens up a novel while he finishes his coffee. Looking at the page, he can't think about the words in front of him as he hears the sharp, sarcastic voice in his head, the woman with dark hair and large dark eyes, and the laughter of her and her friend, taking him back to that terrible morning with Jimmy Montgomery and Bobby Lappeus.

He decides to walk around instead. The women must be staying at one of the Outpost cabins. He takes the trail that leads toward some of the cabins, and another trail past the others. He keeps his ears open for the woman's voice, but the air is quiet except for the buzz of insects and the occasional twitter of a bird.

He follows one trail until it joins a main road, the road now familiar as he and Willard had traipsed several times from the Outpost, heading to one place or another to ask about the missing girl, Bethany Tremain.

Late afternoon, he's back at the Outpost dining room, eating chili and drinking lager. He looks up to see Althea, across the room at a table. On a whim, he grabs his plate and walks over to her. "Mind if I sit down?"

“Derry!” She looks alarmed. “What about the big Pinky?”

“He won’t get back until late, I think. I want to say, sorry he did that to you.”

“You don’t need to be sorry. Not your fault, Derry.”

Chapter 33

Late afternoon Blondie enters the dining area and spots the boy at a table in the corner, sitting across from Althea. Blondie suspects she has the wrong Derry Flanders, this one a New Era boy, and not the other, the son of a prominent citizen from Portland. Blondie waves as she approaches their table and slides in next to Althea.

"Althea!" Blondie says. And then to the boy: "Hey, there, Derry Philanderer. Knew I'd see you again."

"You know him?" Althea whispers to her.

"Not in the Biblical sense," Blondie quips. "Least not yet. Met him last night in the stables."

Althea makes a face. "He's a Pinky, Blondie."

"A Pink? That's too bad." *Or not so bad,* Blondie thinks, since he might still be the Derry Flanders from the newspaper story. Rosa said something about the two Pinkies looking for a missing girl, which makes Blondie think of how Lindy Sue is missing too.

Derry Flanders leans over the table. "What you whispering about?"

"Nothing," Blondie tells him. "Old times. I spent a few months at New Era when I meant to stay a week. Is Althea luring you with her charms?"

"He doesn't dare go down, even for the day because it would anger his boss, even though his boss is over at..." Althea jerks a thumb.

"Nancy's?" Blondie smirks. "Why don't you go there and have a good time, Derry?"

He shrugs. "Don't like that place. Wanted a day away from Willard Stark."

"That's okay." She gets up and steps around the table. He begins to stand, too, but she slides into his side so he can't get out.

"I think I'll leave you kids to your own devices." Althea gets to her feet. "Need to get back to the Valley."

"Just you and me, Derry," Blondie says to him. "I want to ask you about something."

He gulps and takes a sip of his beer.

"Your friend. The one that got stabbed in the North End."

"How do you know..." He twists up his face.

"Read about it in the paper, Derry. Horrible thing. It happened a few blocks from where me and some friends were staying."

He looks at the table. "It was terrible."

"If you ever want to talk about it..." She rubs his shoulder.

"Maybe not now."

She wants to hear his version of what happened. Where were Varla and Rosa when the kid got stabbed? But he's too upset right now to talk about it. "Let's talk about something else," she says. "Who's this girl you're looking for?"

"Her name is Bethany Tremain."

"Bethany Tremain? Her poor family. What's her age?"

"Eighteen or nineteen."

"Really? Would she weigh about ninety pounds?"

He nods. "I think so."

"How tall?"

"Five-one."

"Really?" Blondie has a drag in her voice, an increase in urgency as each fact follows the preceding one. "Hmm," she says in thought.

"You know something?" he asks.

"I might." She leans in closer.

"What do you mean?"

"I don't know. Might not be the same girl." Her voice is low, conspiratorial, as she puts her hand on his upper leg.

Chapter 34

The intimacy unsettles Derry Flanders. Blondie shifts in her seat to put her hand on his upper leg. Her face inches away from his, her tongue flicks quickly over her lips while she stares at him. No woman has ever been so forward with him.

"Do you really know about Bethany Tremain?" He tries to hide his nervousness.

"I can't say more, Derry. But if I did, how much is in it for me?"

"What do you mean?" he asks.

"How much is it worth? For the effort? How much money?"

"I get paid by the week." He feels a sense of shame when he says this.

"Barely paid, while your so-called partner, your boss burns the extra money at Nancy's Nunnery." Blondie chuckles. "Use your imagination. Ditch the big Pinky and his Stinkerton Defective Agency. If you brought her home, how much would the family pay?"

"I don't rightly know. They're paying the Pinkerton Company forty a week, and that's not with guaranteed results. Getting her back alive is the bonus, another fifteen for me. Do you really know where she is?"

"Fifteen dollars!" Her mouth contorts in shock. "Is that all? A rich family's daughter?"

"That's just my cut."

"What if you brought her back yourself?" Blondie asks. "You take her right to the guy that's paying the guy that's paying Willard? Think how happy that house will be, you bring back their daughter, you alone the hero and not Willard or the Finkerton Defective Agency taking all the credit?"

"But that would be..." Derry is aghast.

"What's the big Pinky getting from this? A lot more than you."

"I don't know what Willard makes. He won't tell me. Says it's in the Pinkerton Manual of Conduct."

"How much you think he's getting?"

"I've no idea." He feels stupid.

"A guess?" She smiles at him.

Derry takes a stab. "Fifty. Or fifty-five?"

"I happen to know. A lot higher."

Derry frowns. "How would you know that?"

She smiles coyly, says nothing.

He realizes she's been diverting him. "What about Bethany Tremain? What do you know about her?"

"Can't tell you. I know someone who knows someone. If we make a deal."

"I'd have to ask Willard."

"The big Pinky? When he's making a honey a week."

"A hundred? That high?"

She nods. "Maybe more. And his bonus is based on how much he lowers your bonus, so he gives you just enough to make you feel like you're getting something."

"You think so?" He stares at her as they snuggle together, and at the bar, Ma Gruber gives them the stink eye. Blondie takes her hand off of him and slides over on the seat, but her foot begins caressing his ankle beneath the table.

"You trust the big Pinky? Keeping you on peanuts while he whores at Nancy's every day?" She looks at him as if he's totally hopeless.

"Willard...? You really think he'd..." He thinks he should say something to defend his boss. Willard wouldn't cheat him, would he?

"Their precious daughter, Derry." Her face gets serious. "The joy when you deliver her with the help of me and my friends."

"Friends? What friends?"

"A couple friends."

A shadow appears in the doorway. If Willard walked in right now, he'd beckon Willard over, because Willard would know how to proceed, with her and her friends on one side and him and Willard on the other.

But Willard won't be back until late, on an all-day binge of boozing and whoring, and maybe a nap in between, while Eliza Boggs plays her exotic guitar, and a free girl might sing.

Instead, a woman enters, same red shirt and dark brown leather pants, same cattleman hat from the day before when she rode past him to New Era Valley. In silhouette in the doorway, the sun lighting up behind to dim her features, he is not so sure. His nerves flutter and his heart pounds in his chest.

The woman saunters in slowly, relaxed, like a cat. When she's the same distance away as that morning that Jimmy died, Derry realizes she is the same woman. She will know about the other woman who was there when Bobby supposedly stabbed Jimmy. Even with Blondie next to him, her foot rubbing against his knee and calf under the table, he can't stop staring at the woman.

Chapter 35

At the far side of the cabin, hands and feet lashed to a chair, lips pinched, Lindy Sue glares at Varla who is crouched eye level with her.

"How it go with her?" Rosa asks quietly.

Rosa rises from the bed and steps closer. Varla intensifies her stare into the girl's eyes, face contorted for several seconds of concentrated effort, as her hand waves Rosa to back off. All at once the intensity ends. Varla gasps for breath, echoed a moment later by Lindy Sue's fainter gasp. Rosa thinks of the sexual tinge of a near-simultaneous orgasm.

Lindy Sue sags back in the chair, the bonds chafing her arms and legs, her head lolling against the neck collar as she pants for breath. Varla looks at Rosa with a relaxed smile. "Fine. Only a matter of time."

"Didn't look like that." Rosa takes another step closer. "Way she daggered your eyes."

"Don't worry." Varla holds out her hands. "It's under control. Breaking her down."

"Want my help?" Rosa sneers at the girl.

"Sure, Rosa. But you should check on Blondie. Make sure she's not lollygagging into trouble."

Rosa's gaze flashes between Varla and the girl. She shudders as she remembers when Varla first did the mind thing *kanpa-maindo* on her, and then they had sex, the best ever. Now Varla wants to be alone with Lindy Sue. But Rosa can't think about that. Besides Varla is right, Blondie is the loose bolt in the tripod, and a loose bolt is all that's needed for total collapse.

Varla kisses Rosa passionately on the lips and pushes her gently toward the door. Rosa trudges slowly on the pathway to the front door of the outpost. Entering the room, she spots Blondie at a table in the corner seated next to a man. The man turns toward Rosa before she can duck behind a pillar or back out the door. She pretends not to notice him as she saunters to the bar, but she watches him from the corner of her eye before he's out of view behind a pillar. Where'd she seen him before? Rosa leans on the bar, half twisted toward him, his head mostly visible above the end of the bar. He still has his eyes on her.

Elber Gruber comes rushing in from the side door while his father storms out from the kitchen.

"Give me a sarsaparilla, gramps," Rosa says to the elder Gruber.

"Yes, ma'am. Elber! Back to the store!" As Elber's clumsy footsteps recede, the old man leans across the counter and says quietly: "Don't mind him, he's a good boy, but he's still learning, a little slow." Then he turns to bring her the drink.

The glass clinks in front of Rosa. She grabs it and glances again at her server's worry-weary face. It makes her wonder if she'll look like him and his wife if she lives to that age. These poor grubby Grubers, the vitality of life wrung out of them to make them withered shells, eking an existence in this out-of-the-way outpost. She almost feels sorry for them.

"Thank you," she grunts and saunters toward the table. The closer she gets, the more she's convinced. The same kid from that morning in the North End. The one who ran when the other two attacked Varla. Why is he here? And what's Blondie doing with him?

"What you stare at, kid?" Rosa sits down across from him and Blondie. "Not interrupting, am I?"

"Not at all, Rosa." The top few buttons of Blondie's blouse are undone to flaunt herself at the dope. "This here's Derry the Philanderer."

"I remember you," Rosa says. "You and two drunk

friends. *Molesta* innocent women."

"You and Varla, innocent women?" Blondie giggles.

"That wasn't me," Derry blurts. "I tried to get them to stop."

"Too bad one friend stab the other," Rosa says. "*Cuchilada.*"

"That's not what the papers say," Blondie says.

"That what happened. Isn't it, kid?" Rosa leans across the table.

"I don't know," Derry replies nervously.

"You and Varla were there," Blondie says.

Rosa shakes her head. "We walk away. Kids calling us names. We want no trouble."

"Not me," Derry says. "I told them not to."

"So what you say happen, Derry?" Rosa asks.

He shakes his head. "I don't know. But that other woman must know. The one with you?"

Rosa smiles. "You want to ask her?"

Derry gulps.

"Anyway," Blondie breaks in. "Derry's looking for a girl. You have a picture of her, Derry?"

"It's in the room."

"You should see this picture, Rosa. Derry, go get it." Blondie pushes him out of his seat.

Once the kid has departed, Rosa moves around the table to sit next to Blondie. "Why we care about lost *nina*, Blondie?"

"That picture, it could be Lindy Sue," Blondie says.

"They look for the Hawthorne kid?"

"No. Some girl named Bethany Tremain."

"So?" Rosa looks at her. "All them spoiled rich kids the same."

"That's right. We get the Tremain family pay us for Lindy Sue."

"Makes no sense," Rosa shakes her head.

"Easy money. We bring back Lindy Sue, we don't

know if her family will pay much for her."

"Why not?" Rosa asks.

"She told me things. Evil stepmother holds the family purse. That's what she thinks."

Rosa scowls. "That why you cotton to little Pinky? Your plan is *loco*."

"But it's a plan. If Hawthorne won't pay. We grift the Tremain family, get their money before they realize the girl isn't their daughter Bethany."

"You tell Varla of this... this plan?"

Blondie shakes her head. "Not yet. What do you think?"

Rosa wiggles her hand back and forth. "Eh."

At movement across the room, they both look up. Derry Flanders tromps down the stairs.

Chapter 36

Derry supposes it will be all right with Willard. There are three copies of the Bethany Tremain drawing in a satchel in the bottom dresser drawer. Entering the room, he feels odd. Never before has he handled the pictures. He takes one out, shuts the satchel, and carefully folds Bethany Tremain's face into four corners so he can stuff the picture in his vest pocket.

He moves slowly through the corridor. Their voices are a murmur as he reaches the second-floor balcony and stairs. Willard told him to follow every clue and they haven't interviewed these women yet. Maybe they know something about the Tremain girl.

At the same time, he has trepidation, picturing the one who stood over Jimmy, eye to eye with Bobby, and Bobby's hands all bloody. He, Derry, had sussed out the danger, it hung like an aura around her, and his two friends hadn't seen it, Jimmy now dead and Bobby at the asylum.

With both fear and excitement, Derry starts down the stairs. The women are huddled in a quiet conversation when he approaches the table. He sits across from them and pulls out the drawing, unfolds it, and pushes it across the table to Rosa. "That's her. Bethany Tremain. Missing since April."

Rosa gazes at the image. "Pretty, isn't she?"

"You seen her?" Derry asks.

"Derry, will you get me a sarsaparilla?" Blondie slides some coins across the table.

He picks up the coins. He thinks he could use another lager to calm his nerves. "Sure you don't want a beer?"

Blondie shakes her head. "I stay away from alcohol."

"Anything for you?" he asks Rosa.

"No, thanks." She holds up her glass.

Derry walks to the bar. He turns back to the table, the two women are huddled, heads close together over the drawing, an animated conversation. Instead of a beer or a whiskey, he orders a sarsaparilla for himself as well.

Chapter 37

Blondie asks, "Doesn't it look just like her?"

"Possibly." Rosa looks again at the drawing lying on the table.

"Almost the same weight, same height, same age. See, there?" Blondie taps her finger on some wording in the lower left corner, vital statistics of the missing girl. "Spitting image of Lindy Sue."

"But she is not Lindy Sue."

"Look at the hair. Golden curls."

"You can't tell from the drawing." Rosa scoffs. "It say here girl's hair is dried-wheat blond. And it's straighter. *Pelo Lacio.*"

"We can dye her hair."

"Listen, Blondie. You keep him here. I get Varla. He wants to meet her, and I bet Varla wants to meet him."

"Is that right?"

"And you? I know what you want."

Blondie shrugs and smiles. "He's not bad looking."

"Not bad looking? For a kid." Rosa shakes her head, stands, and walks out the door, eager to tell Varla the latest development. And what of Blondie? Hankering for a Pinkerton? A kid at that. How low can one go?

Chapter 38

Blondie is sitting with Derry at the table in the corner of the main room of Gruber's Outpost. "You're afraid of them, aren't you?"

"Should I be?"

Blondie shrugs. "Don't be nervous, Derry." She steps around to his side of the table and sits next to him.

"They're your friends?" Derry asks.

"What of it?" She puts her hand on his arm. "You got a girl, Derry?"

"Do they really know where Bethany Tremain is?"

Her hand goes lower. She grabs his hand and puts it on her thigh. "I like you, Derry."

Nervously he looks at the counter, but the Grubers are not in sight. Heat wells up in his face. He can feel the firmness of her flesh beneath the thin cotton of the dress. Though a few years older, she's prettier than the girls at Nancy's. He tries not to look at his hand on her leg or her deep cleavage, but he's too nervous to gaze very long into her blue eyes, so instead he glances down at their sarsaparillas in glass tumblers.

"I like you a lot, Derry." She presses down on his hand on her thigh.

Flustered, Derry blurts, "I only have eight bits."

Blondie laughs. "Big Pink keeps you on a short leash."

He twists his face in thought and reluctantly nods.

"And you have the wrong idea. I'm no dollymop."

"I didn't mean to suggest you were."

"So, that morning. You didn't see what happened?"

"Not really. When I looked, Jimmy was stabbed and Bobby had the knife standing over him and that woman was on the other side looking at Bobby."

"So Varla was there when it happened?"

"That the Asian woman?"

Blondie nods.

"She was there. Her name is Varla?"

"Varla Vixen. It's her stage name at the Final Frontier Saloon."

"Varla Vixen." He repeats the name as if to know her name will make her less mysterious. "Is she dangerous?"

"Any person's dangerous the right situation." She laughs. "Maybe we should go now? Run away from her. Run away from the Pinkies."

"What're you saying?"

"I'm messing you. I do think we should go."

Across the room, at the counter, Ma Gruber gives them the stink-eye. Blondie stands up. He stumbles behind her through the dining room. They step outside. It's dusk, the sun almost gone from the sky, and the air cooled by a breeze. She grabs his hand in a firm grasp. "I'm sure she'll be along in a moment."

A voice calls out. Derry looks up the pathway to some of the cabins. A woman strides down the path toward them. Derry sucks in a deep breath and clutches harder to Blondie's hand. He realizes he's scared of the other woman, with her huge dark eyes and black hair, but he remembers how he was also scared for her that day when Bobby pulled the knife. But what happened after that?

The woman looked fierce, facing down Bobby and Jimmy. Now she has her lips in an "O" and a confusion-furrowed brow as she stares at him and approaches.

"You think you know me?" she asks, peering at him.

"Uh huh," Derry mutters.

"That's right." She snaps her finger to make him flinch. "The coward who ran when his two friends threatened me with a knife."

"I told them to stop," he says.

"You want to know what happened? How your friend

got stabbed?"

He nods.

"Follow me." Varla walks up the pathway from where she came. Derry glances over at Blondie, who starts to follow, pulling him along. They head past a couple of cabins, and at the last one on the pathway, Varla pushes open the door. The cabin is small; a single bed, a wood chair, a night table, and a small wood dresser, not even a closet.

"What's he got, Blondie?" Varla asks.

"Eight bits."

"That's enough. You'll give us the eight bits?" Varla grabs her hand around Derry's shoulder and pulls him toward the bed. He's fine with giving them the money; if he doesn't spend it Willard won't give him more, and Willard've paid more to buy him a girl at Nancy's.

"And you'll tell me what happened?" he asks.

"Soon, very soon. We'll give you that and more." Varla smiles, and he almost doesn't recognize her as the same angry woman he saw a week earlier. "Load the pipe, Blondie," she says.

Varla sits on the chair, facing him. Blondie behind her fixes something on the dresser top, her back to them.

"They never should have called you names," he says. "I told them not to."

She shakes her head. "It's sad what happened. That poor boy. I imagine it upended a few lives. It certainly did mine. Yours, too, Derry." Varla grabs the pipe from Blondie. As she inhales from the pipe, Blondie, smiling, bends closer to Derry. Derry lets her plant her lips on his and blow smoke into his lungs.

Derry blows out the smoke. "That's not tobacco!"

"No." Blondie takes another toke from the pipe and gives him another kiss of smoke.

Shapes flicker at the corner of Derry's eyes. What am I getting myself into?

Chapter 39

In the store, between some shelves, Elber peers into the dining area where the blonde from cabin seven sits with the Pinkerton kid. He's sure now that she lied about some big guy staying with her and those other women. She and the young Pinkerton arise and head to the front door.

Elber scuttles toward a window that looks onto the front yard. The couple are joined by another of the women, and the three of them vanish from view, headed toward the cabins.

Elber steps back from the window. The Pinkerton kid isn't even half Elber's age. Elber's mind becomes feverish with excitement and envy. He waits impatiently, moves some cans of beans from one side of the shelf to another, in case his ma or pa are watching. When waiting is too much, he steps into the main room.

The room is mostly empty at that hour, a couple burly men drinking beers at the long table. His pa is behind the bar, engrossed in a newspaper, and his ma is in the kitchen in back, neither of them aware of illicit acts about to be committed. Elber moves quietly to the door. If his pa looks up and asks where he's going, Elber will tell him the outhouse, but his pa continues to read. Elber slips quietly outside.

The air is cool and the crickets are chirping. Elber's eyes soon adjust to the dim light of the stars and the half moon. He walks around the side to the outhouses behind the main structure. After taking a piss, he follows a narrow path the opposite way around the main structure, across the road, and through the brush behind the cabins.

As he pushes past brambles toward the back of Cabin Seven, he imagines being alone in the cabin with the women, where his parents can't pull him away like a dog on a leash. It isn't fair, the young Pinkerton in there with those women. Elber's ma and pa would be furious if they knew the immoral acts that happen in the cabins, some of which Elber has witnessed. He's not doing anything wrong, just bearing witness to the sins of others.

The back of Seven, like the other cabins, has no windows. Years ago Elber drilled spy holes in most of the cabins, close to the ground on the back side, where he can peer in undetected. He'd been lucky enough to catch couples making love or kissing, though most of the time what happened was dull, people yacking or doing nothing.

He has high hopes for this evening's viewing. He creeps slowly through the brush and hears faint noises, which at first sound like sex moaning, but getting closer, he realizes it's the sound of a harmonica and a woman singing.

Music to cover up the sordid sounds of sin. Slowly he edges closer. The clapboard side of the cabin looms directly in front of him. He puts his ear to the side, but he still can't hear anything except the mouth harp and a voice singing quietly, shyly, a familiar tune he can't identify, a tune that should be happy, but there's a tone of sadness in the soft voice and melancholy in the notes blown from the harmonica.

Elber lowers himself onto his belly to get close to the eye hole. Each passing year it's more difficult to get his bulk prone. He pushes some leaves out of the way and puts his eye to the hole, his heart leaping in anticipation.

Disappointment sinks in quickly. At one side of the room, the Mexican, Rosa, plays the harmonica. Almost out of view, another woman lies on the second bed, and she's the one singing. Elber shifts to get a different angle. She's not the blonde or the other woman, and her hands are behind her back, and her legs...ropes around her ankles.

Elber looks again at her face. All at once it hits Elber. The missing girl. The one the Pinkertons are looking for,

Bethany Tremain. The women have her. Perhaps the other women are negotiating with the Pinkerton kid.

Elber watches for twenty minutes and begins to get bored. Carefully, with much effort, he climbs to his feet and slinks away. Ten minutes later, he's back at the outpost. The dining room is now empty. His ma and pa have headed off to their small bedroom behind the kitchen. Only a single lamp illuminates the main room. Horse hoofs clap from outside. Elber glances out a window, to see Willard Stark ride up awkwardly on his horse.

Willard spots him and fixes him with a gaze. "Boy, come out here and stable my steed."

Elber reluctantly walks to the door. Outside Willard stumbles to get off the horse. Even in the dim light, his face is red, his eyes blood-shot.

"Stop skulking and take my horse, you fool."

"I see you're celebrating, sir." Elber grabs the reins of the horse. "Almost found the girl."

"Huh, what're you gab-mouthing? I found a couple of nice strumpets over at Nancy's fuck farm."

"I meant the other one," Elber replies. "Bethany Tremain."

"Just stable my fucking horse, you fat foozler." Waving him away, Willard staggers toward the front door. His boots stomp across the wood floor, loud enough for Elber to hear as he leads the horse down to the stables. Quit with the racket, you'll anger ma and pa. Elber clutches tightly to the reins.

Ignoring Elber when asked about Bethany Tremain, the Pinkerton is keeping Elber out of the loop. Elber was helping the Pinkertons, even thinking he might become a Pinkerton, go away, travel the country on jobs, and escape the dreary complacency of Gruber's Outpost. But Willard Stark, the big Pinkerton, Elber decides he doesn't like him, with his drinking and whoring and the way he snubbed Elber.

Chapter 40

High on opium, Derry Flanders floats above the bed. The cabin room twists and flows in his vision. Varla pulls up the chair and sits down facing him. "You were there. You saw what happened, didn't you?"

"No." He shakes his head.

"You erased it from your mind."

"I don't think so." He sees streams of images come out of her dark eyes and into his, pulses of energy, yet he can't turn away.

"I was there, Derry," Varla says. "I saw you."

"But... I ran away."

"You ran, but you turned and looked when your friend cried out being stabbed."

"I don't remember that." Derry shakes his head, and yet he's not sure.

"The one kid was advancing on me. He had a knife, so what could I do? I stepped backward. The other kid, behind the kid with the knife, he grabs the other kid's coat sleeve as the other kid lunged at me. And the kid with the knife snapped." Varla snaps her fingers.

"What do you mean, snapped?"

"A brain snap. A reaction. Lost his mind for a moment. You looked back and saw it too. The look on his face. The sudden way he spun and stabbed the other boy."

"A brain snap," Blondie exclaims. "I knew that story in the papers stank of hoggledygook."

"Bobby stabbed Jimmy? Why would he?" Derry shivers.

"He's your friend, not mine," Varla says. "Why don't you ask him?"

"But..." In Derry's head is a memory, Bobby Lappeus

and Jimmy Montgomery, the two of them face each other, but no, Jimmy is on the ground his guts spilling out, and Bobby stands above him, not sure why he drove the knife into Jimmy, a half dozen stabs to the gut and the throat as if his mind had shut off and he'd become a killing machine, unaware until it was done.

Bobby's fist clutches the knife. Jimmy screams in pain. Bobby stabs again. Jimmy falls to the ground. Bobby grimaces like he's lost. Jimmy's face peaceful like he's the winner, and maybe he has won, to escape while Bobby's loss will be to live with the terrible consequences for the rest of his life.

"You remember, don't you?" Varla says.

His mind reels at the sight of his dying friend, but she was there too, just beyond them.

"You didn't help him," he says. "When he was stabbed."

"What could I do?" Varla replies. "My word against the son of the Portland Police Chief? You high-tailed it, too, Derry. You're one to talk."

"And you didn't go to the police when they were looking for you," he counters.

"No way. That band of racist thugs? And what if I had? Would you have backed me up? You didn't even remember what happened. You didn't want to believe your friend killed your other friend."

"I think I remember now." The image etched in his mind: Bobby pale white, his story about the Filipino sailors that made no sense, and Derry in doubt though agreeing to go along.

How could Bobby? It's a betrayal, and yet it's always been there in the back of Derry's head, so obvious. The brain-snap, the reaction, a rash act with no way back, Bobby tortured at what he's done, and perhaps that's why Bobby couldn't tell him the truth.

"So you remember," Blondie says. "Bobby Lappeus

killed the other kid."

"I... I think so." Derry nods, and tries to stand, but the room stumbles over him and he falls back on the bed. Hands grab and turn him sideways.

A hush of fleeting ghosts. Whispers of the two women waft across the room but words have lost meaning. He opens his eyes. The two women kiss at the doorway. Blondie turns to him, feasting on him with her eyes. She pulls the blouse over her head and the white lace camisole beneath it. She sashays toward him as the dark-haired one, Varla, slips out the door. Crossing the room Blondie undoes her skirt and lets it fall to her feet. Still lying on his side on the bed, Derry slaps himself in the face to see if he's dreaming.

"Come on, silly." Naked she looks down at him, her blond pube-hairs in front of his face. "Take off your clothes, Derry, and let's have fun."

Chapter 41

Rosa says, "You have a nice voice."

"Thank you." Lindy Sue hadn't meant to start singing, but it felt good and made her forget her hands tied behind her back. When she shut her eyes, nothing existed but her voice and the sounds of the harmonica, each coaching something out of the other. Opening her eyes when the music stopped a moment ago, Lindy Sue was startled to see Rosa with the harmonica. Rosa gazes at her without sarcasm or meanness.

"So what is it like, daughter of big shot doctor?" Rosa asks.

"He's mostly at work."

"They want to put me in his hospital."

"Who did?"

"Doctors. But Varla set me right."

"Why's she trying to hypnotize me?" Lindy Sue asks.

"That what she tries to do?" Rosa asks. "*Hypnotizar?*"

"But I won't let her. I hate her."

"She not one you want to hate, *princesita.* You are *mucho* upset. You blame her, but we bring you home."

"As long as you get paid?"

Rosa smiles and rubs some fingers together. "*Dinero* for time and expense. *Jefe* Doctor JC Hawthorne really your papa?"

"Yes." Lindy Sue nods.

"And he pay we bring you home?"

"Of course he would."

"How much? How much he pay?"

"I don't know." Lindy Sue shakes her head.

Rosa steps closer. "So what you tell Blondie? About your papa?"

"Nothing." Lindy Sue writhes inside.

"And your step-mama?"

"I told her nothing." Lindy Sue glares at Rosa. "What'd she tell you?"

Rosa chuckles. "*Princesa*, you can not trust Blondie with secret. Blondie, she's a *chismosa,* a blatherskite."

A clatter of the turned doorknob, and the door lurches open. Varla enters the room. Rosa rises and strides toward her. Their voices are low, but Lindy Sue makes out the mention of Blondie, as she strains to hear.

"So why not her sleep there, and me and you can...*cochar.*" Rosa points to the bed.

"This is how it'll be." Varla has her hands around Rosa's rear, the fingers sinking into the fabric of the thin cotton shift. She whispers in Rosa's ear. She pulls away from Rosa. "Play me something, Rosa. I could use some music." Varla eases into the armchair and puts her feet on the bed in front of Lindy Sue's face.

Rosa begins to play the harmonica. The song is familiar but Lindy Sue refuses to sing. Over Varla's toes, Lindy Sue makes out Varla's face. Eyes closed, Varla relaxes back in the chair. The melody lopes backward and forward in wobbly gypsy time, Rosa's mouth moving back and forth on the harmonica. Lindy Sue closes her eyes and lets the music envelope her. She sinks deep into it and again almost forgets where she is.

"Move over, Goldilocks." The voice is calm. Hands grab Lindy Sue. A hand jerks hard, she's wrenched across the bed. Varla on top of her, uses fingers to push open Lindy Sue's lips, and the gag is put in place. "Make sure we get a good sleep. Voices carry farther in the quiet of the night when the insects and birds have died down."

Once more Varla's large body is next to her, taking most of the bed. Lindy Sue's skin crawls with revulsion, and she lies in fear until exhausted she slips into fretful sleep.

Chapter 42

The others are asleep, and the lanterns have been snuffed when Blondie, naked, slips into the cabin with her clothes in her arms. She drops them on the floor and climbs into bed with Rosa. The bed is barely large enough for both women.

Rosa grunts something.

"What's that?" Blondie whispers.

"I smell him on you. *Fetidez.* You stink of him."

"Is that such a bad thing?"

"Why Varla let you..." Rosa sighs. She rolls on her side facing Blondie. "You like it?" Rosa whispers.

"I guess so."

"A Pinkerton. Pfff!"

"He's just a kid. It was okay. Not great, though. Nine or ten thrusts. Over too soon."

"Like I want details, you *asaltacunas.* Cradle robber."

"I helped him. He was shy, too shy to convince a regular girl to do it with him. What he lacked in experience, he made up for in enthusiasm."

"You enjoy debauching him?"

"Is that such a bad thing? What would Varla say?"

Rosa stifles a laugh. "You got point."

"I'm waiting to see this Pitts kid."

"Pitts kid? Who's he?"

"His father's in a wheelchair. Lost his legs in a train accident. Little Pinky spilled the beans."

"Varla told me of this."

"And the son, the one who's off his chump? Elber Gruber says he's huge. Biggest man he ever seen. Can you imagine doing the blanket hornpipe with such a man?"

"The *idiota*? That is low, even for you, Blondie. You

have that *babosa* Elber flamadiddle you?"

"No one flamadiddles me, Rosa." Blondie sinks back on the mattress. "But I still don't know what happened that morning. Did Derry see his friend stab the other one, or did Varla make him think that's what happened?"

Rosa doesn't answer.

Maybe even Rosa doesn't know, Blondie thinks. She soon falls asleep, despite Rosa twitching and turning next to her.

Chapter 43

Derry Flanders wakes up confused, his mind moving in seven different directions. He's alone in the cabin. He stumbles to his feet and scrambles to put on his clothes. Making love to the blonde is etched too deep into his head to be a dream and is counterpoised by the revelation that Bobby Lappeus stabbed Jimmy Montgomery and then lied to Derry and the authorities about it.

Night has completely fallen, the air cool enough to make him shiver as he stumbles along the path to the main building. The darkness and cold and even the silence are physical, and everything seems different, unfamiliar, even alien, though he can't place how, except that it has to do with the strangeness in his head and the afterglow of the drugs.

He steps into the empty dining area. The Gruber's are asleep in the small rooms behind the kitchen. Even tiptoeing, Derry's feet make the floor creak loudly. The room is in shadows from the dim moonlight from the windows. He carefully makes his way to the stairway.

He reaches the door to the room shared with Willard Stark, not even sure if Willard is back from the whore house. He can't hear any sounds when he puts his ear to the door. Slowly turning the knob, Derry tiptoes in.

Willard at a window, turns. He's in his drawers and under-vest. Even in the dim light, Willard looks drunk, a dull haze across his face. "Slipping in like a thief," Willard booms.

"Hi, Willard." Derry remains frozen at the door as if caught in the act.

"What you got to say for yourself?"

Derry shrugs.

"Didn't see you at Nancy's, but looks like you found

something anyway."

"What do you mean?"

Willard cracks a big smile. "You can't hide it. It's all over you. One can tell if one knows what to look for. I look at any man or woman, and I know if they've recently been fucking. Just like that. You can't hide something like that, not from me."

"So what if I did?" Derry shuts the door behind him.

"Nothing wrong, kid. I'm just saying...don't try to hide it from Willard Stark. Don't think I'm some idiot you can hide things from. So tell me about it, boy."

"What's there to say?" Sitting on the bed, Derry pulls off his boots.

"Who's the woman?"

"Some woman. Staying here, one of the cabins."

"Huh." Willard eyes him with bloodshot eyes. "Not that New Era slag t'was downstairs this morning?"

"No!" Derry shakes his head vigorously. "A traveler."

"Tell me about this girl."

"It was good. Tomorrow I might ask her to marry."

"You're too young to be married." Willard walks over to the bed. "I'm fucking tired. Got back from Nancy's an hour ago. Wondered what happened to you. Should've figured you were getting some. You sure she's not from New Era? Or one of those mongrel whores who were downstairs this morning?"

"No. I told you she wasn't. Don't have to harp on it, Willard."

"I got all the right to harp on it because I'm your boss. And you don't look right. Like you're staring at me and trying not to smirk 'cause you think you're better than me."

"You're drunk, Willard." Derry sits on the smaller bed and pulls off his outer clothes, dumping them in a pile on top of the boots. "I'm tired." Tired of talking to this boor. He never realized how much he dislikes Willard at times. Staring at him across the room, it's all strange in Derry's head, a veil had lifted from his eyes and he sees the world a new way.

"You should come with me tomorrow," Willard says. "You can't marry the first girl you ever fucked. That's being a stupid kid. You're too young to know what's what."

"I reckon I know I'd rather be with this girl than those whores at the bordello."

"Don't knock it, kid. Tomorrow we got the whole day off, then my friends arrive Monday."

"So?" Derry lies down on the bed. He turns to his side toward the other bed, where Willard lies on his side, looking at him.

"Got something else to mention to you," Willard says. "That fucking Elber Gruber."

"What about him?"

"When I came in, you know what he says to me?"

"Don't reckon I do, Willard."

"He says something about finding the girl. Finding Bethany Tremain."

"Finding Bethany Tremain?"

"Like he's thinking we found the girl. That's what he says to me."

"What'd he mean by that?"

"I don't know, Derry. I reckon he was puffing his chest. Such a stupid thing to say."

"What d'you expect from Elber Gruber?"

"But still. Why would he think we've almost got the girl?"

"Search me. You said yourself, the guy's a zounderkite. Who knows what he's thinking."

"Maybe you're right. Still, got me thinking."

"I'm tired." Derry turns onto his other side, facing the wall, feeling Willard's eyes staring at his back. But Willard says nothing more, and in a few minutes, he begins to snore loudly.

Chapter 44

Sun streams through the window, awakening Derry. He lies in bed and remembers the night before with Blondie, excited to see her again.

"Oh, my head!" Willard moans from the other bed.

"Your head?"

"Drank too much at the fuck farm. Hangover like a son-of-a-bitch." Willard slowly sits up and reaches for his saddle bag resting on the foot rail of the bed. He pulls out a flask. "Best cure for a hangover. A bit of the dog that bit you." He takes a couple of loud gulps and holds it out to Derry.

"What is it?"

"Tennessee bourbon. Good stuff, not like what they have here or Nancy's."

Derry puts a hand in front of him. "None for me. I'm headed downstairs for breakfast."

"Bring me up some too. The menu at the whores is limited."

You get your own damn breakfast. Derry doesn't reply as he trudges out the door and down the steps to the dining area. He gives the old man his order, takes his coffee, and sits at a table.

"Morning, Derry."

Derry looks up from his coffee and griddle cakes. Blondie's smile warms the gloom. She steps deeper into the room, the door open to bright sunlight behind her. Another shape appears at the door, and the other one, Rosa, steps in behind Blondie.

"Morning to you, Blondie. Join me for breakfast?"

Blondie and Rosa walk up to the bar. Mr. Gruber takes their orders. With coffees in hand, she and Rosa head toward him and sit across the table.

Derry beams. "Want to do something today? Go for a ride?"

"Are you not seeking missing girl, *poco* Pinky?" Rosa asks.

"Willard gave me another day off." Derry turns to Blondie. "We can ride to this waterfall Elber told me about."

"Why don't you tell us about the Pitts ranch?" Blondie asks.

"You know about that?" Even as he speaks, he realizes he told them about it the night before, not quite knowing why, spouting it while the Asian woman stared into his eyes. The old man and his son, the train accident, the money. But he can't remember if he told them about the men Willard had sent for, friends of Willard's from the war, a couple of bounty hunters named George Emmett and James Crawford, set to arrive at the outpost the next day.

Derry changes the subject. "What about it, Blondie? A ride somewhere?"

"Like where, Derry? Somewhere romantic?"

"I think dinky Pinky fall in love, Blondie." Rosa smirks. "*Un tonto enamorado.*"

"Derry, I had fun last night," Blondie says. "But..."

"But?" Worry ices into his stomach. "What do you mean?"

"You're a sweet kid, Derry." Blondie reaches over and tousles his curly hair.

That's all she thinks of me, a sweet kid? He takes a sip of coffee, willing the pain out of his face.

"You lucky kid," Rosa says. "We mostly don't cotton to Pinkies."

"Is that right, Blondie? You don't like Pinkertons?"

Blondie holds out her hands in a shrug. "What can I say?"

"What's wrong with the Pinkerton Agency? We help people solve crimes." Derry stares at her, his fork held midway between the plate and his mouth with a piece of griddle cake on it.

Blondie leans across the table, showing off her cleavage. “Break up labor strikes. Hassle poor people. The Pinks are muscle for those rich enough to pay. Justice for the right price.”

“I don’t know about that.” Derry glances from her face to the open neck of her blouse. “Me and Willard, we’re helping these people find their missing daughter.” As he says these words, a memory pops into his head. “You said something last night I can’t believe I forgot.”

“I said a lot of things last night, some that I forgot,” Blondie says.

“You said you might have a clue to Bethany Tremain.”

“Bethany who?” She shakes her head.

“The missing girl.” He tries to remember her exact words, but his head is still soggy and overwhelmed from the previous night’s drugs and debauchery.

“What did I say?”

“You acted like you knew something. Someone who knew where she was.”

“I don’t remember.” Blondie shrugs.

“She fiddle-faddled you, *poco* Pinky.” Rosa snickers. “Words to lure you to her *chocho*.”

Horace Gruber’s frail form slinks toward the table and lays down plates of food in front of Blondie and Rosa. “Ma’ams? Sir?”

“*Si*?” Rosa answers.

“My wife and I will be at the church if any of you good people care to join us. Chapel at the top of the hill.” He jerks a thumb toward one side of the outpost.

Blondie and Rosa shake their heads. Derry follows their lead.

“Our son Elber will see to your needs next two hours, but I warn you, he can’t prepare food.” The old man has a sour look on his puss, perhaps at reconciling his and his wife’s devoutness to their son’s spiritual perfidy.

"That's fine," Blondie replies.

After the old man departs, Derry asks, "You two don't go to church?"

"Why would we?" Blondie says, her mouth full of griddlecake. "Besides, with those two gone, we'll liven up the place. Rosa, you bring your mouth harp?"

Derry points to the sign. "No music."

Blondie calls across the room. "Hey, Elber."

Behind the bar, Elber glances up from his comic book western and leers at her. "What is it?"

"Okay if'n my friend plays a few tunes?" Blondie asks.

Elber walks over to a window with a view of the church up the slope behind the outpost.

"Come on, Elber," Blondie coos. "You're in charge."

"How long they at the church, Elber?" Rosa asks.

Elber turns toward them. "Two hours, I reckon." He saunters back to the bar.

"Then we can't waste time. Right, Rosa?"

Rosa pushes away her half-finished plate and pulls the mouth harp out of her vest pocket. She wets the mouthpiece with her lips and tongue, and with a grin across half her face while she has the instrument at the side of her mouth like a cigar, she blows out a few notes of a melody and then launches into it fully.

"I like this one," Blondie says with a grin. "Sing along, Derry."

Elber pounds a beat on the counter with his hands as he leers at the women. Blondie sings and Derry fills in the parts he knows. Rosa wails on the mouth harp, holding it in both hands. The words echo through the dining area.

"Possum meat so good to eat.
Carve him to the heart.
You always find him good and sweet.
Carve him to the heart.
We pull him in with his funny grin.
Carve him to the heart.

We dragged him home and dressed him off.
Carve him to the heart!
Carve that possum, carve that possum,
Carve him to the heart.
Carve that possum, carve that possum,
Carve him to the heart."

At each "Carve that possum" Derry's voice amplifies.

Chapter 45

In the room, Willard Stark takes another drink of bourbon. His head hurts less; after a bite to eat and a cigar, he'll be ready to return to Nancy's Nunnery. Derry should've been back with breakfast by now. Where is the boy? He seemed off to Willard this morning.

He hears a faint drone from the dining area below. He pulls on his pants and grabs his gun holsters, just in case.

Stepping into the corridor, he recognizes the sound. Voices and a harmonica and someone banging crudely on something, an animal heathenism. The tune vaguely familiar but too faint to place. He walks slowly down the hallway. The tune becomes more familiar, he realizes, but he still can't place it. A fist clenches at his stomach. The cheerful voices become mocking as he reaches the top of the stairs.

That song! It comes to him, freezing his blood, fear he hasn't felt since sixteen years earlier. Before the war ended. He was the squad leader. They had their guns on him. A surprise attack. They killed five of his men, and he, Emmett, and Crawford were prisoners. More galling, their Union captors were a patrol of black men. Savages in uniforms.

Hands tied behind backs, lined up against a wall. Willard was terrified. At one point the captors sang. "Carve that boss man, carve him to the heart." In his memory, they waved large knives in the air as they sang, and they aimed the song directly at him. Carve that white man to the heart. Cut him to pieces. Maybe eat him. So scared he pissed his pants. He still has nightmares of it. His capture and the loss of the war intricately laced that he felt blame for the whole confederacy going up in flames to the boots of Sherman's army.

That cursed song. Willard peers over the rail at the ones

below. A dark-skinned woman, the Mexican with short red hair, blows on the harp, and Derry and a blonde sing, as if possessed by the sounds emitted from the instrument while Elber flaps his arms against the counter-top in rhythm. Derry sings loudly with gusto. The words! The jubilation in their voices at the mockery of the great confederacy burning in ruins, so that inferior people like the harmonica player can act with impunity.

Willard will put an end to this. He can't head back to the room, even there he'd still hear the hated song now that it has contaminated his ears. Not one minute more. The red-haired Mexican is the ringleader, in league with that Mongrel woman she was with the day before. Playing that harmonica and luring the others. There's a reason the Gruber's posted "No Music" in the dining area; some music leads down a path of evil. The white people who were lured to black people's music, poisoning Christian minds with all sorts of heathen heresy. And even Derry, who Willard thought of as a son, is under its sway, him and the white girl and Elber Gruber under the spell of that toxic harmonica blown by that...

As Willard stumbles down the stairs, the words burn into his ears:

"I reach up to pull him in,
Carve him to the heart;
The possum he begun to grin,
Carve him to the heart;
I carried him home and dressed him off,
Carve him to the heart;
I hung him that night in the frost,
Carve him to the heart."
Carve that possum, carve that possum,
Carve that—"

"Willard!" Derry exclaims.

The traitor! The huge smile on his face, as he replaced "Possum" with Willard's name. Willard realizes he can't even trust his own assistant, all the warning signs, his unwillingness to join Willard the previous morning... But most of all Willard needs to stop the musician who controls the others.

"No one's carving me!" Willard shouts as he rushes across the floor. "Stop that noise!" He hurls the harmonica player out of her seat. The harmonica and the woman clatter to the floor, knocking over chairs at the next table.

"*¡No mames*!" she yowls as she rolls shaken to her feet. "What the fuck wrong with you?"

"Why'd you do that, Willard? Elber said it was okay." Derry glares at Willard as if he is the one out of place.

"Don't care what the fuck Elber told you. I hate that song." Willard towers over the couple still at the table. "I told you to stay away from this New Era scum."

"Got problem with me playing, *gran culo*?" The harmonica player stalks toward him, glaring eyes and mouth grimacing.

He looks at her and scoffs. "I'll slap you down again, wench, unless you pick that harmonica up and play Dixie."

"Fuck you, I will." She's large for a woman, but not as large as him, and yet she comes at him in a fighting crouch, with her fists ready to jab. He will show her that she's inferior to him, in fisticuffs and every other way.

He swings and she ducks and returns fast, her fist hitting him in the face harder than he'd imagine possible. Stars shatter in his eyes, and he loses his balance, reeling backward and slamming into a table. He falls to the floor. Though dazed, his anger intensifies. He uses a chair to boost himself back on his feet.

"You want more?" she says, twelve feet away, hands on hips, a big grin on her face.

"I won't put up with shit from you." How dare she treat him this way. And in his own country! The nerve! Her whole face a sneering mask like a big fuck-you to him, letting her get away with that could one day spell the end of the white race.

Willard becomes calm and collected, realizing what he must do next, what didn't happen on that terrible day near the end of the war. Take control of the situation. Willard pulls his Colt double-action revolver from the holster and aims. "You assaulted me! I'm shooting you out of self-defense. Everyone here's a witness."

"Willard, put down the gun," Derry yammers.

"No! She's getting what she deserves."

"No, Willard. Don't do it." Derry reaches for his colt. But Derry wouldn't dare shoot him. Willard begins to squeeze the trigger.

A gun goes off, and then his gun. The dark woman twists. The bullet rips across her upper arm. A pain erupts in Willard's chest. He turns to look at Derry. Derry has shock across his face as he holds the revolver. A wisp of smoke rises up from the barrel.

"How could you, Derry?" Willard looks down. A hole in his shirt, blood leaking out of his chest. It was a very good shot, Willard knows from his war days, a hit to the heart, and he doesn't have long to live.

At the bar, Elber is yelling something, and another gunshot reverberates through the room. The others are frozen in place, Derry half standing with the gun in front of him, the blonde ducked half behind the table, and the red-haired Mexican woman, with a streak of blood on her upper arm where Willard's bullet grazed her. She, like the others, frozen in place at an odd angle, suspended in air where she jerked out of the way of the bullet, which Willard can still see, tracing a path slowly toward the wall behind the woman.

What the fuck is happening? Willard doesn't know how long he's been looking down at the bullet hole and all the blood splatting out of it with each beat of his ever-weakening heart. Why has everything stopped and everyone frozen in place? He can't believe he's dead, but he is.

Chapter 46

Behind the counter, Elber Gruber watches the older Pinkerton storm into the room and shove Rosa out of her seat, stopping the music. Finally some excitement! Been over a year since the outpost had a brawl, and that one ended quickly when Elber's ma blasted off a shot from the rifle set on hooks beneath the bar. But now with Ma and Pa up at the church, Elber thinks as he rubs his palms together, maybe he can watch an actual barroom brawl.

The Pinkerton's face is contorted as he advances, but the Mexican woman, to Elber's surprise, doesn't back away. Fists swing as they leap at each other. The woman slips past the Pinkerton, and he, hurled forward, loses his balance, reeling into a table. The table falls, chairs scatter and a vase of flowers shatters.

Red with fury, the Pinkerton stumbles to his feet while two dozen feet away the Mexican faces him and laughs loudly.

Much as he thrills at the brawl, Elber realizes his parents will be mad if he lets it go any longer and more stuff gets broken. He sidles along the counter to where the rifle hangs on two large hooks, beneath the bar out of sight of the customers.

The Pinkerton reaches for his revolver.

Elber gets alarmed. "No! Stop that! My ma and pa..." Elber's voice comes out as a squeak, and no one pays attention to him as if the action is happening separately from him like those times when he was young and watched actors perform in a traveling theater.

The Pinkerton has his gun pointed at the Mexican woman, a grim look on his face as he screams at her and begins to pull the trigger.

In panic, Elber reaches behind the counter. Grasps the gun frantically. A gunshot booms loudly, and another. As he lifts the rifle in haste, his finger hits the trigger. The long gun jolts from his arms with a loud explosion and skitters across the bar, hitting a post and sliding back toward him.

The Pinkerton still has his gun in his hand. The Mexican woman is on the floor, on the wall behind her blood splattered on a faded poster for medicinal cocaine drops. The other Pinkerton, the young one named Derry, scrambles to his feet, a gun in his hand, while the older one topples and crashes, scattering more chairs.

"What just happened?" Derry stares at his hand and his gun. "Did I..."

"No." Blondie points to Elber. "He did it."

"Yes." Rosa picks herself off the floor, her arm bleeding below the elbow and points at Elber as well. "*Gordito* Gruber kill him."

"Me? But.. but.." Elber stammers for words.

"You're a hero, buddy," Blondie says. "You stopped that horrible man from killing my friend. My big hero." Blondie throws him a smile.

Rosa nods. "Who think the *gordo* had it in him? Save my life."

Derry continues to stare at the body of his companion. Blondie steps next to him and pats his shoulder. "Put away that peashooter, hon. Before our big hero shoots you too."

Derry holsters his gun.

The big hero. Elber puffs out his chest and grabs for the rifle. At the back of the kitchen the rear door bangs open.

"What in tarnation!" The high, piercing voice fills the room. Elber's ma storms past the stoves and shelves of spices and cookware. Elber's pa is not far behind. Their eyes go wide when they see the Pinkerton on the floor.

"Your son just stopped that man from murdering my friend," Blondie says.

"Had to shoot. No other way. He try to kill me," Rosa confirms.

"Elber shot him?" Ma's tone is full of doubt. She doesn't want to believe Elber is a hero.

Elber's pa steps up to the gun on the counter and wraps his fingers around the business end of the rifle barrel. "Still hot, Ma," he confirms.

"You!" Ma points to Derry. "Is this what happened to your partner?"

"I r-reckon so, ma'am," Derry stutters.

"And my boy Elber stopped him?"

"He did," Blondie says.

"I want the Pinkerton to confirm it." Ma's voice drips with suspicion.

"Tell them, Derry."

Derry nods, his face pale while ma peers at him with the full fury of her scrutiny, her face tightened into a wire trap to catch any hint of a lie.

"It was your son, ma'am," Blondie says. "That's the honest truth."

His ma doesn't want to believe Elber's a hero. At least Elber's pa knows what's right.

"Well then." The old man breaks the silence. "What do we do now? Call the sheriff?"

"No need for that." Blondie gestures at the corpse. "Not like there was any crime done, except for that one, and nothing the sheriff can do about him now."

"What about this one?" His ma points to the young Pinky. "You plan to make trouble over this?"

Derry shakes his head. "No, ma'am. Willard was in the wrong. Reckon he got what he deserved."

The front door swings open and Varla strides into the room. "What'd I miss?"

"Everything," Blondie says. "The big Pinker tried to shoot Rosa, and that kid stopped him cold."

"That's right," Elber speaks up. "Wasn't going to let

any crime happen on my watch."

"Put that gun away kid," Pa says. "Got to clean this mess before the coach gets in."

"You want help moving the body?" Varla asks.

"I think it'd be wise if all of you say nothing about this," Ma says.

"None of us want trouble," Blondie replies.

"Let's clean this up." Ma turns to Pa. "Coming down from the church, I think I saw Gus Pitts coming up the road. Be here in ten minutes."

"Gus Pitts?" Pa says. "You sure? Earlier than usual. We'll have to deal with this afterward. Hide the body under that table until we're done with Gus. Then when they leave, we'll bury it behind the outhouse."

Chapter 47

Still shaken, Derry sits at a table while Blondie wraps a bandage over Rosa's upper arm. "In and out," Blondie says. "At least nothing to remove."

"I hate bullets. Hate guns," Rosa grumbles.

"Did Elber really shoot Willard?" Derry asks.

"You were here," Blondie says. "You saw it."

"I saw it but I didn't see it." It happened so fast. He remembers: The colt tugged at his hand as it barked out a piece of lead aimed at Willard. Like a dream, Derry'd only meant to injure but the red hole appeared in Willard's chest as Willard stood in shock and turned to look at Derry. "I think it was me that..."

Blondie puts her finger to his lips. "Let it go, Derry. Keep you out of trouble and a loser like the Goober boy gets to be hero for once. A moment he can live up to his last days."

"It don't sit right with me," Derry says. "It's lying."

"Would it sit more right if they call the sheriff? An investigation? And they bring up the other case, and everyone's wondering how come Derry Flanders happens to be around when Jimmy Montgomery gets murdered, Willard Stark gets murdered. People start to think you have the plague. That what you want, Derry?"

He shakes his head. "I reckon not."

"Now, we got to be quiet." She has moved to a seat near a window. Varla and Rosa are at another window, ducked low, where they can observe the front yard of the outpost. Pulled by a draw-horse with a graying face and bald patches on its rump and shoulders, an old wagon creaks past the front of the Outpost. The Gruber parents are both at the far side of the store, where a ramp opens up at the side, to greet the arrival.

"What's going on?" Derry asks.

"Whoo! Look at that!" Blondie presses her face to the window, her eyes popping out of her head and her mouth gaped.

Derry glances out the window. The man who steps down from the cart is huge, like a seven-foot-tall Paul Bunyan statue come to life. His shirt and pants consist of old gunny sacks crudely stitched together and barely containing the muscles of his huge limbs. He deftly lifts the much older man, wheelchair and all, down from the cart.

"Hoo boy, is he big!" Blondie gushes.

"Cool your horses until later," Varla snaps.

The man in the wheelchair is missing his legs, deflated trouser legs hang from the seat in front of him. He's middle-aged, with a ravaged, angry face. The chair, mostly made of oak, has a wicker back and a solid wooden base beneath the seat. The man uses the large front wheels to propel himself forward with his hands. The giant follows behind him.

"That there is Gus Pitts." Elber has crept up to them as they stare out of the window. "And his son, Butch."

"Hooey, I can't get over how big he is," Blondie says.

"A monster is what he is," Derry says, but Blondie doesn't seem to hear him as she licks her lips and continues to watch the giant.

The old man maneuvers the wheelchair to the loading gate of the store while the huge thing, barely human with its massive features, lopes behind him. The giant pushes the older man up the steep slope of the ramp, and out of view from the window.

"What else can you tell us?" Varla asks, turning to Elber. "How'd he lose his legs? Train accident?"

"Not supposed to tell anyone about that. But maybe, if you give me a peek of your..."

"Elber!" his father shouts from the store. Elber grimaces and slinks away. The others are grinning, but Derry feels a bit sorry for him, trying to impress these women.

"Ta-ta, fat boy! No one wants your flamboozle," Varla chortles at Elber's retreating back.

"So what now?" Derry asks Blondie.

"What do you mean?" She doesn't look up, attention still on the giant loading a gunny sack into the cart.

"I reckon I can't stay here," he says. "None of us can, that's pretty clear. They wouldn't want us, not after what happened."

"You reckon right," Blondie says. "We're riding out today. Another hour or two."

"Maybe I can come with you? We can go together?"

She shakes her head. "That wouldn't work. But you're free, Derry, to go where you want. And maybe later, I'll see you again."

"I don't want to go back to Portland," he says.

"Go to a place that'll make you happy."

"I can't think of a place like that." He catches himself and remembers the people singing and laughing in the field of New Era Valley. "Want to go with me to New Era Valley?"

"No, Derry. I'm going with my friends." She peers closer to the glass. The giant is walking toward the cart, following the old man in his wheelchair. The giant picks up the old man and the wheelchair, lifts up, biceps rippling from the strain, and places him at the front of the cart, where the bench has been cut away to make space for the chair.

Chapter 48

Blondie fans herself with a silk hanky, watching the cart roll out of view from the window with the giant walking beside the horse. "Whoa, I can't stop looking." She glances over to see Derry still eyeing her with a long face.

"Hey, Blondie." Varla's voice quiet, her lips stroking Blondie's ear as she leans close.

"What is it, Varla?"

"Check on our little friend Goldilocks," Varla whispers. "Prepare her for the trip. Rosa and I'll be up in an hour or so. Help them take care of the big Pinky." Varla steps away.

"What did she tell you?" Derry asks, moving closer to Blondie.

"I need to go." She gives him a quick kiss on the lips.

Behind him, Varla reaches out a hand and grasps him by the shoulder. "Never mind her. You need to help us dispose of your friend. We're burying him out in the woods behind the outhouse."

Blondie doesn't look back as she heads out the door. She glances up the road at the giant, Butch Pitts, his shoulders and head still visible over the wagon as he walks ahead of it with the horse.

Chapter 49

Alone in the cabin, sitting on the edge of the bed, Lindy Sue Hawthorne frees her hands and pulls off the mouth gag. She's about to bend down to untie her legs when the door bursts open. She throws her hands back behind her back, not sure if she's been caught.

Blondie enters the cabin and shuts the door. "Leaving today, Cupcake."

"Really? How can I believe that?" Lindy Sue asks.

Blondie shrugs. "Don't matter what you believe. We're taking you back to East Portland."

"How can I trust you? I told you not to tell them."

"What do you mean, Buttercup?"

"You told Rosa about my stepmother."

"I might have said something." Blondie walks to her and towers over her. "We're all from bad families. I figured it couldn't hurt. She liked your singing. She treated you nicer this morning, didn't she?"

Lindy Sue nods. "You didn't tell the other one, did you?"

"You need to stop thinking we're the enemy, Cupcake." Blondie pushes her fingers in Lindy Sue's hair, while her other hand caresses Lindy Sue's cheek. "We're trying to help you."

"What happened? I heard gunshots."

Blondie shrugs. "Man was being a jerk, and another man shot him before he hurt anyone. You know how men are with their guns."

"So it had nothing to do with you or them?"

"Nope."

At least Lindy Sue knows Varla wasn't involved, she was in the room when the shots rang out. That's when she gagged Lindy Sue and quickly departed, leaving Lindy Sue in the cabin alone for the first time until Blondie showed up.

Blondie pulls her hands off of Lindy Sue. “You got your hands undone.”

“What do you mean?” Lindy Sue asks.

“I saw it when I came in.” Blondie sits down next to her.

“The ropes were too tight. My wrists hurt.”

“Ropes weren’t tight enough if you wriggled out of them.”

“Help untie my feet so I can get out of here.”

“You’re not going until the others get back.” Blondie puts her hand around Lindy Sue’s shoulder. “Play along, Cupcake. Be good and you’ll get home.”

“You promise?”

“Yes.”

“And we’re leaving today?”

“That’s right. Now let’s get those ropes back on.” Blondie pushes Lindy Sue face down on the bed and straddles her upper torso. Lindy Sue lets the other woman wrap the leather strap around Lindy Sue’s wrists, while she, head twisted sideways, gazes at Blondie’s naked thigh a few inches from her face.

“Done.” Blondie climbs off the bed. Strong hands turn Lindy Sue over and pull her seated upright. The hands are gentle on Lindy Sue’s face, caressing as if to calm a small startled animal, or so it seems to Lindy Sue. She watches Blondie’s hips sway as she sashays to the dresser.

A flick of a match, and Blondie returns with a lit joint in her mouth. Lindy Sue doesn’t resist. The smoke pushes into her lungs and flutters into her head. She presses her tongue in Blondie’s mouth, and this time Blondie does not back away, instead her tongue is in Lindy Sue’s mouth as their lips mesh. A shiver slides down Lindy Sue’s spine to the valley between her legs and back up to her belly.

Coming up for air, Blondie laughs. “You’re a naughty

girl, aren't you?"

"You were doing it too," Lindy Sue says.

"Does Varla know what a naughty girl you are? She show you how to kiss like that?"

"No! Never!" Lindy Sue makes an ugly face. "I hate her!"

Chapter 50

After Willard Stark is buried, Rosa and Varla, at a corner table in the outpost dining room, huddle together over a map, tracing the route to the Pitts ranch.

"That kid, *grandismo*. Sure we want to do this?" Rosa asks.

"Why not?" Varla replies.

"He is a *goliat. El monstruo de* Frankenstein. *Mucho más grande*."

Varla laughs this off. "Here's how we work it. Blondie will handle the Goliath. Lure him away. You look around. Look for signs of burial. Turned over dirt. The old cripple's got the money buried...or in the house. I'll handle the old cripple, see what I can get out of him."

"And who watches *princesa*?" Rosa says. "Why not take her to *famoso* doctor papa, before we—"

Varla shakes her head. "The big Pinky sent for reinforcements. We get in and out quick. If we go to East Portland first, Big Pinky's bounty hunter friends get the money."

"I still no like it," Rosa says.

"The girl won't be a problem. Remote ranch. Nowhere for her to go."

"You make it sound so easy, Varla. *No hay bronca.*"

Varla folds up the map. "Time to move."

A dozen minutes later, they are at cabin seven, the horses outside the door. Lindy Sue on the bed glares at Varla and Rosa.

"You dope her?" Varla asks.

"Some," Blondie says, packing up the saddle bags.

"I think she needs more. Rosa?"

Rosa grins.

"I can ride my own horse," Lindy Sue says, her eyes fixed on Varla. "I don't want to ride with you."

Varla laughs. "I don't think so. But I tell you what. You ride with Blondie."

PART IV: THE PITTS RANCH

Chapter 51

The wagon creaks and groans. Every trip to get supplies takes the old horse slightly longer. Where the trail tops the hill overlooking Gruber's Outpost, Gus Pitts, seated in his wheelchair, pulls the reins to stop the horse. His over-sized son Butch is in the seat beside him.

"Now, let's have a look, see what's what," the old man says, pulling a spyglass out of a cloth bag at the side of the wheelchair and holding it to his eye. "Make sure none of those Manure Error Valley heathens are there." He chuckles at his little joke. Below the outpost leaps toward him in the eyepiece. The hitching post looks clear, no New Era wagons unloading at the side where the store has a ramp leading up to wide open doors.

"Reckon we're clear, son." Gus shuts the scope and flicks the reins, and they lumber forward over the rutted trail. Butch says nothing, his face without emotion as he stares straight ahead, and Gus is not sure how much the kid understands. Gus often wonders if there's a normal human buried somewhere beneath his son's massive torso, thick limbs, and large block-shaped head. Butch never says anything, which makes up for Gus talking enough for both of them.

They ride past the front of the outpost and around to the side. Horace and Ethel Gruber are at the top of the ramp to the store. Butch leaps down from the cart, and reaches up and lifts Gus down, wheelchair and all, sets him gently on the ground.

"You're early, Gus," Horace calls down to him.

"Reckoned I'd get an early start, Horace," Gus replies. "Before it gets too hot."

"Yep," Horace replies. "Going to be a hot one today."

Once in the store, Gus rolls around the aisles, indicating the various items he wishes to purchase, the usual sacks of millet and flour, three dozen eggs, seasonal vegetables.

He points and the items are picked up and carried out to the wagon by one of the Gruber's or Butch. Elber comes in from the dining area to help out.

"Reckon I'll buy a couple cans of chili," Gus says. He looks over at a shelf of bottles. "And maybe a couple of bottles of red wine."

"Red wine? You planning on visitors?" Elber asks.

"Elber!" his father admonishes. "Don't pry into other people's businesses."

"That's okay," Gus says. "Norman's coming. Today or tomorrow I reckon."

"How's the lad doing?" Horace asks.

"Very good. Working and going to school. Such a smart kid."

"At least one of your boys is doing well," Elber blurts out, eyeing Butch standing stupidly at the doorway.

"Elber, mind your manners," Ethel Gruber snaps.

Gus shrugs. "At least I got one son doing well. Can't say the same for your poor parents, Elber."

"I reckon you're correct about that, Gus," Ethel says, cracking the first smile her face has had in many years. Both she and Horace cackle with laughter while Elber pulls a long face.

The wagon is loaded with food and supplies. Butch walks in front alongside the horse. As he rides, Gus lights his pipe and takes a few puffs before tucking it back in a shirt pocket. "I reckon when that nag dies, Butch, you can pull the wagon, rather than buy another dray."

His son doesn't respond, though his hearing is

exceptional.

In a couple hours they ride up the twisting pathway to the ranch house, a one-story structure of weathered wood on the side of a hill. Because of the sloping landscape, the sagging porch in front is a dozen steps off the ground. Butch pushes the wheelchair up a long ramp to one side. Inside is a large room that combines parlor and kitchen, a small wood table in the center, and toward the back are a couple of small bedrooms. The wallpaper is yellowed and peeling in places. Once the supplies are brought in, Gus sets about directing Butch to bring in some chopped wood, fire up the iron stove, and set a large pot of chili from the cans to a simmer.

Gus at the table reads the several newspapers he picked up at the outpost while Butch sits on a chair near the door, doing nothing. Gus can never get used to that, the ability to sit idly and wait, like a machine or an animal.

"The world's a terrible place," Gus says. "Another murder in Portland last week. A boy only a few years younger than you."

Butch, as usual, makes no indication he comprehends.

Continuing to read, Gus breaks out in a guffaw. "The victim was the nephew of a big railroad owner. Now that changes the story. Not that I suppose the kid deserved punishment."

Butch remains impassive, not even a nod of his big head.

Gus hates the railroads, and anyone who owns one is a scoundrel of the lowest order. The railroad stole his legs from him seven years earlier.

Another article on another page catches Gus's eye. "This is terrible. This guy back east in New Jersey is inventing an electric railway. We're living in scary times, my boy. If anything scares me as much as railroads, it's this electricity thing. Demonic is what it is."

Ten minutes later, as Gus reads about a huge French hunk of copper in the shape of a robed woman to be erected in the New York harbor, Butch arises, floor creaking under him. Gus glances up from the paper. "What is it, son?"

"Sum... brah," grunts the giant pointing toward the door. "Come...ing."

"What's that?" Gus sets down the paper. "Norman can't be here this early."

Butch shakes his head. "Hor's cum." He holds up a hand, four fingers. "Four hor's."

"Four horsemen? Coming this way? We best check it out. Quickly, boy! Wheel me out there." Gus grabs the shotgun as they roll through the front door and down the ramp at the side of the porch.

In the distance, coming up the trail, three or four horsemen. Gus whips out the spyglass to get a better look, unable to focus as the wheelchair bumps and lurches over the dirt pathway until the spyglass hits his eye socket.

"Whoa, there, son! Stop for a moment so I can see, damn it!"

Gus peers through the glass. He shakes his head for a moment, thinking the smack from the spyglass is making him see things. He puts it back to his eye. Three riders, and they're women. He zooms in on the third horse, with two riders, the one behind, smaller than the other women, perhaps a youth. Her mouth is gagged, and her hands and feet are bound in leather straps around the other woman's stomach.

"What in tarnation?"

The riders have stopped on the pathway near where it forks, one fork leading to the house and the other around the side of a small hill down the slope to the water pump.

"Must have spotted us." Gus waves his hand to indicate to Butch to propel the wheelchair. At a cantor, one of the riders turns and heads toward him and Butch.

The woman halts forty yards away and calls out: "Howdy, sir."

"What you doing on my property?" he yells back, his

hands on the shotgun lying across the arms of the chair. He bends sideways in the wheelchair, trying to peer around her to the others at the far end of the path. She stares at him without blinking, her face impassive, arms and legs rippling with muscles. She doesn't appear armed.

"Didn't know anyone lived here," she calls back.

"I do live here, and I don't like anyone on my land!"

"Me and my friends, we reckoned we'd water our horses and cool off. Saw that pump well down that other path."

"You didn't see the no trespassing sign?" he asks, while Butch continues to inch the wheelchair closer. Gus grabs at the wheel to get his son to halt.

She shakes her head. "Must've missed it. We won't be long. You won't even know we're here."

"You from New Era?"

She shakes her head. "Don't know no New Era. We been riding all day from the east."

"Just you and those other three? No one else?"

She shakes her head again. "No one else. Okay if'n we get some water?"

He puts the spyglass to his eye and leans to the side to get another look at the other three women, then lowers it. "I reckon so. Help yourself."

"Thank you, sir." She turns and rides toward the others. He puts the spyglass to the eye and continues to gaze at them.

Normally he'd scare off the occasional intruder since he hated strangers, but these women sparked something inside him. "Look at that, son," he says. "That woman, she looks like something, doesn't she? A man-eater...unless she met the right man. A man powerful enough to tame her."

He aims the glass at the woman tied to the back of the horse, cursing the distance and his inability to see her closeup. The curly golden hair spilling out of the bonnet, the slim figure. But why'd they have her bound and gagged? At that distance she looks like the other one, the girl at the train station the day he lost his legs seven years earlier. His thoughts drift back to that day, the train snorting and belching steam as it began to roll forward, and the woman fell on the tracks and he pulled her out of the way, but not in time for the train to roll over his legs, crippling him for life.

His hand shakes as he tries to keep her image in the scope. The four horses head down the other path to the well, vanishing from view.

"Wheel me back to the house, son. I want to get the more powerful spyglass."

Chapter 52

Lindy Sue is on a horse, riding in the desert, the steady up and down of the animal beneath her. The sun blasts down with its fiery rage. Confused, she thinks she's awakened from a bad dream.

Tommy? She's on the horse behind him, holding on to him, rocking against him to the rhythm of the animal's hooves, riding past tumbleweeds and stunted trees, the land cracked and parch. Where are we?

Where are we, Tommy? Her mouth has something thick in it. Her face is at Tommy's back, but the yellow cotton shirt is wrong, with no collar, and blond hair spills out beneath the wide-brimmed hat. Blondie, she realizes. Her arms are bound in front of Blondie, and her feet, too, bound at the ankles to the saddle horn, her legs bowled about Blondie's waist.

Her drug-dazed mind pulses to the slow steady beat of the hooves. Her feet up in the air, the hiked-up dress exposes her legs almost to her thighs. Lindy Sue is petrified as she looks down at her legs, helpless to do anything about it. She tries to push against the bindings, but movement is difficult. A hand reaches down and caresses her thigh, and Blondie twists back to look at her.

"You stay calm, Cupcake. We're almost there."

But Lindy Sue knows they are nowhere near East Portland.

The horses stop for a moment. Lindy Sue twists around to look past Blondie's shoulder. Thirty feet ahead, Varla walks up to a wooden sign nailed to a tree, and with a grunt, pulls it off and drops it on the ground. She climbs back on her steed, and they continue moving. Several minutes later they stop again.

Varla on her stallion gallops away. In the distance is a ranch house, and some tiny figures, converging with Varla across the dry flat ground. Soon Lindy Sue makes them out, a tiny, old man in a small wheelchair being pushed by a younger man. A part of her wants them to come over and make her captors release her, another part of her doesn't want them to see her, with her naked legs up in the air.

A few minutes later, Varla rides back and waves them to the path. The horses begin to move again, down a trail.

"We're taking a rest, Buttercup," Blondie says. "Let the horses cool off. Could use some cooling off myself."

Blondie reins the horse to stop. Varla walks up to undo the bindings at Lindy Sue's hands and legs, pulling her off the horse with powerful hands. "You behave if I take off the gag?" Varla asks.

Lindy Sue nods.

"Good girl." With a yank, the gag comes out. A dozen yards away is a well-pump, and nearby, a large wood tub, ten feet long and eight wide, made of barrel staves and already filled with water.

"This is great," Blondie says as she undoes the buttons of her blouse. "So ready for a soak."

"You just want to be *nudista*," Rosa remarks, leaning down to splash water in her face. "Give a show to that old *cojo.*"

Varla gives the pump some quick yanks to fill up a couple of large leather flasks.

With the others attentions diverted, it's Lindy Sue's chance to slip away. She looks back up the trail, but she realizes she's too dizzy and weak-legged to attempt to run up the pathway and toward the ranch house. Also the heat burns at her. She takes slow tentative steps toward the tub and kneels down to splash water to cool on her face.

In front of her in the water, Blondie rises up, wet and completely nude. "Come on in, Cupcake."

Jarred, Lindy Sue looks away.

Blondie laughs. Her hands on Lindy Sue's shoulders, she pulls her over the rim of the tub, and she falls into the cold water, screaming.

"Why did you do that?" Lindy Sue sputters, sitting up.

"Doesn't it feel nice?" Straddling Lindy Sue's legs with her own, Blondie is in front of her, too close for Lindy Sue to avert her eyes.

The water does feel nice, completely removing the hot burn of the sun on Lindy Sue's arms and legs; the heat that permeated every part of her body has vanished. Water splashes Lindy Sue's face. She opens her eyes. "Stop that, Blondie."

"You didn't tell me. Doesn't it feel nice?" Blondie sits in front of her, legs spread and back arched, her breasts in the open air, and the lower part of her body barely concealed by the ripples in the water.

"It does." Lindy Sue says. "But I don't think I'd have the courage to take off all my clothes."

"I've nothing to hide." Blondie shimmies her torso to make her breasts jiggle. "Neither do you. You look just as pretty with almost no clothes on."

The wet clothes! The cheap cotton shift and the silk night skirt, translucent, cling to Lindy Sue's skin, her nipples and pubes clearly delineated. She covers up with both hands, blushing.

"Smart girl," Rosa says, scanning the ridge. "The *veijo decrepito* with his peep-glass. Sick old *pervertido*."

"You got that right," Varla says, wetting her face with her neckerchief. "The filthy old ratbag, couldn't keep his eyes in his face and his tongue in his mouth."

"Ugh! Why we not *vamos?* I hate *viejo verde*."

Chapter 53

After a refreshing splash of water, Rosa follows Varla a dozen steps from the tub. Maybe Varla has come to her senses and given up on this scheme. They keep their voices low, out of range of the Hawthorne girl.

"I say we *vamos*, Varla. Pulling this off... Even without the girl..."

"You getting soft, Rosa?"

"No. *Mala espina.* A bad feeling, this whole set-up, that big man-thing..." Butch Pitts scares Rosa. He's like a Golem or an ogre, a creature out of myth. It seems doubtful bullets can kill him, or at least enough bullets before he kills them first.

"Relax, Rosa. Besides, we have company."

The wheelchair rider appears at the far side of the bluff, where it slopes up again.

"I'll meet up with him so he doesn't get too close. The less the girl hears, the better." Varla begins to stroll up the trail. At the far side of the trail, the old man wheels himself down the path. The giant is nowhere to be seen.

Varla and the old man stop, face to face, ten feet from each other, their faces level with the slope between them. She has her hands on her hips and her legs slightly spread, and he tries to peer around at the others behind her. Rosa glances over at the tub, where the horses drink from one side. Blondie and Lindy Sue look up from the water, Lindy Sue coy with her hand over her chest and Blondie giggling and flaunting herself.

Rosa listens to the conversation between the old man and Varla.

"You get around in that chair," Varla says.

"I have to. Keep an eye on my land." He has a deep,

crusty voice.

"That's not where your eyes are looking."

"That girl. Why was she bound and gagged?"

Varla shrugs. "No one's bound and gagged now."

"You didn't answer the question."

"That girl, she's not right in the head," Varla says. "Ever since her boyfriend killed himself. Very tragic. We're bringing her back to her parents. It's all hush-hush. They don't want publicity. You know how that goes."

"Yes," he says. "Reckon I do. I know tragedy. Just the same." He pulls out a spyglass, a foot in length, much larger than the other.

"What're you doing?" Varla asks.

"I need to check up on anyone on my land." He has the peep-glass to his eye, aimed not at Rosa but at the two stepping out of the tub. *Probably putting an image of them in his head to rub one off*, Rosa thinks in disgust. And Blondie, showing it all, she probably doesn't care.

"Listen," says the old man to Varla. "How about you and your friends have dinner with me and my boy?"

"Dinner?" Varla replies. "How sweet of you."

"We rarely have visitors." He still has the spyglass on the tub. "Let's say, in an hour and a half or so?"

"An hour and a half? You're on."

"And..." Distracted, he stares into the spyglass, his tongue flicking over his lips.

"And?"

He puts down the spyglass and turns the wheelchair around. With effort he rolls himself up the sloping path from which he came.

Varla turns and walks back toward Rosa.

"Dinner? *Que carajos.* The fuck, Varla?" Rosa hisses.

"The dirty old lecher's cutty-eyed on Blondie." Varla's voice is hushed as she leans close. "This is ideal. You start looking around for signs of burial, ruts from the chair wheels. Places where the wheelchair can get to."

“You heard him. He get anywhere on this land.”

“You know what I mean,” Varla says. “I’ll look too, while we wait for dinner.”

Rosa follows Varla down to the tub, where Blondie dries off with a towel, and Lindy Sue puts on dry clothes, her back turned to them.

Chapter 54

Lindy Sue quickly and nervously pulls off her wet clothes, to put on the dry ones Blondie has set out for her. The skirt is too short, not even to the knees, and both it and the blouse are too large.

She hears the footsteps of the other two women.

"What'd the old dotard want?" Blondie asks.

"Invited us to dinner," Varla replies. "Hour and half from now. Keep an eye on Goldilocks. Rosa and I are moseying around."

"I will, Varla." A moment later a hand falls on Lindy Sue's shoulder. "You hear that, Cupcake?" Blondie asks.

"Dinner?" Lindy Sue is stricken. "Why don't we leave now? If we wait, we won't reach East Portland before dark."

"It'd be rude, Buttercup. Nice man let us use his water. We can't mizzle on him. One kind gesture deserves another."

"But he was staring at us with that telescope. He aimed right at us."

Blondie shrugs. "Poor guy's a cripple. All he's got's his eyes and his brain. Don't give it no mind, Cupcake."

"Another thing," Lindy Sue says. "Why've we been traveling east?"

"What do you mean?"

"Where the sun is. Seems like we've gone east, not west."

"Taking a different route, that's all. We've been mostly going west."

"That's not what it seemed like."

Blondie grasps Lindy Sue's hand and brushes the fingers of her other hand through Lindy Sue's wet hair. "You're confused, Lindy Sue."

Smiling to Blondie, Lindy Sue has her attention on the horses, hitched to a post in the shade where the bluff forms a cliff side, fifty feet away.

"I don't think so." Lindy Sue pulls her hand from Blondie's fingers and heads toward the animals.

"Cupcake, I wouldn't go over there." Blondie's voice is far more relaxed than Lindy Sue would think it would be. *They can't keep me here.* Now that Lindy Sue is refreshed and Varla and Rosa are gone, perhaps kissing the way she kissed Blondie, perhaps doing what Blondie and Varla did in the bedroom of the other ranch when Lindy Sue was tied to the chair.

Her horse Chillins, like a pony next to the larger horses, grazes on some grass behind the others. As Lindy Sue gets closer, Varla's horse, the large black stallion becomes alert, bares its teeth facing her, and snorts through its quivering nostrils. When she steps to one side, the steed steps that way too, guarding the other horses. She hears Blondie's laughter behind her.

"Come back, Buttercup, before you hurt yourself."

Lindy Sue glares at the black stallion. Why did she think it could be that easy? To get on Chillins and ride off. Even if she did, the other horses are faster and stronger and they'd quickly catch her.

"Damn you!" She shakes her fist at the stallion. Trudging to Blondie, she turns to look at the horses.

The big stallion eyes her suspiciously.

"Run away, Cupcake, you get me in trouble," Blondie says.

"Why don't you help me? I can distract the stallion, and you can get our horses."

Blondie shakes her head. "I don't want trouble."

"You can come with me."

"This again." Blondie rolls her eyes. "Put these fantasies out of your head."

"Why not?"

"I'm not ready to leave."

"Are you afraid of her?" Lindy Sue stands face to face with Blondie. "Afraid she'll track you down?"

Blondie laughs. "Of course not. Varla's my friend. Not afraid at all."

"Then why do you do this? You're not like them."

Blondie puts her hands on Lindy Sue's shoulders. "What're you getting at?"

"You and me. You don't need them. We could be..." Flustered Lindy Sue has no words, and she's not even sure what she wants to say.

"I like you, Cupcake. I'll make sure you get home safe, even if I have to ditch the others. Let's go up and see our host, Old Man Piss."

"But dinner's not for an hour and a half."

"So? I want another look at the big guy." Blondie grabs Lindy Sue's hand and starts up the trail they came down. Soon they round the bluff and the old ranch house comes into view, at the far end of the other path, three hundred yards away.

Blondie pulls her to a halt, and faces her, putting her hands on Lindy Sue's shoulders. "Listen, Cupcake, you behave. I don't want you feeding any flamadiddle that upsets our host. You got that?"

Lindy Sue nods.

"You behave, and be a good girl. Do it for me, Lindy Sue."

"I will."

Blondie bends down to kiss her on the lips. A moment later Blondie straightens, staring into her eyes. "I can trust you, can't I?"

"Yes."

"Good." Blondie clutches her hand and starts to stride the path toward the ranch house, pulling Lindy Sue along.

Lindy Sue begins to strategize. Perhaps the old man can help her, though she can't think how. Blondie's hand is firm in hers, but Blondie seems lost in thoughts, staring straight ahead at the house. To one side, and set back from the house on a flatter patch of land, is a barn, half the roof collapsed, a shed, and a stable. Closer to the house, is chopped wood scattered around part of a tree, the handle of a large hatchet sticking up from a three-foot thick trunk. Clad in weathered boards like the barn, the house, too, looks ready to fall apart, as it juts up from the side of a hill. At one edge of the porch steps is a long wooden ramp, and the porch front is eight feet up from the sloping ground. The front door is open. The old man wheels himself out on the porch to watch them approach. As they get closer, Lindy Sue's anxiety grows.

Chapter 55

Hiking up the pathway with Varla, Rosa glances back at Blondie and the girl, near the water tub and pump.

"Varla, you trust her to watch the *princesa*?"

Varla turns and shrugs. "Blondie? Why not?"

"She got big eyes on the big guy."

"So what? She'll soon head up to the house, She and the girl will distract them while we search for the money."

"Bah," Rosa says. "A needle in a haystack." As she says this, she notices some broken leaves of sheep fescue at the side of the trail. She stoops down closer.

"Find something?" Varla asks.

Rosa nods, scanning the ground. A faint trail appears, hinted at by the rocks, the dirt, broken plants and snapped twigs, branching off from the pathway.

"Knew you'd find something." Varla crouches down to get a better look. "You have the eyes of a hawk."

They slowly work their way along the mostly hidden path. A large boot print in some dirt, from the giant no doubt. At one stretch, where the ground is baked hard by the sun, Rosa and Varla circle back and forth before they pick up the trail again. They're about two hundred yards off the pathway when they both stop and look at each other with smiles. In front of them, signs of earth being turned up, digging.

"Might be easier than we thought," Varla says. "I'll get the shovels. We have an hour before dinner."

"Maybe we don't stay for dinner if we have the chingching, Varla."

Varla shakes her head. "No. He'll be suspicious."

Varla heads back to where the horses are hitched, to grab the shovels they purchased earlier at the outpost.

Chapter 56

From his spot overlooking the pump and the soaking tub, with the spyglass to his eye, Gus Pitts becomes more and more convinced. The girl, she's the spitting image of the other one from seven years earlier. The same golden curls, the same oval face and pale skin. Through the more powerful spyglass, a closeup of her face, her eyes aimed directly at Gus, her mouth opened slightly, rounded in an "O" as she crouches in the water. He can't tell if she's naked like the blonde standing in the tub over her, but just the thought of it makes his hand tremble and his groin tingle.

He puts away the spyglass. He begins to move the wheelchair down the trail to get closer, but the black-haired woman appears in front of him, preventing him from moving any nearer. He invites them to supper, he'll have to wait to get a better look. He trades smiles and words with the big one with black hair, still blocking the trail. He spins the chair away and labors himself up the hill and back to the house.

He flashes back to that terrible day seven years earlier. At the station at Oregon City to see off his son, Norman, who was taking the train south to college. The train grunted and snorted, preparing to leave the station. Gus, still mourning the loss of his wife, sixteen years earlier, had been eyeing this beautiful girl-woman, eighteen or nineteen years old.

It was love at first sight. He walked up to her. She smiled. They began to talk. His heart pounded in his chest. He could see his life change before him, this angel pulling him from misery. She stumbled on the track in front of the train as it began to move. He leaped to save her, to push her out of the way, but not fast enough to save himself. The train shrieked to brake, but not fast enough as the wheels sliced across his legs. He was pulled away from the track. Blood sprayed from the crushed limbs, dripping from the bottom of the engine car, splattered on the iron of the wheels. Pain shot through his entire body. A doctor fashioned tourniquets around both his thighs above the knees and gave him morphine to make the pain go away.

For one moment he was a hero. He sacrificed his legs for the life of the girl. God had granted this for him so that she would be grateful to him, she would share her life with him, the life she now owed him. It made the pain easier, the thought of their life together, as he sat on the floor of the platform, propped up on pillows, her sweet words of thanks, the way she nodded when he said he wanted to marry her.

The train announced it was ready to go again. Not even a good-bye from her. Grabbed her bags and raced to get on the train. Not even a glance back, she hurried to board, pushing herself past the two or three others on the platform.

It was a one-two punch. Even worse than when his wife died giving birth to Butch. He was devastated. The Lord giveth and the Lord taketh away. But why was he always on the taketh away end of things?

With the help of his son, Norman, smart as a whip, even at eighteen, he sued the railroad. They won a big settlement, but it didn't take away the pain, the defeat. It simply meant that he could survive. Legless, and living with an imbecile kid, alone and bitter in the ranch house where he grew up. For many years he lived this way. Talking only to the Grubers on his weekly trips for supplies. He had all that money, but what was the point? It didn't buy happiness, it couldn't bring back his legs or his wife or that beautiful girl.

But finally the Lord has come through, he reckons. These women showing up. Something suspicious the way they had the young one tied up. Something wild and unsavory about these women, like they were godless heathens. And the young one, the spitting image of the one he saved seven years earlier.

"I tell you, son, she's just like the other," he gushes to

Butch when he returns to the house. “Just as beautiful. It’s a miracle. We have been blessed by the Lord at last. Get the other table in here, we’ve got four more for dinner.”

Butch grunts with a small smile.

“That’s right, boy. Those girls are joining us. And we got to get that young one away from the others. Rescue her from those other women. The Lord has given us a second chance. This time, I’ll make sure she doesn’t slip through my fingers. Can’t let that happen again. I’ll save her from those she-devils and she’ll be mine.”

Butch utters “Gir,” standing near the stove stirring the pot of chili.

“That’s right. There’s a girl for you too. That big one, with black hair. Never seen such a wild creature as that one. From the Amazon jungle, no doubt. She’ll be yours. No other man is strong enough to tame a woman like that. Think of it, Butch. We’ll have a double marriage with our new brides. This will turn our life around. We’ll have a reason to live. Bring this ranch back to life. Buy livestock and plant crops. Who knows, maybe Norman can marry the blonde or the redhead.”

Butch nods and grunts something. He looks at the door.

“What’s that?” Gus asks.

“Guh...uhh. Cuh.”

“They’re coming?” Gus glances out the open doorway. Two shapes are at the far end of the path. He wheels out to the porch to get a better look. His heart beats faster. Holding hands with the tall blond, the golden-haired angel floats toward him. *The two are like sisters*, he thinks.

He couldn’t ask for anything better. The young one, each step bringing her closer. More and more he’s convinced she’s the spitting image of the girl in his head, the one who dumped him after he saved her. And he finally gets to examine her up close, without the black-haired she-demon standing in the way.

Chapter 57

Lindy Sue and Blondie are a hundred yards from the house. "You act polite, Lindy Sue, and don't tell him anything. He won't believe you anyway."

Lindy Sue doesn't reply. The old man's eyes are glued to her, moving up and down in his head to take her in. He has a smile on his face. When she and Blondie reach the steps, they lose sight of him behind the porch steps above their heads, and then he reappears as they ascend.

"Welcome, girls'" he says. "You're early. Feeding time not for another hour."

"That's okay," Blondie replies with a smile, letting go of Lindy Sue's hand. "I'm not hungry yet, least not for food." Blondie peers past him into the house at Butch, who stands inside the doorway. Her eyes move up and down, her tongue licking her lips. "What's your son's name?"

"That's Butch," the man says. "Come out and greet our guests, Butch."

The giant treads warily onto the porch, floorboards groaning with each footstep. Standing outside the door, his face emotionless, he glances at Lindy Sue and Blondie and turns to his father.

"He's not much for words," the old man says. "My name is Gus. Gus Pitts."

"I'm Blondie, and this here is Goldilocks," Blondie says, not taking her eyes off Butch Pitts.

"Pleasure to meet you, Goldilocks." The old man lingers on the pronunciation of her name. He looks at Blondie. "And your name is Blondie?"

Blondie nods.

"Those are not your real names, are they?" His eyes narrow.

"No, but that's what everyone calls us. Your son, he sure is a big one."

Gus nods. "He's strong too. He pulls trees whole out of the forest for our firewood. About the only thing he likes to do is chop wood and lift weights."

"Lifting weights?" Blondie lights up. "People pay money for that."

"He'll give you a show for free." The old man shifts in his chair. "Boy? Show the nice lady your lifting."

The giant grunts and turns to where his father's finger points.

"That's right, boy. Take her to your work-out shed."

Blondie steps closer to the old man. Though her voice is low, Lindy Sue makes out Blondie's words: "Did my friend tell you about her? A bit out of her head. We're taking her back to the asylum."

"Yes. She mentioned something like that." Gus nods.

"Keep an eye on her."

"I will." He nods more vigorously.

Blondie steps up to Lindy Sue. "You hear that, Cupcake? You stay here with Gus."

Linda Sue lets herself be pushed hurriedly by Blondie to a wooden chair, along the wall a few feet from the open front door. "And don't tell Gus any tall tales."

Lindy Sue sees that Blondie has one thing on her mind, one thing only, and that thing she now swaggers toward with an exaggerated gyration of her whole body. She grasps his large hand with far more enthusiasm than she grabbed Lindy Sue's hand twenty minutes earlier.

"Yes," Gus says. "That's right, boy. Go to the shed with her. And I can keep an eye on the child."

"I'm not a child!" Lindy Sue blurts out, watching the backs of Blondie and the giant step off the far end of the porch, where the slope has negated the need for steps.

"And you...you tell me about yourself and your friends." The old man wheels his chair to face Lindy Sue.

Any hope of Blondie helping her has shattered. Lindy Sue looks at the man. “Can you help me?”

“What’s that? Let me get near so I can hear you.” He rolls the chair closer, floorboards creaking, until the wheels press at her knees.

“My dad’s a doctor,” she says.

“So?” He shakes his head.

“Dr. JC Hawthorne.”

“Dr. JC Hawthorne? I’ve read of him. Doctor who runs the loony house in East Portland.”

“Yes!” Lindy Sue exclaims. “He’s my father.”

“You’re confused, Goldilocks. But don’t you worry none. Neither those she-devils nor that doctor will ever put their hands on you again. You’re safe with me. Such a pretty young thing. Gus will protect you from all of them.” He edges his chair closer. “Tell me all about it.”

Lindy Sue glances past him to see if the women are approaching. She might not have much time and she doesn’t know how to even begin to tell him of the ordeal she’s been through the past several days. “Me and Tommy,” she chokes. “She killed him.”

Chapter 58

Blondie notices how the old lecher has an eye for Lindy Sue. The perfect opportunity for Blondie to get to know the gargantuan gollumpus better. His big strong hand in hers makes her feel like a little princess, taking her back to the first few times when she fucked men and not peepee-fumbling boys her own age. Blondie throws caution to the winds. Varla wants her to watch Lindy Sue, but it's worth the risk, for a chance to make out with the big guy. Old Man Piss can't keep his eyes off Lindy Sue, and Lindy Sue'd be a fool to run away this far from civilization.

Also he has a shotgun, attached by some straps to the side of his chair. That'll stop her from fleeing.

Guilt quickly fades as Blondie and the colossus enter the shed, an eight-by-ten structure with one side open. Inside on the back wall is a full-length mirror and a few images taken from newspapers, yellowed advertisements depicting circus strongmen with huge biceps and handlebar mustaches, in loincloths, and leopard sashes or sleeveless shirts, lifting barbells above their heads. Blondie has heard tell of this new circus sensation but hasn't seen it yet. On the floor of the shed are several large iron kettlebells.

The giant grabs a pair of the kettlebells and slowly lifts them over his head while looking in the mirror. "Haaa!" he says.

"You could be a strongman in the circus, Butch," Blondie says. "You'd be like them." She points to the pictures of the strongmen. The giant places the kettlebells on the floor and lifts them over his head again. Blondie tries to lift the smallest kettlebell, but it seems bolted to the floor it's so heavy.

The giant has put down the weights, and he now stares

at himself in the mirror, his arms up, flexing his muscles. Blondie steps up behind him, unable to resist putting her hand on his arm. The muscles in his arm are like massive cords as hard as gristle. What else was there to do? Not like they could carry on much of a conversation.

"Such big powerful muscles you have, Butch. You know any other tricks besides lifting anchors and looking at yourself in the mirror?"

No reaction. His face emotionless. He does nothing when she wraps both her hands on his chest and feels how solid it is, rubbing her hands against his rough skin. She peers out from beneath his armpit at the mirror in front of them. He neither pushes her away nor encourages her advances.

He's like a big mannequin or a wax museum creature, Blondie thinks, but one made of flesh and not wax or wood. Or like a male version of the Dutch Wives that Japanese sailors brought on long sea voyages.

The real question, the one she's been wondering since setting eyes on his out-sized size several hours earlier, is how big he is down there. She snakes her hands slowly down his abs, watching his face for any change of expression. Her hands linger at the top of his burlap shorts, tied by a thin rope, and then she glides them down over the rough surface. She feels the lump at his groin, not at all as big as she imagined, what would be a decent size on a normal man actually seems small for such a large man.

No reaction from him. He looks down at her hands, a slight look of confusion on his face. His penis remains flaccid, unresponsive to the probing of her fingers. A complete lobcock.

A woman's scream erupts from the direction of the house. Blondie freezes. Lindy Sue!

Chapter 59

The chair rolls closer, the wheels creaking on the weathered wood slats of the porch. The old man is in front of Lindy Sue, close enough to reach over and put his hand on her shoulder.

"You tell Gus all about it, sweet angel."

"Tommy..." She remembers that Tommy is dead and tears well up in her eyes, blurring her vision. She wipes them away to see the old man leering at her breasts.

"Such a pretty young thing. You don't worry none. Gus'll help." He leans forward, places his hand on her knee.

"Tommy... murdered...with her bare hands..."

"Tell Gus all about it." He leans over in the chair. The hand crawls up her thigh, pushing away the skirt.

"What are you..." Alarmed, she brushes away the hand and begins to stand.

He grabs her wrist with his other hand. "Don't get up, Goldilocks. You have to trust me. Let me help you."

"Let go of me!"

"You be sweet on me and I'll save you from those women. I may have lost my legs but I still have something down there." He pulls her hand toward his groin.

"Stop it!"

"No! You won't get away this time." His other hand grabs at one of her breasts. Lindy Sue screams and jerks back, tipping over her chair, at the same time smacking him in the face as hard as she can. Gus falls out of the wheelchair with a yelp, letting go of her. Lindy Sue leaps away from him, glancing down at him sprawled on the porch.

This is her chance, and she doesn't hesitate. She turns and rushes down the steps. Instead of heading toward the horses, she veers around the side of the house, opposite the way Blondie went, and begins to run as fast as her legs will carry her up the hill. The adrenaline pumps through her. In moments she reaches the brush where she won't be seen from the house. Her heart hammers in her chest and after a few minutes she slows slightly to a pace she can keep. Past scraggly evergreens and jagged rocks, up one slope and down another, feet slapping the hard ground. She doesn't dare look back. She has no idea what'll happen next. Maybe find a road that leads to a town? Another ranch? None of that matters as much as getting away from Gus, escaping the Vixen Outlaws, putting as much distance as she can between herself and the insanity.

She has no idea how long she's been running. Across open spaces, past sagebrush and through long tall grasses above her head. Along the edge of a creek for several hundred yards before it veers into a small canyon. Her knees and ankles hurt and her heart thunders and her hands and legs are scratched from brambles and thorns, but she doesn't dare slow. Birds, snakes, and small rodents scatter in front of her. At one point she thinks she's on the edge of collapse, but euphoria floods into her and she picks up her pace. On a small hill, she risks a glance over her shoulder, expecting to see Varla, Rosa, and Blondie on horseback in pursuit, but there is nothing.

Gasping for air, she continues to run. The sun is lower in the sky. Her legs are in pain. She finds herself flying down a hillside, stumbling into a pathway and almost colliding with a horse and rider. The horse rears with a loud whinny, nearly throwing the rider. Lindy Sue loses her footing and falls into the dirt.

On her hands and knees on the dusty path, she looks up in fear, expecting to see Varla. But instead, the rider is a man in his mid-twenties. He leaps down from his horse. His voice is gentle. "Sorry I almost ran you down. Are you okay?"

Lindy Sue begins to sob uncontrollably.

Chapter 60

In the weight-lifting shack, "Better see what's up," Blondie says to Butch, not that she knows if he understood, though his face contorts slightly, mouth gaped open at the sound of the scream. Blondie sighs. "Can't leave her alone for five minutes without trouble."

She hastily buttons her blouse as she rushes out of the shed and up the path to the porch, where the old man lies sprawled a few feet from his wheelchair, and no sign of Lindy Sue. Blondie scans the terrain with a rising sense of panic.

She stands over the old man. "Where is she? Where'd she go?"

Gus moans, twisting his head to glare up at Blondie. "Damn girl's dangerous. Almost killed me."

Blondie suppresses the urge to kick his face with the tip of her boot. "Dangerous? How can she be dangerous when you have a damn shotgun. What'd you do to make her flee?"

"Me? What could I do? I'm helpless."

"I bet. Real helpless." The sarcasm drips from her voice. "I need to find her fast."

The giant must have finally realized something is wrong; he stomps across the porch bellowing. "Pwah! Pwah!" He grabs his father off the floor by the arms, and lifts him up and sets him back in the wheelchair.

"She ran that way." Gus points to the far end of the porch. "My son can help you track her down."

"The clodpate colossus?" Blondie shakes her head. "Seriously?"

"Yes. He has exceptional hearing."

"We don't have much time." Blondie glances over at the trail to the water pump, but so far neither Varla nor Rosa have appeared.

"Boy?" the old man says. "Can you hear her footsteps? The young girl. Can you hear her running away?"

The giant stands over his father, cocking his head one way, then another.

"Boy, you go with this woman and find that girl. Find her and bring her back. You understand, boy?"

The giant nods. "Fine'... Guh. Brin' here."

"That's right, son. No time to lose. Bring her to me."

The giant runs to the far side of the porch, and Blondie follows. As she steps down, she sees Varla emerge at the far side of the trail, heading toward the house on foot at a rapid clip. *Anything to delay a confrontation with Varla*, Blondie thinks as she follows the giant up the hill and into the brush.

The giant pauses, a hand to his ear, looking one way and then another while Blondie catches up.

"You hear her?" Blondie asks.

"Guh. Don' wan' hur' guh."

"Don't want what?"

"Hur' guh."

"Hurt girl?"

He nods vigorously with his huge head.

"No one wants to hurt her," Blondie says. "We need to find her so she doesn't hurt herself."

The giant grunts, and begins to run toward a patch of small stunted trees. Blondie races after him, struggling to keep up with the speed of his long legs. He's dozens of feet ahead of her when she reaches the trees.

"Hey! Wait up!" At her shout, he doesn't pause, look back, or even slacken his pace. After another minute he's almost out of sight, and when she emerges from the woods, where the land slopes down and back up, he's a small shape, many hundred yards away, running up the steep hillside.

"Fooey!" Blondie watches him vanish over the side of the hill. She stops to catch her breath. No point in trying to follow him, she'll just get lost. She turns back, to see Varla emerge from the woods.

Blondie gulps a deep breath and strolls toward her. Varla doesn't look angry, not that that means anything. Hands on hips, she waits for Blondie to get closer.

"What the hell, Blondie? You were supposed to watch her." Varla jerks her hand and Blondie flinches. The hand grabs Blondie's arm, and the other hand yanks her close, face to face with Varla. She can't look away from Varla's eyes.

"The big guy'll catch her," Blondie says, glaring at Varla, waiting for the blow. It comes open-handed across her face and nearly knocks her down, but with a yank on her arm, Varla keeps her on her feet.

"I ought to spank you."

"I deserve to be punished."

"Spank you like your daddy used to do when he found out you watered his liquor when you were nine years old," Varla says. "Spank you so hard that cute ass turns to sausage meat. Come here, Loretta. You been a bad girl."

A rush of fear, Blondie trembles. Her father, holding the bottle to the light, looking from it to young Loretta, a bit tipsy from what she's drank that night and knowing her father sees it in the way she has trouble standing still and facing his violent gaze.

"You old enough to drink, you're old enough for other things too. You bad girl. Too bad to be a daughter of mine." His arms on her, pushing her into the shed behind the house to punish her. The pain wells back up in her, and she shakes and squirms in his arms as he pins her to a wall, but then she realizes she's against a tree, Varla in front of her.

"Why did you..." Weak, far weaker from the memory than from Varla's slap, Blondie staggers and almost falls. "You know how painful those memories are?"

"More painful than what I can do with my hand," Varla says, grinning. "You shouldn't have let her get away."

Blondie shrugs, trying not to cry or look weak. "The gargantuan gollumpus will catch her."

"Let's hope so," Varla says. "Who knows what he'll do to her when he does. Why aren't you with him?"

"I couldn't keep up. I don't think even you could."

"Sure as a gun I could. What were you thinking? Leaving her with the old cripple?"

"I figured he'd watch her for a short while. I didn't think she'd be stupid enough to run away and he'd be stupid enough to let her."

"Come on." Varla grabs her hand and they trudge through the woods toward the house.

"Have you found the money yet?" Blondie asks.

"Maybe. Rosa's following some clues."

"Why don't you get it out of the old lecher with your mind flummery?"

Varla shakes her head. "Not so easy. Getting into his head, too much ugliness and misery. Too risky."

"Too risky? For you?" Blondie glances over at Varla.

"His brain's too messed up. I try to get inside it, it'll make me that way too."

"You mean someone is more messed up than me?"

"He's had a long time to accumulate that. Most people that age, have things more figured out."

"Well, that's swell," Blondie says. "What about Lindy Sue?"

"What about her?"

"She messed up too? That's why you can't read her?"

"That's another matter. Only a bit more time."

"Or maybe you're losing your touch, Varla."

These words sting Varla. Blondie can feel it in the flinch of Varla's hand on hers. "Shut up," Varla says. She yanks Blondie around to face her. "You want me to—"

"No." Blondie shakes her head.

"Okay. Let's not fight. We need to work on getting that money."

They head back to the house, Varla pulling Blondie beside her. The smattering of trees offers a bit of respite from the hot sun, but ahead the trees thin out to an empty field.

"I have an idea," Blondie says. "That old cripple, you see the way he looked at Lindy Sue?"

Varla nods. "At first I thought it was you, but you're right. He has a big thing for her."

"I was thinking, maybe we can get the money out of him that way."

"What do you mean?" Varla asks.

"See how much he'd give us if we gave him the girl. A trade. So we don't have to get the money out of him some other way."

"But then we don't get the reward."

"Which won't be much," Blondie says. "I told you what she told me. Her stepmother holds daddy's purse strings."

"She doesn't think much of herself. But we don't know what her dad'll pay for her, stepmother or not."

"But that cripple, I think he'll pay a lot. He's obsessed with her."

Varla nods. "True."

"He's been hoarding this money for years. Waiting for something to spend it on. Waiting for a moment like this. He has nothing else to live for. I think he'll give us most of it if we hand her over to him."

"Interesting idea, Blondie. If Rosa hasn't found the money, your plan might work. We make a deal, and when he goes to where he keeps his stash... But that won't happen unless the son finds her and brings her back alive."

They emerge from the woods. The old man is at the side of the house, putting the spyglass in its sheath while he waits for them to approach.

"You wait," he says when they reach him. "My boy, he'll find your missing girl. And bring her back, carrying her over his shoulder like a sack of grain."

"You'd better hope so," Varla says. "Her parents'll pay a lot of money to know she's safe. They'd be very upset if she's dead."

The old man turns his wheelchair and heads toward the porch, and the two women follow.

"Say, where's your friend?" the old man asks. "The red-headed one?"

"She'll be here soon," Varla replies.

"Don't like people creeping around my property. Not proper behavior for guests."

"She's tending to the horses and taking a dip in that tub."

"Is that so?" he mutters, his fingers rubbing against the spyglass, in a cloth sack at one handle of the wheelchair.

"Look, here she comes now." Varla gestures with her hand. Rosa appears at the far end of the trail, striding quickly toward the house.

The old man sighs. "I'd better check on that food, make sure nothing is burning. Sure hope Butch gets back soon."

Chapter 61

On her hands and knees on the dusty path, Lindy Sue can't say anything as she gasps for breath, feeling pitiful with her sobbing. The man kneels down next to her. "It's okay. Just let it out, if you need to." He pulls a cotton kerchief from his shirt pocket and holds it out to her.

"Thank you." She dries her eyes and hands it back to him.

"What were you running from? A cougar?"

She shakes her head. "Murderers. Three women."

"Huh?" He glances around. "I don't see them. Nothing to worry about now. Want some water?"

She nods. He hands her a canteen and she takes a drink, the water washing the dust and grit from her mouth. When she hands it back, he pulls the kerchief back out, wets it, and hands it to her. She wipes the dust off her face, the wetness refreshing.

"Don't worry," he says. "No one will hurt you. What's your name?"

"Lindy Sue."

"Mine's Norm."

"Thank you, Norm." She struggles to her feet. A hand on her arm, he helps pull her up.

He shields his eyes, looking west toward the sun. "It'll be dark in a few hours. You shouldn't be out here alone. You live around here?"

She shakes her head. "East Portland."

"I'm headed back in that direction in a couple days. I can take you there."

"You don't mind?"

"Not at all. Nice to have company on the trip. I'm headed over to see my family. Come along. You'll be safe there."

"That's okay?" she asks.

"Sure."

"That's so kind of you, Norm." She tries not to sound weepy.

He hoists himself back on the horse and then leans down to help her on the horse behind him. With a twitch of the reins, the steed begins a steady trot along the trail. He twists his face toward her. "So you live in East Portland?"

"That's right," she says. "My dad runs the hospital."

"Hospital?"

"The asylum in East Portland."

"I know of it. I'm studying psychiatry myself. Hope to get a job there. You say your dad works there?"

"Yes. Dr. JC Hawthorne."

"You know Dr. Hawthorne?" He glances back at her, a look of surprise.

"Yes. He's my dad."

Norm nods. "I heard he had two or three daughters."

"I'm one of them."

"Isn't that something," he says. "Maybe you can put in a good word for me when I go for an internship."

"I'll do that."

"You still haven't explained why you're out here alone."

"These three women. They kidnapped me."

"Three women. Okay. Why'd they do that?"

"They killed Tommy."

"They killed someone?"

"Yes. Tommy, my fiancé. She murdered him with her bare hands. They were taking me back to East Portland to make my dad pay a ransom."

"Is your dad wealthy?"

"He owns the hospital."

"That's right. Dr. JC Hawthorne." He chuckles. "I'll get you home safely, Lindy Sue. And no worries about ransom."

Finally, someone who can help me, she thinks, even if she suspects he doesn't quite believe her story. She puts her arms on his chest to steady herself to the gentle up-and-down of the saddle. He's not as strongly built as Tommy, but certainly no weakling. His shirt is of a rough cotton, a cheaper blend than what Tommy would wear. She leans forward to let the brim of his hat shade her face. They continue to ride, through the dry hilly landscape of runty trees and tall sage grass while insects drone in the heat and a lone raptor floats high overhead, circling once and then away.

"You awake?" Norm asks.

Lindy Sue realizes she nodded off. "I am now."

"Almost there. My family'll have a nice meal. Looks like they have other guests. You must be hungry, Lindy Sue."

"Yes." She glances over, the landscape vaguely familiar, a flat dry plane with bits of crabgrass and brush. Then she sees an old barn, with part of the side caved in, and in front of it, scattered wood and the ax. All at once the alarm rises up in her. She twists sideways to look past Norm, and the alarm becomes full-blown panic. There, gathered in front of the ranch house, Varla, Blondie, and Rosa, and Gus Pitts, all of them watching the horse approach.

"No! That's them! Turn back, Norm!"

"What's that?" He twists around, confused.

"You have to turn back. They're the ones who murdered Tommy. Why're you taking me here?"

"Calm down, Lindy Sue. This is my home."

"You... live here?"

"Yes. That's my dad over there."

"That man in the wheelchair?"

Chapter 62

A short distance from the front of the house, Blondie and Varla meet up with Rosa coming from the trail. Blondie can tell from the grim look on Rosa's face that she's not found the money. They stand in a circle.

"So what'd you find?" Varla asks.

"No money. Nada. Buried out there, some animal. Maybe not animal. I won't dig more to find out. Buried four months ago. Rotting bones. *Fetido.*"

"What kind of animal?" Blondie asks.

"Maybe you should've dug further," Varla says. "He could have a dead dog to guard his loot. Some crazy superstition like that, who knows."

Rosa's face wrinkles up. "Not digging further. Dead body out there. More than one."

"I still think we get the old cripple to buy Lindy Sue," Blondie says. "Instead of sneaking around. It could take days to find the loot."

"We don't have days," Varla mutters. "The big Pinky's bounty hunter friends arrive at the outpost tomorrow. With that blabbermouth Elber Gruber..."

"You like it here, Blondie?" Rosa says. "So you can *chingar* ugly giant."

Blondie shakes her head. "I'd rather leave this creepy place."

"Me, too," Rosa says.

"He'll take Lindy Sue off our hands," Blondie says. "I bet he pays almost everything he's got. Everyone happy. No one gets hurt."

"Sell the *princesa* to the old *cojo*?" Rosa nods, her forehead wrinkled in thought. "Good idea, Blondie. Easier than we take her to East Portland. What you think, Varla?"

“If we can’t find the money another way. But leaving her with these...” Varla becomes quiet at the sound of the wheelchair rolling onto the porch.

“You becoming *blandito*?” Rosa asks. “Getting soft?”

“No!” Varla scoffs. She turns and waves to Gus Pitts, on the porch with the spyglass to his eye. He puts down the spyglass and begins to descend the wooden ramp at one side.

“Good news, ladies! My son’s found her. Over there, look.” He points toward the trail. In the distance, a horseman rides toward them.

“How can that be your son?” Blondie says. “He’d break the back if he mounted a horse. He’d have to ride an elephant or rhino.”

“No, my other son. Norman. Right on time for dinner.”

The other son, the one who was supposed to be away at college? The three women share a look before they turn to the far-off horseman with another rider in the saddle behind him.

Chapter 63

Lindy Sue grabs the reins from Norm's hands to get the horse to make a one-eighty degree turn but he slaps her hand away. "No! Take me somewhere else."

"Stop that," he cries out. "What's wrong with you?"

The panic completely takes over. Lindy Sue pushes herself off the horse, rolling quickly in the dirt to avoid the back hoofs clattering inches from her legs. She stumbles to her feet, but too late, Varla's strong fingers coil around her arm and pull her standing. Norm leaps down from the horse.

"What's going on here?" Norm looks from Varla to his father and back to Lindy Sue.

"They murdered my boyfriend," Lindy Sue says. "And then he tried to..." She points at the old man as she squirms in Varla's grip.

"Be quiet, will you?" Varla says. "Or must we gag you again?"

The fingers on Lindy Sue's arm tighten until she gasps in pain. Afraid, she clams up and the fingers loosen their grip.

"Thank you, Norman," Varla says. "She escaped the asylum in East Portland."

"These women work for the asylum," says Gus Pitts, a drooling leer on his face. "That's Varla, and the others are Blondie and Rosa."

"She claims she's Dr. Hawthorne's daughter," Norm says.

"I am his...ow!" Lindy Sue is cut off by Varla's strong fingers squeezing pain into her arm.

"How absurd is that?" The old man laughs and points at Lindy Sue. "She's not quite all in the head, Norman. You should know that with all the money spent on that damn school." The old man glances around. "Norm here wants to be a brain doctor." He chuckles dismissively.

"Do we need to put a leash on you to make you behave?" Varla says to Lindy Sue.

"Or maybe pull your britches down for a public spanking," Blondie says. "In front of all these people?"

Lindy Sue glares at Blondie and turns to Norm, pleading to him with her eyes. Surely he'll see the meanness of the others and take her side. Mouth gaped in confusion, he stares at her. The fingers around her wrists slacken. Lindy Sue quivers her lips, please help me. His eyebrows raised, his mouth pursed, he rubs at his chin.

"Her story did seem a bit wild," Norm says.

"And you believed her?" old man Pitts scorns.

"Well..." Norm shrugs helplessly.

Any shred of hope sinks completely. Norm is on their side, just as Blondie is; all of them united against her, looking at her with pity and contempt. Standing in front of them, exhausted from running and riding, in a slight daze, she begins to wonder who she is. The house in East Portland, her father, Maggie, Tommy, it's all so far away, more like a dream than reality. And yet, she knows what happened.

"I can prove they murdered Tommy," she says, trying to keep her voice calm and level. "He's at a ranch his father owns."

"Tommy who?" Rosa and Blondie ask in unison.

"Tommy Mitchell. Senator Mitchell's son." Her eyes on Norm, Lindy Sue's ready to cry, and she will if that makes her more sympathetic without seeming mad.

"The senator's son? That'd be in all the papers if it happened," the old man says.

"There's proof. They murdered him. His dead body. All you need to do is—"

"Enough of your flummadiddle." Varla pushes a gag in Lindy Sue's mouth, while Norm, ten feet away, does nothing but stare.

"We can at least hear her story." Norm steps closer.

"You can later," Varla replies. "We'll ride west with you."

"She's acted crazy ever since her man bit the ground," Blondie adds.

"I reckon we know too much about death here," the old man says gravely. Butch Pitts appears from the side of the house, striding toward the group on his enormous legs. "That one there..." The old man points at the giant. "He was gargantuan, even as a baby. Killed his mom when she birthed him."

Lindy Sue has never heard it said that way and it repulses her. She looks over at the colossus, his face expressionless, but maybe he feels inside, this cruel dig from his father. She thinks about her own mom, who died giving birth to her. It's like Gus Pitts has just accused her of killing her mother. His words reverberate in her head. "Killed his mom when she birthed him."

"Time for someone's medicine." Varla pushes Lindy Sue over to Rosa. "You do the honors, Rosa. And check on the horses."

Rosa grabs Lindy Sue's arm. "*Si. Medicamento.* Come, *Pingo*." She pulls Lindy Sue on the pathway toward the trail to the water pump where the horses are still tethered. Lindy Sue twists her head around to the others. They stare at her as Rosa leads her away.

"Run off like that, you ninnyhammer," Rosa says. "You want die in desert? *Chica muerta?*" They are fifty yards from the group in front of the house. Rosa tightly grips Lindy Sue's arm and Lindy Sue stumbles to keep up with Rosa's long legs and fast gait. Rosa glances over her back and halts, yanking Lindy Sue close to her, face to face. The Mexican unties the gag and pulls it out of Lindy Sue's mouth.

"You're all liars!" Lindy Sue's voice quavers with anger and fear.

"*La Verdad,* the truth is what we say." Rosa wrenches on Lindy Sue's arm to start them walking again.

"That's crazy. You can't say something and make it so."

"I no take off the gag for you to argue." Rosa slows her pace.

Lindy Sue says nothing. They reach the path down to the pump.

"Is it true?" Rosa asks. "What Blondie say? Stepmother hold purse strings, not pay to bring you home?"

"If it's true, you'll let me go? I won't tell anyone what happened. And you weren't the one who killed Tommy. Let me ride away and save everyone a heap of trouble."

Rosa grins and shakes her head. "You're a clever one."

"Why not? If you helped me... I'd be thankful."

"What I do with your thankful? Not worth a peso. Now, you sit." Rosa points to the ground, loose dirt and small scraggly plants poking out of the crusty earth. They are past the water pump and the tub, thirty yards from the horses, who watch them idly.

"Sit?" Lindy Sue says. "There's nothing to sit on."

"Your *culo*." Rosa pushes her down. Lindy Sue lands with a gasp, her rear end painfully hitting the hard ground. Rosa stands over her. "Stay here."

Rosa walks to the steeds. The large black stallion in front of the others watches her warily but does not make any of the threatening moves it did to Lindy Sue earlier.

"Good boy, Storm." Rosa pats the animal's head. She walks over to Lindy Sue's mare, Annabelle, with the extra saddlebag load, and pulls out some treats, which she gives to each horse, the others whinnying in anticipation. Then she goes to the black stallion and extracts a small black cloth sack from the saddlebag.

Lindy Sue watches, not daring to move. On her feet, how far could she run before Rosa catches her? Without a horse, her chances of escape are nil.

Rosa strides toward her, a smile softening her face. "Good girl." She kneels down in front of her. "Time for *medicina*."

"You don't have to do that. I'll behave."

Rosa shakes her head. "No take chances, *chica carino*. You bad girl today." She pulls a small vial from the bag.

"Are you trying to poison me?" Lindy Sue asks.

"Why we do that? You worth nothing dead."

Lindy Sue struggles, but Rosa, her hand on Lindy Sue's jaw and her fingers at Lindy Sue's cheeks, forces her face upward and lips open while she drips some of the tincture into Lindy Sue's mouth. The stuff is bitter to the tongue.

"Swallow." Rosa drops the vial and has her other hand on Lindy Sue's throat. She lets go of Lindy Sue's face and hands her a leather canteen. Lindy Sue drinks the taste from her mouth with several large gulps of water.

"Stuff take half hour to kick." Rosa says. She has a pipe in her hand, which she lights and inhales.

"No. You don't have to." Lindy Sue struggles to avoid her lips. Rosa pushes her backward on the ground and climbs on top of her. Pressing her lips to Lindy Sue's, Rosa blows the smoke into Lindy Sue's lungs, its heat radiating into her torso. Despite her fear, Lindy Sue has an exhilaration, a tingle between her legs as if a man was lying on her the way lovers do, Rosa's large body pinning her to the hard ground.

Rosa rises up, clamping her hand on Lindy Sue's mouth until Lindy Sue begins to convulse in a coughing fit. Still straddling Lindy Sue's thighs, Rosa's dark eyes stare at her through the wisps of pungent smoke that drift between them. Lindy Sue lies still, her hands out at her sides, feeling the smoke in her lungs push fingers into her mind. She becomes aware of her breath, her chest rising and falling, her heart beating rapidly, Rosa above her, the intensity of Rosa's large dark eyes on her.

Rosa relights the pipe, not taking her eyes off Lindy Sue. Lying back down on Lindy Sue to give her another dose, meshing her lips into Lindy Sue's while she blows the smoke deep into Lindy Sue. Lindy Sue closes her eyes and pretends for a moment she's kissing, surrendering herself to a man, to Tommy, or Blondie, or Maggie, another hugging her to the ground, pressing warmth and strength into her. She's giddy, relaxing herself to let the flesh press in closer to her own. Rosa pulls herself upright again. Her brow furrows in confusion. Tendrils of smoke linger between them.

"Why you look at me like that?" Rosa asks.

"Like what?"

"*Me deseas.* You desire me." Rosa's fingers caress Lindy Sue's cheek, chin, and throat while her thumb, tasting of sweat and hot spice presses between Lindy Sue's lips.

"No," Lindy Sue says hesitantly. The tingle in her groin spreads into her thighs and up through her torso, that same tingle she got with Blondie, and before that, hinted at that time with Maggie. Rosa, with her muscular arms, her hand on Lindy Sue's cheek, is how Lindy Sue imagines making love to a man would feel, if Tommy had ever gotten intimate with her that way, and while she denies Rosa's accusation, she rubs her cheek into Rosa's firm palm.

"Varla, she make love to you?" Rosa asks.

"No! Never! I hate her."

"Blondie told me you kiss women, *tortillera*?" Rosa pushes her thumb past Lindy Sue's lips, rubbing inside between the cheek and teeth.

"I..." Lindy Sue closes her eyes. The thumb in her mouth tastes of salt and earth.

"You are *morrita,*" Rosa says. "Sexy girl. *Taco de ojo.* And you *jarioso*. Full of desire."

"I'm not." Lindy Sue tries to shake her head.

"You can not lie." Rosa smiles. When she leans down, Lindy Sue closes her eyes and puts herself into it, using her tongue this time, her heart pounding. Rosa's mouth is lemony as her tongue pushes into Lindy Sue's. For half a minute Lindy Sue forgets where she is as she kisses the other woman.

Rosa sits up straight. “You can not lie, *zora*. You want *el delicioso*. You desire sex.”

“What are you...” Lindy Sue gasps. Rosa has her hands on Lindy Sue’s breasts, fingers pinch the nipples through the thin cotton of the cheap shirt.

“*Pezones duros* give you away,” Rosa says. “You *excitada encholada*.”

“Stop it.” Lindy Sue gasps, her throat thick. The fingers on her make her body tremble and sing as if this is something it has waited for, not knowing the lack. She squirms beneath the strong hands.

Rosa laughs. “You’re a *cachanda zorra.”* She pushes her hand down between Lindy Sue’s legs while staring at her face. “You wet down there.”

“Stop that!” Lindy Sue shudders, trying to gasp out the words, trying to freeze her thighs to not respond to the pressure of the palm of Rosa’s hand. Rosa grabs Lindy Sue’s hand and begins to rub it against her own groin, while her hand rubs on Lindy Sue. Soon they are side by side on the ground, and Rosa pushes Lindy Sue’s hand down inside Rosa’s pants, down to the wetness between her legs, while Rosa continues to squeeze and rub her other hand on Lindy Sue’s groin. Lindy Sue loses control, gasping, the flood of ecstasy between her legs, barely aware of Rosa’s own grunts and gasps. Then it’s over, their hands at their sides, the only sound their heavy breaths and the nickering of one of the horses over the insect drone.

Rosa pushes herself up on one shoulder, looking down at Lindy Sue. “You like, *si*?” Her face is softer, relaxed.

Lindy Sue speechless merely nods. It took her mind off her problems, if only for twenty or thirty minutes.

Rosa rises from the ground, standing above Lindy Sue. “I like you, *chulita.* See why Varla like you.”

“She doesn’t like me. She hates me and I hate her.”

Lindy Sue pulls herself off the ground. On her feet she feels dizzy, from the sex and the drugs, and almost falls back down before Rosa catches her, hugging her, kissing her on the lips.

"Silly one. We go to house, *chulita.*"

"Do we have to? Why don't we just leave? You bring me home and my dad pays you." Lindy Sue gazes into Rosa's eyes, her hands on Rosa's tight biceps. "I like kissing you."

"Silly *pingo.* I like sex with you, but you think I desert Varla?" Rosa laughs, grabs Lindy Sue's hand and starts to pull her up the trail to the ranch house.

Chapter 64

Norm Pitts watches Lindy Sue, if that is her name, be dragged away by the Mexican woman. He sympathizes with the young woman, the turmoil in her mind and the way she got agitated at the sight of the others. He has the urge to stop Rosa from taking her away, to find out more, but he's confused, a swirl of questions in his mind.

"Can you imagine that?" Gus chuckles, spyglass to his eye, leering at the departing women with his tongue lolling from his jaw. "Telling us a senator's son was murdered."

"It's no laughing matter, father," Norm replies. "That girl has gone through something terrible. Why is she taking her away?"

"The girl's medicine is in the saddle bags," Varla says. "Our horses are hitched near the water pump."

"These women work for the Hawthorne crazy house," Gus says. "They might put in a good word for you, Norm, if you finally get that degree."

"I'm almost done," Norm replies testily. "End of this year."

"Sure. Then you go back to school for something else. What'll it be this time? Saddle tanning?"

"Stop it, Father." Norm glares at Gus. "My legal degree came in handy, didn't it?"

"No more talk about that." Gus glares back before a fake smile crawls across his face. "Why don't we all go inside and check on dinner? It must be almost ready." He gestures to Butch and points toward the front door. "Boy! Bring me up on the porch."

Butch walks over and pushes the wheelchair toward the long ramp at the side of the porch steps.

Norm faces the two women, both nearly as tall as him. The three stand in a triangle. “You two work at the asylum?”

“That’s right. We’re nurses,” Varla says.

“You don’t look like nurses.”

“We only wear those uniforms at the hospital. Those white-and-grays show too much dirt when we’re in the field.”

He turns from her to Blondie. Both women stare at him, *an almost hungry, predatory look*, he thinks, far more bold than other women he’s met. Who are they? Why are they at his father’s ranch? What is up with them and the girl, Lindy Sue? So many questions roil around his mind he doesn’t know where to start.

“So your dad says you study medicine, specializing in mental abnormalities,” Varla says.

“That’s right. Let me talk to the girl, Lindy Sue. Use some of my learning to figure out her problems.”

“You had time to talk when you brought her,” Varla replies. Her eyes gleam from the shadow beneath the brim of her hat as she steps closer to him. “Why didn’t you ask her then?”

“I... I didn’t know...she seemed normal...”

“After failing to recognize the illness, you want to use her as a guinea pig? Is that all you want her for?”

“What do you mean?”

“Come on. Sweet young thing like that.” A wicked grin flashes across her face.

“If you’re insinuating...” He stares at her in shock.

“I’ll tell you about her.” She draws close, her voice hushed and smoky. “You can talk to her later. We’ve got all evening and tomorrow morning.”

There is something fascinating about Varla’s eyes, something in them that comes at him. Startled, he pulls away and glances down at her chest, and yet her eyes are still swirling in his head. How strange. Perhaps the exhaustion from the all-day ride. He looks back up, embarrassed to be staring at her breasts. She smiles and steps closer, her eyes more vibrant, swirling with little lights.

"You've had a long trip, Norman. And you haven't put away your horse or saddle."

"Chester." He'd completely forgotten about his horse, who gazes at him with a look of woe a dozen feet away. "Poor boy." He steps over to pat Chester's long face.

"Why don't I help you get Chester settled," Varla says. She has followed him, stands with her hands on her hips and her legs slightly spread, a warm smile on her face. "And we can talk. I think you want to talk to me."

"I do want to talk to you." He keeps his voice as low as hers. He has assessed that she's in charge, and he wants to know more about Lindy Sue, and this whole situation. He takes a deep breath, sensing her at his side. The saddle and bags he unbuckles and takes off the horse, giving it a toss to the bottom of the porch steps. He grabs the reins as Varla steps beside him, puts her hand around his shoulder, and starts leading him away from the house with the horse following.

"Oh, fooey," Blondie mutters, behind them.

"The stable's over there." He points to a structure at the side of the barn.

"Now we have a chance to talk, Norman," Varla says, clutching his hand.

"Call me Norm," he says. *Varla.* That is her name, but who is she? He's never seen anything like her, nor read about any such woman in any of the journals on abnormal personalities, but this woman, Varla, she's different from the few women he's known as if she's part man with her assertiveness and command of herself. At the same time, her hand on his, the way she looks into his eyes and smiles, seducing him.

"I like you, Norm."

"You...do?" He glances over his shoulder at Blondie, now sulking and trudging up the porch steps. Blondie is very pretty, he admits to himself he thought that, as soon as he rode up to them, but now he begins to feel the same way about Varla. With most women, he's afraid of their fragility, but there's nothing of that with her.

"Yes. I want to help you, Norm," Varla says.

"Help me? How?"

"You don't always say what you want to say or do what you want to do."

"How do you know anything about me?"

"I see a lot...what hinders someone's mind. Just like you can, with your training."

"You've never studied abnormal mental behavior."

"How do you know?" Varla asks.

"Have you?"

"Would that surprise you? That something women shouldn't do?"

"That's right," Norm says. "Women can't study medicine." They reach the horse stable, and he lets the horse inside a stall and shuts and latches the door.

"Wouldn't a woman better understand the ailment of another woman?"

Norm shakes his head. "Not the way it's supposed to be. Women don't have the constitution and stamina for medical science or any type of science."

Varla laughs. "You think I don't have the stamina?" She pushes him against the side of the stall and gazes into his eyes. Thoughts come to his head, strange thoughts pulled from the darkness of his mind, the image of Lindy Sue lying in the dirt when he came upon her on her hands and knees, the concern he felt for her now tinged with lust, her slender body, her breasts pushing against the thin cotton of her shirt, her riding behind him to the ranch where three more women awaited, each attractive in their own way.

"I've never met anyone like you," he says, unable to escape her grasp or look away from her eyes. He's never felt such feelings of lust, and he wants to quell it and not act on it like his father would. “Maybe we should go to the house before we do something rash?”

“Is that what you really want, Norm?” A mischievous smile twists her lips.

Chapter 65

Blondie watches Varla lead Norm away, leaving her alone in front of the ranch. “Fooey.” Norm is older than Derry, and slightly larger, which in Blondie’s mind means he’s most likely a better, more experienced lover. *Maybe I can find out*, she thinks, once Varla is done with him. The sun is already low in the sky, so they’ll spend the night at the Pitts ranch.

Now what? So far the whole trip a piddle. Too many dead bodies, not enough lovemaking. And now Varla is off doing the blanket-hornpipe with Norm, and Rosa and Lindy Sue are down at the horses, maybe making passionate love, leaving Blondie with the choice of staying out here alone or hanging out with the unresponsive brute and the decrepit old man.

If only the brute had the old man’s passion, she thinks. She walks up the steps and enters the house, where the old man sits near the table and the brute stands at the stove, stirring a large black pot.

“We’ll eat when the others get here,” Gus Pitts says. “For now you’ll have to spend some time with me and Butch.”

“What a thrill,” Blondie says sarcastically. The kitchen stinks of beans, bacon fat, and flatulence, a stench ingrained in the walls, floor, and ceiling. She finds a wooden chair to sit on and takes in the yellowed, peeling wallpaper, a clutter of pots and pans in the sink, dirt and crust on most of the surfaces.

“We’re simple people, as you see,” the old man says. “And the place needs the hand of a woman.”

“It does at that.” Her eyes alight on a bottle on a shelf near the sink. “Is that bourbon?”

"Yes. Good idea." The old man rubs his hands. "A drink before we eat. I could use a glass myself. Celebrate new friends. Bring it over here."

She stands and strides to the bottle. It has been two years since she had a drink, and a voice inside her, Varla's voice, tells her to put the bottle back and walk away and yet she's bored and angry at Varla and besides, one small drink won't hurt. On another shelf are four small glasses, all of them smudged with grease.

"I think I'll just drink from the bottle if that's okay."

"Yes, let's do that," the old man says, waving her back.

With the bottle she returns to the chair and pulls it closer to the old man's wheelchair and the table. She uncorks the bottle and puts the mouth up to her nose. "Mmm." The first small sip tastes wonderful, as if she'd been waiting for it these last two years. She follows it quickly with a larger one and hands the bottle to the old man. He wipes his mouth with gusto and places the bottle on the table.

"Can I ask something?" Blondie gestures toward the brute. "What's up with your kid there?"

"What do you mean? That boy could be a circus strongman."

"Well he's lacking in one way," Blondie says. "He turns into a scared little boy around women. An over-sized lobcock."

"Oh, that." The old man chuckles a raspy staccato. "He's had some bad experiences in that department. Doesn't know what to do, really. Needs me to coach him."

"I don't want to know any more." Blondie cringes. She reaches for the bottle and takes another drink.

"As I said, we don't have a woman around here. We could really use one. More than one."

"Don't look at me. I hate housework and I'm not the domesticated type. But we might be able to arrange something. I noticed you have an eye for Goldie."

"What do you mean?" he asks defensively.

"You can't fool me, Gussy Piss. She'd make a nice little domestic servant, don't you think? Or maybe a wife, for you or one of your boys?"

Dumbstruck, he gapes at her. "What you're saying?"

"If we bring her back to the crazy house, her rich parents will pay us well. A lot of effort to find her. But really, is the asylum the best place for her? You've heard the stories."

"Yes, I believe I have." He nods.

"This pretty flower, she fled that place for a reason. And once she's back, they won't let that happen again. Can you imagine her in that place?"

He shakes his head. "Too terrible to contemplate."

"An asylum is a torture chamber. Throw away the problem child and forget they ever were."

"But why would the family do that?" he asks.

"Can you imagine what she'll look like in a few years in that place? The ones in the crazy house...they quickly lose their looks. Their looks and their minds. Come out crazier than they go in."

"Then why take her back?"

"We get paid. But maybe we can find a different future for her. A loving home. A family that cares about her. Hard work to build character." She takes another drink of bourbon and hands the bottle to him.

"That would be better, wouldn't it?"

He nods vigorously, before taking a drink.

"It sure would. But it took months and months of hard work to find her. And we have contacts to pay. People who helped us. We need that money. It's terrible, as much as we want her in a nice home, we can't unless we get paid. So the parents get their way."

"Maybe the parents can be talked to. Their minds changed."

Blondie shakes her head. "Her dad wants to hide her, afraid she'll sully the family name."

“Who’s her dad?”

She gives a small laugh, shaking her head. “That’s confidential, Gush Piss. A name you would know from the papers.”

“But if she married, and had her name changed?” Gus asks.

“You think her father’d want that to get out? That she married some legless rancher old enough to be her great-grandpappy?”

The old man frowns and takes another drink from the bottle. Blondie takes another too, enjoying how her words sink into the old man.

“Of course, she could marry. Find the right man. Someone who can relieve us of our expenses. We haven’t yet sent word to her father. He doesn’t know we have her.”

“He doesn’t know?”

“We wanted to surprise him. No time to send a telegraph.”

“Don’t know why you tell me all this,” he says. “As you see, we’ve nothing. Bank won’t even let us do a mortgage. But I do wish to help the girl. How much are her parents paying to bring her home?”

“Does it matter? If you’ve no money... Sometimes people have a bit of money they never bothered to spend, lying around. A cache of cash, in case the opportunity of a lifetime comes around.” She observes him closely, she can almost see the machinery of his mind, the small grin on his face.

“Let me think,” he says. “There might be something. What if I did have money, or remembered where I could find some? What would stop the girl from running away? She ran away from the asylum, she ran away from here.”

“That’d be your problem. But it won’t since you got no money.” Blondie takes another large swig of booze.

The old man’s face twisted in thought, he’s taken the bait. “Reckon you’re right. I might remember where I can get some money. How much you say the father was paying?"

"Not at liberty to say, even if I knew. Varla and Rosa handle finances. I have no head for numbers, except two, three, and *soixante-neuf*."

Chapter 66

Varla tells Norm Pitts, "we have time for that later. Right now I want to know you better." She stands in front of him, his back to the stable wall.

"What do you mean?"

"You know precisely what I mean." She gives him that thither-and-yon look of a seductress on the cover of a lurid pulp. She arches her back to give her breasts more emphasis; they're directly beneath his eyes and almost touching his chest.

He trembles in front of her, his hands twitching helplessly at the ends of his arms. "I reckon I know what you mean, but we shouldn't."

"Why not, Norm?"

"It wouldn't be right."

"Why not? We both want it. Who would be harmed? Some imaginary white-beard in the clouds? A dead corpse nailed to a couple boards? Come on, Norm, we're too smart for all that honey-fuggle." She presses into him, pinning him to the wall of the stable...and kisses him.

Years of suppressed lust stir inside, pulled up into his head from the shadows of the subconscious, pulled up by her eyes.

She hasn't had a good fuck with a man in a while. Rosa doesn't like it, so it has to be done on the sly, and Varla realizes how much she misses it, at the same time knowing it will weaken his resistance, open his mind further to hers to reveal where his father has hidden the money.

She kisses him. "Tell me, Norm... Why's a nice guy like you cottoning to that freak show?"

"What do you mean?" he stammers.

"The dirty old man and the big idiot?"

"They're my family."

She kisses him again, this time with far more passion, pressing her body into his.

"That why you studied madness? To figure out how you could be connected to those two?"

"I reckon so." Norm swallows. "I want to help them."

"Even when they commit murder?"

"You know about that?" His eyes go wide.

"Isn't it obvious? How many women buried around here?"

"I don't know. I've only suspected."

She pulls him into a vacant horse stall, and pulls him to the ground scattered with hay, where he lands on top of her. Her hands rub his back and rear. "They both should be institutionalized."

"What can I do? They're my family."

"Family? You think the old gimp cares about you? You work your way through college, taking jobs to pay for it, while the old miser hoards all that money."

"He does help out a little. It's..." Norm stiffens. "You know about the money too?"

"Money you helped him get...with your knowledge of legal affairs. Isn't that right?"

He nods.

"Money just sitting there. That miserable old man doesn't know how to spend it."

"How do you know about the money?"

"Your little brother...big brother? Told me."

"Butch? You talked to Butch?"

"Never mind that. Shouldn't some of that money be yours?"

"I never thought of it that way."

"Why not? You're the one who got it for him." They roll on the ground until she's on top of him, straddling his torso. Her vest is unclasped. She pulls his hands to her breasts, dangling above him. "Where does he keep the money? A bank?"

"No." He shakes his head. "My father hates banks. Doesn't trust them at all."

"Then it's buried somewhere here at the ranch. Or hidden somewhere in the house." She's got her pants around her legs and his around his. While he squeezes her nipples, she runs her hand along his stiffening erection.

"Yes. He's gotten it hidden somewhere."

"Where, Norm?"

"I-I don't rightly know. I...I've never done this."

She gets on top and lowers herself to get him inside her.

Norman gasps.

"Think, Norm... You're the...smart one. You...got to... Have a clue." She gasps as she pushes herself up and down on him.

"I just...don't know."

"You...don't...know?"

"He doesn't...tell me...to know."

"Why...not? Doesn't...trust you?"

"Doesn't...trust... Oh, god...no one."

"You...really...don't know?" She stares him in the eyes as they continue to fuck.

"No." He gasps. "Don't...know...oh."

How useless. He doesn't have a clue, and he's beginning to flag, confused, suddenly realizing he's being used, his face curling with anger. He looks up at her in panic and fear.

Damn! She might as well get a good fuck out of him if she can't get anything else. She puts her hands to his neck, pressing thumbs deep into his throat as she continues to ride him, heaving herself into his neck with each stroke.

His eyes and mouth go wide in fear. He smacks at her hands and her face, gurgling out a suppressed scream. The lack of blood to the head sustains the erection, even as his face turns pale and blue and his eyes bulge from his head. Varla closes her eyes and orgasms and continues to ride his cock until it becomes flaccid.

She pulls herself off him. A bit of remorse that he couldn't enjoy it with her, but it would not do to have him around. She pulls on her clothes and strides out of the stable. They will have to find the money another way. If Blondie's play of selling the girl doesn't work, they'll torture it from the old man, which will not be fun.

Chapter 67

Reaching the front doorway to the kitchen of the Pitts Ranch, Rosa notes the absence of both Varla and Norm. She steps through the door, yanking Lindy Sue in behind her. "There you are, Goldilocks. Sit here."

Lindy Sue grunts and flops into a large chair. Rosa looks over at the half-empty bottle on the table, and then at Gus Pitts and Blondie, sitting near each other.

"Dinner's about ready." Gus Pitts points to the stove where a blackened cast iron pot simmers and, on the sideboard next to it, several wooden bowls are in a stack. "Soon as Norman returns with your friend, we eat."

"What's going on here?" Rosa's eyes flash from the bottle to Blondie to the old man.

"Come join us," Gus says. "We're taking turns sluicing our gobs."

"Blondie, you been drinking?"

"Loosen up, Rosa," Blondie says with a slight slur. "Only had a shlip or two." Then she burps.

"You are *jarra.* Drunk floozie." Rosa's eyes dagger Blondie.

"So what, Rosa? Might as well get roostered up. Nothing else to do." Her eyes glued to Rosa, her face insolent, Blondie reaches for the bottle, takes another drink, and pounds the bottle back on the table. "Besides, you're pissed because your main squeeze is pirooting a man."

Rosa turns red with fury. "You shut up, drunk *ramera.*"

Blondie laughs. "I won't cotton to your crap, Rosa. And speaking of crap, I need to piss." She stands and stumbles toward the door.

"We've an outhouse out back," Gus offers. but Blondie's already on the porch, her booted footsteps loud on the wood.

"You." Glaring at Gus, Rosa points to Lindy Sue. "Keep eye on her. But you place hand on her and I hurt you."

"No. No one wants anyone hurt," he replies.

Rosa turns and steps outside, where Blondie is a dozen feet from the porch, squatting and urinating.

Varla appears from behind the barn, striding toward them. When she nears, Rosa can smell the man on her, the acrid stench of their lovemaking.

"What's wrong, Rosa?" Varla asks.

"He tell you where the money is?"

Varla shakes her head. "He didn't know."

Rosa glares at her. "What you mean?"

"The old cripple never told him." Varla smiles. "But we'll get it out of him, one way or another. Maybe Blondie's idea...offer the girl to him."

"Also, Blondie's *boracha*. Blootered."

"Are you serious?" Varla frowns

Rosa nods. "Passing the scamper juice with old Pitts."

"Getting him drunk too. Smart move. Where is she?"

"There!" Rosa points. Blondie has passed them and is now behind Varla, almost to the barn.

Chapter 68

Blondie staggers toward the barn. Not much hope, the man has probably been sated by Varla, but why not give it a try? While Varla and Rosa converse, heads close together, Blondie reaches the barn. "Norm?"

Another few steps and she's around the back, at the stable, where Varla came from. She freezes. He's in a stall on the ground. Eyes wide open. Pants down. On his back, looking up at the sky.

"Norm?" she calls out. He's not sleeping but he's not responding, either. His face is not quite the color of flesh, and he seems smaller than she remembered. Pants around his lower thighs, his penis is semi-flaccid, with bits of dried cum on the head. His hands are at his side. *Varla must have fucked him good,* Blondie thinks, but she freezes, at the red marks at his throat.

It hits her all at once. He's dead. Varla strangled him with her bare hands. Blondie staggers backward, away from the stable.

Varla murdered him. Just like she murdered Tommy Mitchell. And that boy back in the North End? Varla murdered him too and made Derry think it was the cop's kid who done it.

Murder. Cold-blooded murder. She knows Varla is not a good person, but then who is? But this. Murder. No way this could be an accident. And it all makes sense, like the pieces of a puzzle clicking in place. Varla a murderer, and she and Rosa kept it from Blondie. Their little secret. Varla kills and Rosa gets off on it. A death thrill, this is too deep for Blondie. She stumbles back toward them. Beyond them is the trail that leads out past the yard to where it forks with the other trail that goes to the water pump and where the horses are tied.

She will walk down there. Pat the horses and give them some turnip slices she purloined earlier from the Pitts' kitchen, and untie Chillins and ride away. The sun is almost setting, but she can make it back to Gruber's Outpost in the starlight, might get there before midnight. She doesn't care about the money anymore. The money has death on it, the slow death of the old man, and the other deaths, Norm Pitts, the Pinkerton shot by Derry, and who knows, the old man and the brute once Varla and Rosa are through with them. Blondie wants nothing of this blood money.

"Blondie!" Varla calls out. "Come here."

She turns to face Varla and Rosa a dozen feet away. "Why should I? Because you said so?" Then she turns and walks away.

"Where are you going?" Varla asks.

"You can't leave," Rosa says.

Blondie turns to face them. "Why not? It's a free country. There's easier ways to get thrills. For once in a long time I feel free. Maybe I need a break from you two." The anger in their faces, Varla giving her an intense stare, and she feels Varla in her head, even across the space of fifteen feet, trying to manipulate her to change her mind.

"She can't go, Varla," Rosa mutters. "She knows what you did."

"You can't stop me," Blondie says. "Like I said before, maybe you've lost your touch, Varla." She turns her back on them and strides toward the path to the horses. She can't wait to return to the North End and pick up where she left off. Maybe head down to San Francisco. Find a few nice men and women to make love to. And being drunk like this. How much she missed it.

"Blondie! Come back!" Varla's voice has a tinge of desperation.

Blondie turns to look at her. "I don't care about the money! I'm done!" She turns and keeps walking. She hears their voices behind her, growing farther with each long stride. Something hard hits her back, and she begins to fall forward, as she twists her head toward the house. The sun, low on the horizon, sets the whole tableau in an eerie light, long shadows, even her own in front of her, stretching out toward the pathway to the horses.

The old man at the bottom of the ramp pulls his shotgun from the side of his wheelchair, his mouth open in mid-yell. Butch looms at the top of the porch. Both have shocked looks on their faces as they stare at her, though she's not really sure why, the world has become frozen, the sounds of the birds and insects becoming one monotonous drone, the setting sun, a couple birds shooting toward the sky while the ground flies into her face.

Chapter 69

Half-awaken, Lindy Sue hears voices. The angry one that stirred her from sleep, and another voice too, followed by the clatter of footsteps on wood. Her eyes closed, her mind moving in circles, she can't think where she is, and then it sinks in at the sound of Rosa's voice.

"You hurt her and I hurt you!"

The heavy odor of ham fat and beans from the kitchen pushes into Lindy Sue's nose and mouth. Another set of footsteps clatter toward the door and then out on the porch, fading down the steps. Lindy Sue opens her eyes. The squalid kitchen, grease and splattered food on the walls and ceiling, the large black pot boiling on the stove. The giant stands near the door, and much closer is the old man in the wheelchair.

"Sleeping beauty awakes," says the old man, leering, wheeling his chair closer. "They got her doped up, so she won't skedaddle."

The giant grunts incoherently. Lindy Sue is sprawled in a chair, her head against a cushion. She tries to move her hands and legs, but her body doesn't respond. The old man warily moves closer.

"If we make a deal with those women, we oughta get a look at the merchandise," the old man says. His chair is in front of her, the side touching her legs. She tries to squirm away as he leans forward. He grabs the front of her shirt with both hands and tugs apart, sending buttons flying. With another yank and a loud grunt, he rips it open all the way, and then he backs away half a turn of his wheels to gaze at her.

Lindy Sue's breasts are exposed and she feels herself redden with shame and she can't even bring up her hands to cover herself while the old man stares, his eyes and mouth wide, his tongue lolling on his lips.

"Stop...stop it!" she tries to yell, the words jumbled in her head.

"I think I like this deal," he says. "Look at her, boy. You won't be layin' a hand on this one. We need to keep her. We can't have an accident, the way you were too rough with those others."

The giant grunts again. "Uhh." He points to the door. Voices raised in anger outside.

The old man turns his head to the door too. "Something's happening out there. Boy, don't let the girl go anywhere." The old man moves toward the door, the wheels creaking on the wooden slats of the floor, and then the porch.

Lindy Sue is alone with the giant. His big face is passive. He glances at her and turns to keep an eye on the door. Poor thing, the old man treats him like an animal. That he never knew his mother makes her feel an affinity, and even sorry for him in an odd way.

"My mom...died...when I... was born," she chokes out, feeling more power in her vocal cords, but still not sure if she's speaking coherently.

The giant's face lights up. "Uh..."

"That's right. But my dad remarried. Guess that's better than no mother at all."

The giant grunts again, the word almost sounds like "sad" to her.

"I reckon it is sad. Not having a mother... Me and you are so different and yet we both have that. Never knowing our mother."

Her limbs begin to regain strength, a tingle in her fingers, arms, and legs. She drags one arm across her bare chest to cover up.

"Muh..." he grunts, which she thinks is either "me" or "ma." He points to her. "Yuh... Muh ah yuh like."

"You're almost making sense."

“Muh...” He points to himself. “Nah hur’ yuh.” He points to her.

“I hope not. Will you help me get back to East Portland?”

“Yuh?” Confusion on his face. “Guh...woe.”

“Get away from your mean father? He’s no good, and my father, he can help you. He knows how to help people. We need to get away from your father and those women.”

He cocks his head, but his face is expressionless. “Yah? Mah?”

“If you take me there... They can help you. Your father hates you.” An image in her mind, riding on his shoulders all the way to her father’s home, and a moment later she begins to giggle at the absurdity. But is it so absurd? If only she had more strength in her arms and legs—

“Boy!” Even at a distance, the old man’s shout is loud. The giant stiffens at the sound. “Get out here, boy! Grab my rifle!”

“Pah?” The giant stampedes across the floor, and out the door.

Lindy Sue tries to stand, but her legs are too weak and the room moves in every direction around her. She falls on her hands and knees. She begins to crawl toward the door. As she gets closer, she sees outside, toward the side of the house, Blondie walks away, only her upper torso visible above the edge of the porch.

A wet thunk. Mid-stride, Blondie jerks to a halt and vanishes from Lindy Sue’s sight.

Chapter 70

Moments earlier, Varla stares into Blondie's glassy eyes, seeing repulsion as Blondie looks back at her.

"I don't care about the money! I'm done!" Blondie's words slice the evening heat.

Anger and betrayal flare up in Varla. How can Blondie do this? And blurting out about the money, completely revealing their plans to the old man. Blondie's drunkenness and insolence, and what infuriates Varla even more is her own loss of control, of Blondie, of the complete situation. Blondie turns to leave.

"She can't leave," Rosa mutters, her voice rising in panic. "She knows too much, about you and me. You stop her."

Without thinking, in complete grip of anger, Varla glances around, and pounces on the ax, sticking up from a log a dozen feet away. She yanks it free, straightens up, draws it behind her head, and lets it fly.

As soon as the ax leaves her hand, despite that it's an excellent throw, Varla has a pang of regret. How she wishes she could stop the hatchet, spinning through the air and speeding toward Blondie's back almost forty feet away. The blade hits with a thunk. Blondie gasps, jerks at the impact, and falls facedown, the ax handle jutting above her neck like the hand-grip of a life-sized stick puppet.

"*Chinga tu madre!* She's ratted us." Rosa grimaces and makes a dash for the ax.

The old man yells and raises his shotgun. His son bounds down the steps. Rosa reaches Blondie, about to grab the hatchet. The old man fires, pulling the trigger twice. The shotgun thunders, and Rosa sprawls across the ground, a few feet from Blondie.

Varla rushes toward the ax since there's nothing else she can do. If she can grab it and hurl it at the old man before he reloads...

"Boy! Stop her!" screams the old man. The brute bellows and runs toward Blondie and Rosa. "Damn it! I need my rifle!" The old man wheels around to the ramp. "Goddamn it, boy! Get the other one! While I get the rifle!"

As Varla races toward the bodies, the giant races toward her, face contorted, teeth bared and jowls puckered. She reaches the ax, but not in time to pull it out before he smacks her away from it. She rolls into a crouch onto her feet and rushes him again.

At least he's not smart enough to grab the hatchet from Blondie's back. He comes at Varla full speed. She slides beneath him as they collide, flipping him over her back. He crashes to the ground with an agonized groan, but quickly resumes his feet and rushes again. He grabs at her and she slides under him again and sends him tumbling with his own momentum.

This isn't going to work, Varla thinks, watching him quickly get to his feet. This time he's more wary, coming at her more slowly as she tries to circle around to get the ax. Meanwhile, the old man eggs on his son as he rolls up the ramp to get the rifle leaning next to the front door. As Varla faces the brute, the old man's voice grates on her nerves. "Subdue her, boy! I'll be down there with the gun!" the old man booms hoarsely.

She flies at the brute with the same blow that killed Tommy Mitchell, but her hand slams into thick muscle on his neck barely making an impact, and he smacks back at her, sending her reeling a dozen feet, causing stars to flash in front of her eyes.

Dazed, she climbs to her feet. She begins to have a barely remembered sensation, one she's registered in the minds of others many times but has not felt in herself in several decades, the sensation of fear.

The giant's mind is too empty for Varla to make eye contact and worm her way into it. He has the strength of a bull, doesn't matter that he doesn't know how to fight, her blows and maneuvers are useless. Once the old man has the rifle, it won't matter if she reaches the hatchet.

The giant hits Varla again. She reels, loses her footing, and falls backward. As she rolls back on her feet, a huge fist slams into her face, another flash of stars. He's on top of her, crushing her legs. His face contorted in fury he smacks her in the face, stars bursting in her eyes. He reaches for her neck with both hands, but she has no way to stop him. His fingers are steel cords. He could probably squeeze her neck and break it and keep squeezing until her head pops off her body and rolls down the hill.

He yells up at his dad as if to ask the dad for permission to strangle her. She stares up at the empty eyes. She's never been so afraid in her life. If only she'd listened to Rosa, if only she hadn't given in to anger, if only...if one could only set back the clock... She smacks at his arms, tries to reach up to blind him but his head is out of reach, and his face wavers in her vision as the fingers crush pain into her throat and his head and arms and the blue sky beyond him begin to fade, and in the distance, the crack of a rifle.

Chapter 71

Lindy Sue is on her hands and knees in the doorway, unable to stand up because the porch in front of her moves up and down like she's on the deck of a ship in turbulent seas. Noises of fighting, grunts and smacks and the crash of a wooden structure collapsing. Down below, Varla and Butch go at each other, smacking and throwing each other, two indomitable forces colliding again and again.

"Hold her down boy...'til I get the gun." The old man's excited voice is nearer. His head appears from the ramp, the wheels of the chair squeaking as he slowly pulls himself up the incline, past the switchback at the middle. His head twists toward the combatants as he approaches Lindy Sue. "Keep on fighting, boy. Wear her down. I'll soon be there with the rifle."

The rifle is propped against the wall next to Lindy Sue.

"You do it, boy. She's tuckering out. Keep it up and if you don't finish her off, I'll blast her to pieces with the rifle." The old man reaches the top of the ramp, and he turns his wheels to face Lindy Sue.

"This rifle?" Lindy Sue grabs the rifle and sits back against the wall.

The old man's eyes go wide. "Better hand that over, little angel, before you hurt yourself. You even know how to use it?"

She reworks the lever to put a round in the chamber and cocks the gun the way Tommy once showed her.

He smiles at her. His voice softens. "Now come on, Goldilocks. Stop fiddling and paw it over."

"Why should I?" She glares at him. The way he leered at her earlier, tried to grab her, ripped open her shirt.

"You wouldn't shoot a defenseless, paralyzed old man,

would you? Hand it to me." He inches the wheels closer. The fighting has stopped, silence beyond the porch. Lindy Sue doesn't know if she can pull the trigger. As much as she hates the old man, fear tingles in her hand, finger on the trigger, the other on the back of the gun, trying to steady it against her wavering vision.

"Pah!" The son breaks the silence.

"Keep on her, boy!" the old man yells. "Don't let up!" Then he lowers his voice to a hiss. "Don't anger me, my bride. Give it here now." He rolls closer, reaching out his hand to grab the gun. The same hand that reached earlier to grab at her, the same leer on his ugly mug.

She pulls the trigger. His face explodes and he's pushed back, across the porch and off the stairs. The gun slams her against the wall. The old man and the wheelchair crash down the porch stairs, wood shattering into splinters.

Everything gets silent for a moment, then shattered by an unearthly howl that penetrates to the bone. "PAAAHHHH!" The enormous brute in the yard forty yards away has his eyes on her. "You...kill...Paaaaahhhhhhhh!" Another ear-shattering wail.

He runs toward her. Her heart pounds in her chest. She works the lever and cocks the gun. He's coming up the steps when she pulls the trigger. The gun knocks her back against the wall. The bullet hits the brute in the chest and he screams again, but he keeps coming up the steps more slowly. She chambers another bullet and fires again. He's near the top of the steps, lumbering closer. She aims at his head and fires another shot. Part of his face falls off in a spray of blood but he keeps on coming, more slowly now, his eyes fixed on her as he continues his banshee scream.

Her back to the wall, she fires again. Another bullet to the head, one of his eyes now gone, bone exposed and blood splattering across his torn shirt. He's at the top of the stairs when she fires again, another bullet in the face between the eyes. He stares at her with his one good eye and screams.

Then he falls backward, the porch shaking when he crashes down the steps, splintering them on impact.

Lindy Sue gasps for breath, dropping the gun, the panic still gripping her. The brute and his father at the bottom of the steps. Further lies Varla and past her Blondie and Rosa. No one is moving. The setting sun leaves an eerie glow over the tableau in front of Lindy Sue.

PART V: RETURN TO PORTLAND

Chapter 72

Lindy Sue crawls to the top of the stairs and looks at the carnage. The old man and Butch are at the bottom of the porch steps, and the three women farther away, bodies sprawled and splattered with red. The air is thick with the smell of gunpowder and blood, its metallic tinge causing her gums to ache. The last bit of sunlight casts the yard in long shadows. The only sound is a faint breeze rustling the dry leaves. Lindy Sue doesn't see Norm.

"Hello?" she squeaks out, then much louder. "Anyone out there? Norm? Can you hear me? Hello!"

A few crows squawk from the scraggly trees and the roof of the barn. Nothing but dead bodies, ghosts. Fear grips her.

"Anyone hear me? Norm? Blondie? Rosa? Is everyone dead?"

"Not everyone," a voice says. Varla sits up slowly, her face purple with bruises.

"You!" Lindy Sue reaches back to grab the rifle off the porch and sits at the top of the stairs. "I ought to shoot you."

"Go ahead," Varla mutters. "I probably deserve it." Battered body slumped on the ground, Varla looks up at her, lips tightened in a wince.

"You do!" Lindy Sue raises the gun, aims it at Varla's head. The panic that caused her to shoot the old man and his son has subsided. Lindy Sue even has a twinge of empathy for the injured woman on the ground in front of her.

Varla shrugs. "Go on. Pull the trigger."

"Don't bait me or I will." Lindy Sue looks past her to see if anyone else survived. Now that she's not being threatened, she doesn't think she can pull the trigger. Not on someone injured, even someone as evil as Varla.

Varla shrugs, her eyes darting below Lindy Sue, to the dead bodies at the bottom of the porch stairs. Her eyes open wide. "So that's where he had the dough," Varla chuckles. "Bottom of his wheelchair." Beneath the seat of the wheelchair, the wooden base is cracked open; gold coins and large denomination federal bank notes have spilled onto the dirt.

Ignoring her, Lindy Sue uses the ramp railing to pull herself to her feet. Still dizzy, she steps carefully down the stairs, past the dead bodies, carrying the rifle with her. Using the gun as a cane, she makes a wide arc around Varla. Varla, on her hands and knees, crawls slowly toward the porch.

Night has fallen, the stars twinkling on as the sun vanishes completely beyond the hills. A half-moon hangs low in the sky to her left, and a few night crickets have begun chirping. Lindy Sue will try her luck getting back to the outpost, though the closer she gets to the horses, the more this plan sounds foolish since she's not sure if she can retrace their steps, even with the stars to indicate directions.

Another problem arises. The large black stallion stands between her and Annabelle. She tries to circle around, but the stallion moves in the way, snorting and bearing its teeth, blocking her from the other horses. She calls to Annabelle, but the mare merely looks at her, content to be in like company. Lindy Sue glares at the stallion and trudges back to the ranch house, her legs slowly regaining strength.

"You're back," Varla says, sitting near the bottom of the stairs, stuffing money into Norm's saddlebags while his belongings: clothes, books, little trinkets picked up in college are scattered at the bottom of the steps near her. "Grab those greenbacks over there." Varla points to some bills, which have blown a dozen feet to catch in a clump of sagebrush.

"That's stealing," Lindy Sue says.

"Old geezer can't spend it, where he's going. Ours now, Goldilocks."

"Ours? Or yours?"

"I'll give you half. I need help. Too banged up to get out of here alone."

"It's not right, taking money not ours. You came here to steal that money, didn't you?"

"Easy for you to say. Your father has money. How much he steal from the state every year with that hospital?"

"He earns his money."

"And we earned this," Varla says. "We worked hard for it, just as hard as your father works to bilk the state. I lost two friends for this money."

"But it's not right. It's not our money."

"And shooting someone, is that right?" Varla asks. "You want to explain to the sheriff how you shot a poor cripple off his own porch? And then pumped several more bullets into his son?"

"He attacked me."

"He was unarmed. You had a rifle."

Lindy Sue hasn't thought of that. "You really think they would..."

Varla tries another smile on her battered face. "You saved both our lives killing the old cripple and his son. We got to skedaddle."

"Why should I help you?"

"The Pinkerton's friends. They'll be here tomorrow afternoon."

"The Pinkertons? The ones looking for the missing girl?"

Varla nods. "That's right. You know them?"

"The kid. Derry."

Varla shakes her head. "Not the kid. The other one. Got friends coming here. Bounty hunters. I know his type. Bitter they lost the war, but these ones are stone-cold killers. We got to scram before they get here and kill us. If you help me to my horse—"

"No way." Lindy Sue starts to walk away. But she reaches the top of the trail down to the horses, and she sees the big stallion, eyeing her, even from a hundred yards away. She realizes she has no other choice. Heading back, she sees that Varla has up-righted the wheelchair and sat down in it, but she's too weak to maneuver it.

"You're back," Varla says. "To get out alone, you'd have to shoot Storm to get to your ride. But I don't think you can, can you?"

"Shoot a horse? No!" Lindy Sue is horrified.

"Then help me down there. We'll leave together."

"How can I trust you?"

"You can't, but neither of us has a choice, do we?"

"Are you telling the truth about the bounty hunters?"

Varla nods. "I wish it weren't so. But we can't stay here, Goldilocks."

Chapter 73

With the help of Lindy Sue and the wheelchair, Varla flops herself on the black stallion. They ride slowly in the dark, Varla grunting with pain as she hugs her horse, Lindy Sue beside her on the trail, and the other two horses with supplies behind them. The night is bright with stars and silent except the clip-clop of the horse hooves and the rustle of dry grasses. Over an hour they ride, until Varla reins her horse. "I need to rest. I'm camping here." She indicates a spot off the trail, beneath a clutch of juniper trees. "You want to go, I'll give you a share of the money."

Lindy Sue has no idea where the trail ahead leads, though she knows from the stars they've mostly traveled east, farther from the ranch and the outpost. And she's very sleepy, it catches up to her, now they've stopped. She follows Varla to the spot where they'll camp.

"We can't build a fire," Varla says. She falls off her horse, trying to get down. Lindy Sue feels sympathy for her, lying helpless, wincing in pain. Lindy Sue pulls the animal skins off Rosa's horse and lays them on the ground near Varla.

"Can you do something for me?" Varla asks.

"What?" Lindy Sue grumbles.

"There's turnip pieces in one of the saddle bags. For the horses."

Lindy Sue finds the turnips and pulls out four pieces. The big stallion whinnies appreciatively and rubs its head on her shoulder, no longer threatening her. She pats each of the horses affectionately as she feeds them, returns to the blankets, and sits down on the edge. Varla, lying on her back, looks up at her. The night is quiet but for occasional far away sounds of an animal or an owl, too far to be anything but a slight smear on the silence.

"Thanks for not riding off," Varla says. "Wouldn't blame you if you had."

"You got pretty banged up."

"Bit off more than I could chew. Now my two best friends are dead. But you, you surprised me, Goldilocks. Way you took care of the cripple and his son. Didn't think you had it in you." Varla cracks a smile.

Lindy Sue looks away, embarrassed at the praise, unsure herself how she did it.

"Your dad really the famous doctor?" Varla asks.

"Uh huh."

"They wanted to put me there. My mom's second husband. My dad died in the war, when I was seventeen. But he showed me things. Showed me how to get inside the minds of others. That was a gift he had, or maybe a curse, to see in the heads of others. It got him kicked out of Japan, kicked out of China. Getting into people's heads. Maybe something like your dad?"

Lindy Sue shakes her head. "I don't think my dad can do that. He just tries to make people think better."

"How can he if he can't get inside their heads?"

"You can really do that?" Lindy Sue's curiosity perks.

"Sometimes. Not always."

"Were you trying to do it to me?"

Varla replies with a sheepish grin. "Not successfully."

"How does it work. Is it hypnotism? Mesmerism?"

"You know about Franz Mesmer?"

"I read about him in one of my dad's books."

"Something similar to that, but no magnets. My dad called it *kanpa-maindo.* He taught it to me. I have no idea how it works. I look into someone's eyes, project myself into their head. It can't be explained with words."

"And you got into my head?"

"Like I said, doesn't always work. Some people, their

heads are too full of crap."

"Are you saying my head is—"

Varla chuckles. "Not at all. You resisted me. That's all." She yawns and closes her eyes.

Lindy Sue pulls a skin over her, but the cold leaks through, and in spite of her exhaustion, sleep doesn't come. She thinks of the way Varla stared at her, in the ranch house and the cabin at the outpost. Soon clouds darken the stars and the moon and the nocturnal sounds become tangible and threatening in the emptiness beyond their campsite. She doesn't know which to fear more, the night or the woman snoring next to her.

Chapter 74

As soon as Lindy Sue drops off to sleep, dawn creeps across the mountains and hills. She opens her eyes. Varla is still asleep. Lindy Sue plods to the horses, ten feet away. The black stallion nickers and nods its head, not threatening. Annabelle looks at Lindy Sue with her yellowish eyes. *I could leave now*, she thinks, ride away. She returns to the sleeping woman, trying to decide.

Varla opens her eyes. "Good morning, Goldie. You saying good-bye?"

"I don't know. Trying to decide. Were you serious about those men coming?"

"Dead serious. Arriving at the outpost today. Derry told us. Good kid."

"You look too beat up to travel."

"I think you're right," Varla says through gritted teeth. "But we got to keep moving. I know where there's a cave we can hold up. I think we can get there today. But first, maybe you can help bandage me up? I don't think he broke anything, except maybe a couple of ribs when he threw me."

An hour later they're on their horses. They ride slowly, putting more distance between themselves and the ranch. At times the trail narrows along a slope or ridge, and they go single file, and at other times it widens along flat dry plains. White-peaked Mount Hood rises up in front of them, and then to their left as they reach the foothills.

In two hours it'll be dark. Shadows cross the side of the mountain as the sun sinks beyond it, turning the forest on the slope below them from green and brown to gray and purple. Above their heads, several buzzards ride the sky, nearly touching the low-floating clouds. A pair of the buzzards circle back toward them, while the rest continue onward toward the direction of the Pitts ranch.

Varla looks at the sky as they ride. “Damn, carrion birds. They have sharp eyes. They see the fear of death, like they have forgone knowledge from the grim reaper.”

“I never liked buzzards,” Lindy Sue says. “They look mean and ugly. When most birds are so pretty.”

“They can’t help the way they look, Goldilocks. Not every creature’s a pretty bird like you.”

Lindy Sue grimaces at this remark.

Varla laughs bitterly. “Thing is, those buzzards’ll give away our location to those men. But you can’t shoot them. Shoot them just makes the others your enemies. They’re like crows that way, they never forget an enemy. And me, I’ve made enough enemies in this life to not have them lurking in the sky above me.”

Chapter 75

In the early afternoon, the two riders slow their pace as they approach the Pitts ranch. Both men are in their mid-forties, their faces shaded by their confederacy slouch hats.

"Can't be good," grunts James Crawford, the taller and lankier of the two men. A thick dark beard covers most of his brooding face where it's not sunburned.

"Buzzards having a feast day," George Emmett drawls in his high, soft voice while rubbing at his blond van dyke tuft. A cherubic face, blue eyes, smirking lips, and curly blond hair, spilling beneath the hat brim lend him a boyish charm.

In moments, they spot the dead bodies, more dead bodies than either have seen since the war. Not that dead bodies concern either of them. What concerns them are the few blood-splattered twenty-dollar notes on the ground near the dead men at the foot of the porch stairs.

"Someone got here first, Emmett." Crawford groans.

"Whole can of someones. Recent too. Fresh meat, what I see. Most likely, not even a day. Buzzards haven't yet started to rip them open. Bodies don't stink yet."

They ride back and forth, checking the various corpses, while trying to calm their nervous steeds. "You see Stark?" Crawford asks in his gravelly voice.

"No. None of these for sure. That one there..." Emmett points, "bigger than all shit. This one's the old codger lost his legs, but where's his wheelchair? A couple dames over there. I reckon they too far gone for some horizontal refreshment."

Crawford nods, gazing glumly toward the corpses of the two women. "I reckoned the same."

"A pity," Emmett sighs. "They look to be a pair of fine wag-tail."

They leap down off their horses. While Crawford looks around, Emmett gathers up the three bloody double eagle notes in an old handkerchief. Barely enough to make the ride worth it. Crawford returns, slinging a thumb over his shoulder. "Another one behind the barn over there."

"But no Stark," Emmett says. "Shee-it."

"What'd we do now, Emmett? Get more out of the big mouth kid?"

When they had arrived at Gruber's Outpost several hours earlier, they found that Willard Stark was gone, but they immediately sussed out Elber Gruber as a big-mouth know-it-all. He told them Stark and Derry Flanders, his Pinkerton sidekick, had left the previous morning, maybe with a couple other men. With some prodding, they got Elber to tell them the way to the Pitts ranch.

Emmett shakes his head, scanning the skies. "A huge fight here. Whoever Stark got away with, maybe some of them are wounded. We follow the buzzards. See where they take us. If that don't work, then we go back, talk to the kid."

"And you think they got the money?"

"If they left behind a bit of it, you know damn well they got the money." Emmett pats the shirt pocket, where he's stashed the three twenties.

"Why you reckon Stark did this to us? After all we had together." Crawford spits on the ground.

"Never know with people. But if he ain't dead, he will be when I run into him again." Emmett strides to his horse.

"You got that right." Crawford nods, flashing a rare grin. Soon they are back in the saddle and riding and scanning the sky with their spyscopes.

Chapter 76

Half awake, a hard surface beneath her, Lindy Sue is aware she is not in her bedroom. The smell of burning wood, a small campfire crackles several feet away. She breathes in the cold, brisk air. She snuggles closer into the spoon of his body for warmth. As he shifts behind her, his arm falls across her waist.

"I had the weirdest dream, Tommy," she says quietly, so as not to wake him if he's asleep. She dreamt he lay dead on the ground, but she can't tell him that. Her head cobwebbed in confusion, but she remembers riding east with him to an abandoned ranch.

"We're alone, Tommy, out here. Just you and me." Her voice sounds small in the darkness.

A wisp of his voice is in her ear: Lindy Sue?

"Mmm, Tommy. This feels nice."

Tommy murmurs sleepily and shifts his body. His hand slides to her leg, the thigh above the knee. She's excited and slightly fearful where this might lead.

Outside past the flat, dry terrain, an owl coos sweetly to its prey. Whooo, the owl asks. Who wants to die? A coyote yelps from farther off.

Past the flames of the campfire, a big cold world out there. She snuggles deeper into Tommy's arms. She enmeshes her fingers into his large hand and pulls it to her breast. It'll be better this time. We were both afraid that other time, at the ranch house, the disappointment, but she doesn't want to think about that.

She presses the hand down, the fingers brushing across her nipple. She rolls slightly, to position his other hand closer to her groin, and starts rubbing against it like she does when she's alone, or the time with Maggie. Perhaps Maggie is getting ready to do something similar with Handy like she and Maggie had discussed a couple weeks ago, to do this thing before the summer ended. She can't think of Maggie at a time like this.

He mumbles again. "Huh?"

"Are you awake?" she whispers.

"Want me to keep going?" His voice sleepy, muffled.

"Yes!" She gasps.

She has a pang of guilt, at the amorality of their act. Is it less wrong if we both do it? Only half a sin for each of us, if in fact, it is a sin. She's not sure about this, and now she doesn't care as the fingers come to life, fluttering around her inner thighs like curious birds.

"It feels good," she moans. His fingers find the place which makes her trill.

"You like this?" His voice sounds odd, not at all nervous like before, instead calm and quiet.

"Yes. Keep going."

He's far more confident, his hands move smoothly and firmly than those times in her bedroom, or at the ranch, which might have been last night or a month ago.

The thumb and fingers do things down there she's never experienced before. He sticks a finger inside her while he rolls the thumb on top. His other hand crosses to the other breast. He tweaks her nipple in his fingers, makes it go hard before he smooshes it down with the palm of his hand as she pulls into the softness of his torso. Her body trembles uncontrollably. His fingers slowly pull something up from inside her which opens a plateau of pleasure beyond any experience she's had, and floods her with an orgasm that causes her to gasp out, her voice echoing off the rock walls.

"That was... Oh!" She opens her eyes. She's unsure if she's awakening from a dream, but now she's awake. "And you didn't even...use your..." *He can if he wants to*, she thinks. Your man-thing. Where are we?

They are in a cave, she realizes, not the abandoned

ranch house. A small fire flickers. A dozen feet away, a large black stallion eyes her with mild curiosity. Behind him, Annabelle is with two other horses.

"Tommy?"

His body tenses. She remembers suddenly. Tommy is dead. Then who? Faces dredge up from her confused mind, Norm Pitts, who gave her a ride, Derry Flanders, the young Pinkerton who looked at her with concern. Confused, she stares down at the arm on her breast. It's hairless and smooth in the firelight and darker than her own. "Tommy?"

"You sure got off," a voice says.

She cringes. It's not Tommy. She pulls out of the arms and shifts around to face him. "Where's Tommy?" She squirms away. "You... You're..." Memories slam into Lindy Sue's head. Tommy lying on the ground. Injured, maybe dead! And this woman... Varla. The outlaw!

"You caught me off guard, Goldie," Varla says groggily, her dark eyes shiny in the flickering campfire.

"But...but..." Lindy Sue recoils, clambering out of the animal skins and on her feet, standing naked in front of Varla, her clothes scattered on the ground.

"Don't tell me you didn't enjoy it."

"No! You took advantage of me! You—"

"Me?" Varla shakes her head.

Lindy Sue shudders. The skins pulled off, Varla lies sideways, one of her huge breasts falling vulgarly out of the thin cotton shift.

Lindy Sue's anger overcomes her fear. "Better not do that again! My head..." She's dizzy; the walls of the cave do not stand still. She shivers as the cold seeps into her bones. Reluctantly, she staggers back and crawls under the edge of the furs and draws herself into a fetal position as far from the woman as possible. She wants to sob. She listens to a coyote bay and another respond.

"Whoo?" an owl asks somewhere beyond the cave.

Chapter 77

The black steed whinnies as Lindy Sue approaches the cave entrance. Beyond the cave, the valley at early dawn is nearly silent except for the low hiss of wind and a slight creaking of a runty tree near the cave.

"Goldie?" Varla calls out from the blankets.

"What?"

"Going somewhere?"

"No. Just outside to—"

"Outside to what?"

"You know..."

"Outside to what? Piss? Shit?" Varla chuckles.

Lindy Sue glances back at her. "Why are you so vulgar?"

"What's so vulgar about something we do every day, Goldie?" Varla snickers derisively.

Lindy Sue steps outside. The sun has almost emerged from the horizon. Beyond the cave, a vast expanse of arid nothingness stretches toward distant hills. Cacti and twisted brush throw long shadows across the barren, cracked earth. An occasional tiny flower flickers purple or yellow in the desolate terrain. And the coyote is out there again, calling out a long "howw youuuuu."

Now is the time to make a run for it, Lindy Sue thinks. While Varla is recuperating, a sprained ankle swaddled in wrappings. But they are too far from anything, and Lindy Sue fears being lost in this wilderness. Instead, she relieves herself and steps back in the cave.

How did it happen? Lindy Sue thinks. Last couple days Varla was at her mercy, and she felt in control, but now it is changing. Did Varla get into my head with that mind manipulation? Why didn't I ride away that first night, or the next morning? Why am I staying? At least Varla isn't treating her the same way as before, but still... She can't trust Varla. Not in any way.

The day goes by without incident. Varla doesn't mention what happened the night before, and Lindy Sue wants to forget about it, pretend it never happened. When night falls, Lindy Sue's at the edge of the bedding, staring into the small fire, while Varla snores behind her. She looks at Varla with hatred. Taking her away from Tommy and her home. And last night, the shameful way she let Varla take advantage of her and her own complicity in the carnal act.

Never again, she tells herself. I won't let her violate me again. The idea of that cruel woman with her vile hands... A shudder runs through the length of Lindy Sue's body. She lies down as far as she can from Varla, on the edge of the bed matting. She shivers from the cold leaking in from the edges of the furs as she tries to squeeze herself into a ball. Though only the second night in the cave, her home and East Portland seem far away, like something from a dream.

Maybe I'm dead and this is hell. God punishing me for giving myself to Tommy before we wed. She lies there and listens to Varla breathe.

I won't let her do it again, she thinks.

But later in the night, she lies half-awake and shivers in the cold, and she remembers the night before. Varla lies on her back under the blanket a few feet away. Her large breasts heave up and down as she sleeps, her face relaxed.

Lindy Sue snuggles closer to the woman she hates. *It's only for warmth*, she thinks, and yet she can't stop thinking about the night before, like a terrible itch inside her, as she snuggles between the arm and the body, and pulls the hand on top of her. It feels more comfortable than that time with Tommy, lying in the bed of the abandoned ranch, his body with sharp edges in the wrong places.

Chapter 78

Before dawn Varla extinguishes the fire so the smoke won't be visible, leaving one small piece burning. Like the previous morning, she loads up a pipe with something from the tin.

The odor of burnt maple syrup wafts over to Lindy Sue. "What is that?"

"Opium. Helps with pain. Want some?"

"I'm not in pain."

"It can help with pleasure too. Fucking on this stuff is fun, long as you don't overdo it and get addicted."

"I don't know about that." Lindy Sue reddens with shame, remembering how for a second night in a row, she let herself succumb, and this time neither she nor Varla was half asleep.

"Come on. Smoke some with me. Not like there's anything else to do today, sitting around here in the cave." Varla smiles. "You know you want it."

Lindy Sue shakes her head. Varla stares at her as she lights the pipe, and Lindy Sue can almost feel Varla inside her head, some force behind the eyes pushing into her own eyes and into her thoughts. The phrase comes to her, *kanpa-maindo.* Lindy Sue remembers the times before. Kissing Blondie. The way the opium let her float to the ceiling of the room. She leans toward Varla, her mouth open, and lets Varla kiss the opium into her.

Somehow it feels even more shameful in the daylight, with the sun streaming through the cave entrance. The opium brings urges into Lindy Sue. Varla sucking on her down there, using tongue and lips to make her groan and gasp uncontrollably. Varla pulls Lindy Sue's face into her own groin, presses down on the back of Lindy Sue's head, and the aroma of Varla's vagina fills her mouth and her nose. At first, she's slightly repulsed by the dank taste and feeling weird, but also thrilled.

They lie back on the animal skins, sated.

Chapter 79

James Crawford and George Emmett ride their horses through the dry range, past tumbleweed and sagebrush, at the foot of Mount Hood at their right and some hills further to their left. “We could chase buzzards for weeks and not find them,” James Crawford mutters. “Too many ways to die out here in this damn desert.”

“Where there’s life, there’ll be death,” Emmett replies, glancing back at him.

“I say we head back to the outpost.”

“In a day or two, Crawford.”

“Did I tell you? A horse in the stable. At Gruber’s Outpost. Looked a bit like Stark’s horse.”

“And you’re telling me this now?” Emmett shakes his head.

“I didn’t think about it until now. Maybe we head back?”

“You sure you don’t want to visit the cat wagon back that way?” Emmett smiles.

“That’d be nice too. Why not?”

“Like I said...” Emmett snorts. “We’ll head back in a couple days. If Stark cut out and we go back now, we might lose them, and we don’t want that.”

“No, I reckon not,” Crawford mutters.

“Buck up, Crawford. We get our hands on that kelter, I reckon it’s enough to land us the sweet life.”

“That’d be daisy. Bounty work’s paid crap last few years.”

“Not like the good old days,” Emmett says. “They used to pay for injun scalps. Ten or twenty apiece.”

Crawford grimaces. “Messy work. I don’t mind killing a man, but...” He remembers how Emmett enjoyed the knife work once one of them made the kill.

"Were not talking men, Crawford." Emmett chuckles and then gets serious. "No future in bounty hunting. Federal supreme court claimed it legal a few years ago, now too many greenhorns and fops."

Crawford doesn't reply, in awe of Emmett's unfathomable knowledge of the workings of government and law. As they continue to ride, Crawford has a niggling feeling in the bottom of his spine that they are being watched. He scans the plain to their left and the slope to their right and back. He considers telling Emmett, but he can't be sure, maybe just the buzzard above them, slowly floating, circling once and then onward where he and Emmett can see specks of a couple others. He glances back the way they came, and again at the steep foothills that lead up to the mountain, and soon the tingle in his spine dissipates and he wonders if he's getting too old for this sort of thing.

Chapter 80

Varla sits at the cave entrance with the spyglass. "I see them. Come look."

Lindy Sue pulls herself off the furs and strolls to her. "Who?"

"The Pinkerton's friends." Varla hands her the spyglass and points. "Over there. On that small ridge."

Lindy Sue scans the ridge until she spots them through the lens. Two men on horseback, both wearing slouch hats with one flap up, and even at that distance the look on their faces is grim and determined. One is tall and gaunt with a dark beard, the other with a mustache and the hint of a goatee and curly blond hair. Farther away are some specks in the sky.

"Following the buzzards," Varla says. "Maybe a dead bison. Good thing they aren't headed this way."

Lindy Sue puts the spyglass to her eye again. The men are barely perceptible as they vanish into the foothills, following the buzzards who follow the demise of some hapless animal beyond her view.

"If I wasn't banged up, I'd ride out there to confront them," Varla says. "Hate leaving loose ends. Loose ends can trip a person up later, maybe even hang you."

Varla staggers back to the animal skins, using a stick cane. Lindy Sue follows her and lies down beside her. All at once she thinks of Tommy, lying in the dirt, like that animal somewhere out there, lying dead, though she no longer remembers the details, her head confused, still dazed from the opium. No one helped him, though Varla, Blondie, and Rosa were all there. She knows what happened is in her head, but she can't quite summon it into her consciousness. Now, as she lies in Varla's arms, it no longer has as much importance, as if Tommy is part of a dream, something far away.

Did she love him once? She wanted him to propose to her, and she remembers that night, unsatisfied, lying in an unfamiliar bed while he slept.

Lindy Sue traces the scars across Varla's back with her fingers, older ones and new ones. Like so many horse trails and train tracks, different stories, and so many of them. Another whole life in those scars, an endless series of stories, compared to the one scar Tommy has on his arm from playing football.

"You want to know how I got most of those scars?"

"You don't have to tell me."

"But you want to know, don't you?" She doesn't wait for Lindy Sue to answer. "When I was younger, they tied me up and whipped me."

"That's..." Lindy Sue has no words.

"The ones who did this, I made sure they were sorry. No one does that to me again." Varla turns and looks at her. "Tomorrow we head back to Portland."

"Really?"

"That's right. I'll be well enough at least. And those bounty hunters... Need to put some distance. Looked like they headed east, so we go north."

Lindy Sue's not quite sure she believes Varla. Are they really headed to Portland? Can she trust Varla? Perhaps it's a trick. *She'll sell me to the Mormons. A blackmail letter to my father. For ransom.* Varla would try something like that.

Too many people know me in East Portland, Lindy Sue speculates. When we ride into town, they'll recognize me and rescue me. If we don't run into a search party first. By now her father and Tommy's father, the senator, will be worried and have notified the law. They might be out there now, beyond where the carrion birds circle the sky. They've probably found Tommy's dead body.

Lindy Sue is still dazed from the opium, but not just the

drug. She thinks about kissing Varla, Varla's hands and legs around her. To think about earlier that day makes her blush, to have those memories in her head in the full light of day, and when she wasn't half-asleep. And she enjoyed it. Tommy never took her to that place of ecstasy, not even close.

"We have a long ride next couple days," Varla says, brushing her fingers through Lindy Sue's hair. "We'll head north, around the east side of the mountain and follow the river back."

"That's so much longer. Why not the direct route? Back the way we came?"

"Through East Portland? You'd like that, wouldn't you, Goldie?" Varla laughs at her. "Will anyone know you in Albina?"

"Some might. Everyone knows my father."

"The famous Dr. Hawthorne and his crazy farm."

"You shouldn't call it a crazy farm. It's a Hospital for the Insane."

"Yeah, trying to throw me in there. Can you imagine? I'm one of the few who's not crazy. Isn't that right, Goldie?"

Lindy Sue does not reply.

Varla lies down on the furs, looking up at the cave ceiling. "Is it crazy to take what you need? Crazy to not put up with people telling you what to do? Tut-tutting Bible-punchers and fat sweaty boss men with grabby hands... Men with badges and the ones behind desks, making the rules... I don't hanker to these highfaluting flannel-mouths like other folk, letting that pack of four-flushers run their lives when they should be scoffed out of their churches and towers. That make me crazy? To do what I want? To not let them tell me who I am? The world is crazy. Not me."

Lindy Sue stares at her. Is Varla insane? Am I? What would my father and the other doctors think if they knew what we had done together?

Chapter 81

Lindy Sue awakes. Daylight streams into the cave entrance. The crisp air clings to the flesh. Varla pulls herself into her black leather riding suit. "Getting out of here. Ready for Portland, Goldie?"

"Uh-huh." She nods. By now, pictures of her and Tommy will be in the newspapers, even the ones in Albina and downtown Portland. Once someone recognizes her, she'll be rescued, and Varla will be thrown behind bars or locked up in one of the padded rooms at one corner of her father's hospital. Her father and Tommy's father are too important to the community of East Portland, and the entire Portland area to have their children missing.

As she thinks this, Varla stares at her, as if Varla can see inside her soul and read her mind, as if Lindy Sue is hollow like a wooden doll.

"Riding into Portland in a couple days. Won't it be sweet, Goldie?"

"Yes." she nods. "Better than this cave."

"Except I won't be riding with you."

"What do you mean?"

"You know I can't ride into town with you. Your puss plastered in the papers by now. Whether they found your boyfriend or not."

"Maybe in East Portland, but not Albina."

"They'll see you ten miles away with that golden hair." Varla reaches down to her leg sheath and pulls out a ten-inch dagger. She takes a slow step toward Lindy Sue. "I can't be seen with you."

In a panic, Lindy Sue scrambles to her feet and backs into the wall. "No. Please." Last night's conversation about insanity wells up in her head. Varla is crazy, capable of cold-blooded murder. Lindy Sue, the only witness that Varla stole the money from the old man in the wheelchair. One side of a saddle bag is stuffed with US greenbacks, twenties, fifties, one-hundreds in bundles, and another has gold coins. Varla can't bring her into town, she realizes with fear. Varla comes at her with the dagger.

"I have to do it, Goldie."

"Please, Varla. Don't hurt me."

"Hurt you? Is that what you think?" Varla grabs her by the hair at her scalp and yanks her away from the wall. "You want me to hurt you?"

"No!" Her eyes closed, she prays to God, though what good is God against Varla who not only doesn't believe in God but scoffs at the notion of religion.

"Sorry, Goldie. I have to do it."

"You don't have to. I won't tell them anything."

"I must, Goldie." Hand on Lindy Sue's hair, she forces Lindy Sue to the ground, face in the dirt. She straddles Lindy Sue's back, one hand on the knife, the other on Lindy Sue's hair.

Lindy Sue panics, her blood racing. "Please don't..."

"Hurt you? Just cutting off your hair. Hold still or I will stab you." Varla puts the blade half an inch close to Lindy Sue's left eye. "Hold still! Don't want an accident."

She yanks a swath of Lindy Sue's hair and hacks away. Several tresses float down in front of Lindy Sue's face. She is paralyzed with fear as the knife pulls pain at her scalp with each slash. And with each slash, her panic diminishes.

An hour later, Lindy Sue looks at the unrecognizable image of herself in her pocket mirror. Her hair hacked off, her scalp burns from the harsh blade and her exposed head is cold and weightless in the sharp dawn air. Varla also smudged ash from the fire on her face and hair. Lindy Sue wears a pair of too-big field work pants and a threadbare button shirt with torn pockets.

"What have you done to me?"

"Shush, Goldie! A long ride ahead."

"Are you really taking me home?"

"Sooner or later, but first, we go to the North End."

The North End. Those words evoke a shudder from Lindy Sue Hawthorne. The North End is the most crime-ridden section of Portland and no place for any woman except nude dancers and prostitutes. On the other hand, once they leave, Lindy Sue is grateful to put distance from the cave and to have the familiar feel of Annabelle between her legs.

Within several hours they reach a trail along the east side of Mount Hood, headed toward the Columbia River. Lindy Sue is dazed from the previous days in the cave. *It's the opium,* she thinks, but not just the drug. She gazes at Varla, ahead of her on the trail. Thinking of the previous day makes her blush, to have those memories in her head in the full light of day, and she imagines crawling into Varla's hug for more in the coming night. But she wants to go home to her father.

When the trail widens, they ride side by side, Lindy Sue asks. "Why the North End?"

"Because I said so."

"Why can't you take me directly home?"

"Not until I'm done with you."

"Done with me?"

"A room with a large comfortable bed."

The trail narrows and the conversation ends as they go single file. Lindy Sue doesn't know if she's Varla's lover or her prisoner. Does Varla want her as a sex plaything, for ransom, or for some other nefarious purpose?

Chapter 82

Climbing down from their steeds, George Emmett and James Crawford enter the cave, hands on their guns. The interior smells of campfire ash, sweat, and another odor, flowery and sweet.

"Told you those were horse tracks," Crawford says.

"A fire." Emmett crouches down and rubs his fingers into the ashes. "Reckon they left a day or two ago. But where'd they go? If they'd headed north toward the Columbia, they'd have to pass that trading post at Dee Flat, and the man there this morning said it was only a couple women went by, a mother and daughter, last several days."

"You reckon he pulled a long bow on us?" Crawford asks.

Emmett shakes his head. "Why would he?" He picks something out of the fire pit and holds it up to his eyes, a single strand of hair, half-singed. He finds several more. Silken, hair from a girl or young boy. Rubbing the strands in his fingers and thumb, he closes his eyes and imagines grabbing the hair of a young whore's head, ready to push her throat around his erection. He lets the hairs fall back into the ash.

Crawford frowns. "Those damn women were here."

"I reckon so." Emmett stands.

"Does that mean..."

"Might have nothing to do with it, or they might..." Emmett smiles. "You ever shot a woman?"

Crawford shakes his head. "No. Have you?"

"Sure. No different than shooting a man. Pull the trigger, bang, and down she goes. It don't bother me none, and you can't let it bother you, if it comes hither." Emmett thinks for a moment. No way two mere women were all that survived the massacre at the Pitts ranch.

"So now what?" Crawford mutters. "Back to the outpost?"

Emmett nods. "Get more out of the fat boy. I don't reckon he told us the right story. We're looking for Stark and some other guys, but we don't even know who or how many with Stark, or if we're even looking for him."

"I told you that's what we should've done," Crawford says. "And that horse—"

"Tell you what. After the outpost, we head over to the cat wagon...check out the wagtail Stark told us about. Spend one of those bloody twenty notes."

Crawford breaks out a rare smile. "I could use a night with a girl."

"Sure. All work and no play. But only after we make the fat boy sing."

Chapter 83

Sunrise. "You want to trade up rides?" Varla asks. "Chillins or Rusty? They're both finer animals than that nag."

Lindy Sue shakes her head. "No. Annabelle would be so upset."

"I figured as much. When we get to the river, I'll find good homes for the other two." Varla pats the heads of Chillins and Rusty.

For most of the day they ride, first on a harrowing cliff trail along the lower slope of Mount Hood, and then another trail with hairpin curves through the forest to the Columbia River, where the air becomes cooler and breezy, and the wagon trail widens as it skirts between the river and steep cliffs.

By nightfall they are with Varla's friends outside a small cabin in a clearing overlooking the river, a mile from the wagon road. The voices are hushed over the crackle of a campfire. The man and the woman have dark skin, like Varla, but they are nothing like Varla, with their mellow voices, which sing the words when they speak. They are a few years older than Varla, and they wear loops of beads on strings around the front of their shirts, and their hair is long and braided in two tails.

"You look good, Varla. Staying out of trouble?" the woman says.

"Much as I can."

"I hope so. You replaced Rosa with this one? Is Rosa well?"

"She's at peace at least."

"I suppose it's one way she'll get rest, though I'm sorry to hear," the woman says. "And this one? She's not your type, Varla. Barely enough of her and so young."

"Her name is Goldie. She got lost and I'm bringing her home. Isn't that right, Goldie?" Varla looks at Lindy Sue.

Lindy Sue nods.

"Good to meet you, Goldie," the man says. "My name is Sam."

"And I'm named Spring Bloom," the woman says. "You can call me Bloom."

"That's because she's no longer a spring bloom," the man jokes.

"Are you Indians?" Lindy Sue asks.

The man looks confused. "Do we look like we're from India, halfway around the world?"

"No. I didn't mean that."

"She's still young and a little stupid, but she's a fast learner." Varla snickers and rubs the top of Lindy Sue's near-bald head.

"We are qwi-whey-poom people, Goldie," the woman says.

"They're Klickitat, Goldie."

The woman lights a colorful wooden pipe with a long stem and passes it around. The smoke is pungent and ropy, neither tobacco nor opium. Lindy Sue recognizes it: ganja. She hands the pipe to the man, who takes a long pull from it and passes it to Varla, who does the same. Varla gives the pipe to Lindy Sue.

"Have some," the woman says. "Make you feel good." Lindy Sue sucks in some smoke and hands the pipe back to the woman.

"You want to stick around a few months?" the woman asks Varla. "Settlers come through here every day this time of year. Money to be made."

"No, we'll just stay the night."

"We heard you and Rosa went legit, Varla," Sam says. "Dancing in some tavern in Portland."

Bloom says, "You, Rosa, and a white girl, in the North

End, like we did at that crimp club in Astoria."

Varla laughs. "Almost twenty years ago. That was where we met, at that crimp club. Terrible place to work, but at least I met you and Sam there."

Bloom nods. "Wild days. Sam and I, we're a bit more settled now, but you..." Bloom meets eyes with Lindy Sue. "You wouldn't believe some of the crazy times we had with Varla. She's a hell-raiser."

Lindy Sue nods and looks at Varla a few feet away. She feels the effects of the cannabis now, as it tickles into her thoughts and scrambles some of the meanings, and in a different way than the opium from two nights ago. Varla has a twinkle in her eye as she gazes across the fire at the man and the woman.

Beyond Varla, across the Columbia River, is the dense wilderness of the Washington Territory. On this side, across from a bight in the river, a tall mass of rock juts high above at the end of a spit of land, caught in the few remaining beams of sun that spill across the river. At that moment Varla, the man, and the woman erupt with uncontrollable laughter after the man says something. Watching them roll on the ground makes Lindy Sue laugh too.

"Unless you are born rich and white and male, raising hell's the only way to get anything out of this so-called civilization," Varla exclaims. "They rig the works and get upset when we try to get our fair share. Speaking of which..." Varla digs into a black leather pocket bag at her side and pulls out a wad of twenty-dollar U.S. notes and some gold coins.

"A gift from me." She grabs Lindy Sue's arm and places the clump of currency in Lindy Sue's hand. "Paw this over to Bloom." Lindy Sue stares at the greenbacks and gold pieces, over six hundred dollars grasped tight so none falls in the fire. She leans toward Bloom with the money held out.

"Thank you, Varla." Bloom stuffs the money into a leather bag without counting it. "So you fell on a bit of luck, did you?"

"Maybe in more ways than one," Varla replies. "Also I wonder if you can take a couple horses."

"Sure thing." Bloom nods.

"Salmon almost done," Sam says. "What you staring at, Goldie?"

"That rock over there." Lindy Sue points to the slab of rock jutting up above a swampy inlet.

They all turn to look.

Bloom asks, "What does it look like to you, Goldie?"

"An icebox?"

"It's called Cock Rock," Varla says.

"Cock Rock? Why's it called that?"

"It's one big hard cock. Every woman's dream."

"Every man's dream too," Sam quips as he pulls the fish grill out of the fire.

"Not one like that. The one out there is the un-fuckible cock."

"Ohh!" Lindy Sue gasps at the turn in the conversation to sheer vulgarity, and then she giggles, looking over at the rock, a dark shadow against the starry sky, imagining the giant cock.

"Look at Goldie blush," Bloom says. "Listen, Goldie. That rock over there's been called something like that for generations among the various peoples who come along the river."

"Never mind. Here's some fish." Sam hands flat wooden platters down to her and Varla, each with a hunk of salmon and some greens. He sits down and Bloom hands him a platter, as well. Lindy Sue is about to ask for silverware, but the others begin to dig in, pulling off pieces of salmon with their fingers. Lindy Sue watches them for a moment and begins to do the same. The salmon melts in her mouth, still warm from the fire. The greens have a sharp tang that cuts the rich, lulling headiness of the bites of salmon. She remembers as a child she liked to eat with her fingers.

"Taste good?" Sam asks when everyone is done. The others murmur affirmative. "How about you, Goldie? You like it?"

"Yes," she says. Her stomach full, the warm fire and the talk among the others, exploits and people from their past, make her drowsy. She catches herself closing her eyes and about to fall forward a couple times, and she leans sideways on Varla's arm. She opens her eyes to find her head on Varla's lap and the voices continue above her while the fire crackles.

She gets stirred awake as Varla scoops her up in both hands. Sam makes a remark about Varla robbing the cradle. Varla follows the couple into the cabin. Sam and Bloom climb up to a loft while Varla lies Lindy Sue down on an animal hide, slides down beside her, and pulls over the blankets. Lindy Sue snuggles to Varla for warmth and quickly falls asleep again.

Chapter 84

The dining room of Gruber's Outpost is empty in the late morning between breakfast and lunch. Wiping the counter, Horace Gruber glances at the sound of the door. "Elber! Where you been? Missing all afternoon, worrying your Ma sick."

Elber waddles into the room, and two men file in behind him, both in slouch hats, the one tall and gaunt, face etched in a frown, the other with curly blond hair and a smile. Horace remembers these two from several days earlier, and he can think of why they're here, with their confederacy hats and similar CS pins like the one worn by the dead Pinkerton on his overcoat.

"What you doing with these two?" Horace asks Elber.

"We were at the Pitts ranch, Pa," Elber's fat round face is pale, his words stuttered. "Someone done murdered the Pitts."

"Murdered Gus Pitts?" Shaken, Horace clutches the counter with his bony fingers and stares at the two men, still at the doorway. "How we know it wain't these two scoundrels?"

"Wasn't us." The blond man strides across the floor. "Happened before we got there. My name is Emmett, and over there is Crawford." He jerks a thumb over his shoulder at the other man, then holds out his hand. Horace reluctantly shakes it.

"We're looking for our friend, and your kid told us he'd gone out that way."

"Your friend?" Horace asks.

"A Pinkerton. Stayed here a week. Willard Stark. His horse is still in your stable."

"Willard Stark?" The old man shakes his head. "I don't

remember..."

"Your son already confessed. You got Stark buried out back behind the outhouse." The man grins.

Ethel Gruber steps out from the kitchen, pinch-faced, peering suspiciously at the two men. "What's going on, Horace?"

"These men are saying someone murdered Gus and Butch."

"It's true, Pa," Elber says. "Saw it myself. Shot them dead and robbed them."

"I told that old fool to not keep the money out there, waiting to be stolen," Horace mutters. "And you, Elber, shooting off your damn mouth."

"I din't tell no one," Elber blubbers. "Except these two men after they took me there."

"Anyway, we know Willard Stark is buried in the back," Emmett says. "We served with him in the war. Don't seem right, war hero in an unmarked grave."

Trembling, Horace looks to Ethel, his lips flapping wordlessly. Ethel's shriveled face tightens.

"We don't want trouble," Ethel says. "He tried to kill another customer. Whole thing was an accident."

"Stark did have a temper," Emmett agrees. "And I know you wouldn't want this getting out. Bad for business. We might be willing to overlook it, isn't that right, Crawford?"

"What's that?" The tall gaunt man has sat down at a table near the door.

"We'd much appreciate it," Ethel says. "And we'll give you a free meal."

"A free meal and some of..." Emmett peers over at the bottles on a shelf behind the other end of the bar. "That stuff in the red label."

"Yes." Horace nods profusely and rushes over to grab the whiskey bottle with the red label and a pair of glasses. Emmett sits down at the table with the other one, Crawford.

Horace reaches the table with the bottle and two glasses. After pouring the drinks, he recaps the bottle.

Emmett smiles. "This is fine for now. Kid told us the till was low. But we'll want more, and we want to help you too. The kid has some great ideas."

"The kid? What kid?" *Derry Flanders*, Horace thinks, *or Norm Pitts*, who stopped in a few days ago for an ice tea before riding out to his father's ranch. Whatever went down out there. Horace doesn't believe Elber's story...they're all dead.

Emmett wipes his mouth on his sleeve. "He wants to make this place more lively. Bring in entertainment. Make this a destination, not a pass-through. When you retire, he has ideas... Bring this place to life."

"Elber said what? He never told Ethel or me."

Emmett throws his hands in the air. "Entertainment. Music. Dancing. Laughter. Stuff to get the stagecoach traffic to stay instead of moving on." Emmett finishes his whiskey and jumps to his feet. "Which reminds me. We want to see his room." The tall man, Crawford, also rises, tapping his empty glass on the table.

"His room?" Horace asks.

"Stark's room."

Ethel steps out from behind the counter. "I'll take you up. We haven't opened it since he vanished."

The two men follow her. Horace strides over to Elber, standing near the counter. Elber shrinks back, his hands clutched in fists.

"You big blabber-mouth, Elber. What're these plans you keeping from me and your ma?"

"It was an idea," Elber says. "People would stop here for that stuff he said, instead of going into dangerous Portland. Music and dancing."

Horace shakes his head. "Music? That stuff'll make us dangerous like Portland. Darn music killed one person, already, Elber. It's evil."

"Listen, Pa." Elber scrunches up his body, his hands stiff at his sides. "Those men can help us. They're getting a reward for saving a kidnapped girl, and they're getting the money stolen from Old Man Pitts."

"They're probably the ones that hooked it."

"No. It happened after those girls left. When I went with Emmett and Crawford, two of the girls were dead at the ranch but the other two weren't around. The big tough one with black hair and the other one, the prisoner."

"Prisoner? What prisoner?" Horace asks.

"I saw her when they rode away. Tied to the back of a horse. And they had her in Room Seven, hands tied behind her back."

"How you know this, Elber?" Horace asks. Elber has a problem with fabricating tales. "You peek in the window?"

"No! I-I mean, I didn't mean to when I heard a noise. The other one, the big one with black hair... She's a big outlaw named Varla, is what Emmett reckons, and she kidnapped the other one."

"Kidnapping?"

"That's right, Pa."

"I reckoned those women were bad news. At least they're a long way gone from here. We don't want to know anything more, Elber. We've enough trouble with these two thugs."

"Thugs? Why you say they're thugs?" Elber says. "They're war patriots. Fought for all of us."

"They only fought for half of us against the rest of us. And they lost."

Elber sinks forward on the counter for support, his head down and his voice slightly muffled. "It was terrible what I saw, Pa. Not one dead body, a whole bunch, blood everywhere, and one of them, half his head split open, the blond girl with an ax in her back."

"Enough, Elber." Footsteps on the stairs, Ethel and the two men return from Willard Stark's room.

"I reckon we have what we need," Emmett says. "And we'll take Stark's horse. Bring it home to his widow."

"Go ahead. We're tired of feeding the damn animal," Horace mutters.

"Good luck. For the sake of that poor girl." Ethel looks to Horace, her emotions lost in the shadows of the room. Emmett and the other, Crawford, soon ride away. Ethel approaches Horace, still at the window though the two men and their horses are no longer in sight.

"They're taking over for Willard Stark," she says. "Looking for that missing girl. They're headed to New Era to talk to the other Pinkerton, Derry Flanders."

"As long as they don't come back here."

"I hope they don't come back. We need to pray they won't, or they will. And they'll want more than a meal and a glass of hooch."

Chapter 85

At the busy Mitchell Street Two dock on the Albina riverfront, shirtless laborers don't notice Lindy Sue beneath the ill-fitted farm-boy clothes. Varla has also wrapped a cloth around Lindy Sue's torso and waist to disguise her feminine figure. Varla has on a gray wig beneath an old bonnet, a frayed cotton dress of faded gray, and a stained apron, top low enough to accentuate her cleavage, much to the discernment of many desperate eyes on sunburned faces.

Varla has one hand on a boxy black cabin trunk and the other tight on Lindy Sue's hand, pulling Lindy Sue rapidly along the dock, past departing passengers with their newspapers folded down, past other news pages trampled on the deck-wood beneath them.

They've just walked down from a farm where they stashed the horses and saddlebags. The farm, a few miles away on the hillside at the edge of the Sullivan's Gulch forest, belongs to Varla's friend Betsy, a spry, gray-haired woman with a motherly smile and a gentle voice.

Lindy Sue has a leather pack with a strap on her shoulder. The newspapers will have her disappearance by now, though she can't see it on the front pages. She glances around pleadingly for someone who might help her, someone who can take her directly home, as Varla drags her toward the ferry.

Twenty feet from the end of the embarking line, Varla stops, voice softened to golden honey. "No funny stuff. Play along, and in a day or two I take you home. Your trap shut. No talking to strangers or drawing attention."

Lindy Sue nods, her eyes darting at the people beyond Varla.

Varla smiles. “But I can’t trust you, cunning little Cupcake. Not right now.” From the large pocket in her apron, Varla pulls a device the size and shape of a stiffener for a smaller fedora, two curved slender metal bars with a pair of smaller slats of wood at one side. Varla’s other hand grabs Lindy Sue’s face, her fingers dig into the cheeks in the space between the back teeth and the crook of her lower jaw.

“What are you..?” Lindy Sue bursts out, indignant and startled, her words cut off by the pressure of Varla’s fingers.

“Did you know the jaw bone is the largest and strongest bone in your face?” As Varla holds Lindy Sue by the cheeks, she fits the contraption over Lindy Sue’s mouth, forcing the wood pieces between Lindy Sue’s lips and teeth. Holding the device in place with one hand, Varla reaches around to clasp a strap at the back of Lindy Sue’s head to fit the device snugly in place. A few clicks of the ratchet on one side pushes the wood slats farther apart against Lindy Sue’s teeth, prying her jaws wider with each click.

Lindy Sue’s eyes go wild, but she can not say anything but animal-like grunts, a sense of helplessness overwhelms her. She glances upriver to her left, toward East Portland, which seems as far as ever. Varla grabs her hand and the cabin trunk and pulls her toward the boarding line.

“Doctor says you got to wear it on the ferry, son, so’s you don’t grind your teeth to stumps.” The shrill voice of piercing intensity jolts Lindy Sue.

“One adult, one lad? That’ll be three bits.”

Varla slaps the coins in the conductor’s hand. “Thank you, sir,” she says in the same high-pitched raspy voice. She turns to the captain, standing next to him. “I apologize for my son, sir. He fears water. His first time taking the ferry.”

“No apology needed, ma’am.” The conductor puffs out his chest. “He’s nothing to fear. This ferry is the safest in all the Northwest Territories.” He gazes at Lindy Sue. “Won’t take long, my boy. Half an hour we’ll be there.”

Lindy Sue is terrified. With her jaw forced open by the

device, it's like the inside of her mouth is exposed to the harsh smells of Mitchell Street Dock Two, sweat and flatulence with the sweeter smell of wheat, piled up in burlap sacks at one end of the dock, and the less compromising pungency of the deck.

"Take this off, please! Take this off!" she wants to scream, unable to articulate the words. She stands on the deck with her mouth wrenched open like a gaping yokel. Children stare at her, and adults surreptitiously take looks of pity or revulsion. She glares back at them, embarrassed and angry.

"Poor kid," a silver-haired man in an expensive suit says as he lights a pipe and puffs on it. He glances at Varla's breasts and back at Lindy Sue.

"I wish he didn't have to wear that thing," Varla says in the screechy voice. "It's called a Whitehead Gag. A new contraption...invented by the famous doctor Walter Whitehead in Europe. My son has to wear it on the boat. He's so afraid."

"He looks petrified. Ma'am. What's your son's name?"

"Gollen, sir."

"Gollen?"

"It's Irish. His dad was an Irishman, died in a famine."

The man looks at Lindy Sue with what he must think is a comforting look, but comes out as an insipid smile, made even more insipid by his crooning voice. "Don't be afraid, Gollen. The Willamette River is safe. We'll be in Portland in less than half an hour." Lindy Sue wants to ask him for help, signal him with her eyes to let him know she's Varla's prisoner, but he turns to Varla, again, twirling his waxed mustache and ogling her cleavage. Angry at his obliviousness, Lindy Sue hates the man.

"How old is your son?" he asks.

"Fifteen. Taking him to a specialist doctor at Fourth and Alder in Portland."

"You should have taken the ten o'clock to Alder. This

one only goes to F Street."

"We don't have enough money for that one. We can walk the rest of the way."

"Stay along the docks until you get to Stark. You don't want to go too deep in the North End."

"Thank you, sir, and God bless." Varla beams a smile at the man.

Lindy Sue looks away over the rail. To the right, a dozen or more junked steamships in various states of disrepair, abandoned and abused, creak and groan along the side of the river. She remembers a ferry trip with her father, him pointing and telling her about the shipyard, owned by the Oregon Steam Navigation Company and known as the "Boneyard" where steamships go to die. Farther along the river bank, is their destination, the dock at the end of F Street at the edge of the North End.

At the dock, the stench is stronger, rotten vegetables, urine, and excrement assault Lindy Sue. The clatter of feet on wood, soon they're on the gangplank to the dock. A couple boys hawk competing papers to the passengers getting off. Lindy Sue can't see the headlines, but the news hawkers yell out the top stories.

"Two hundred drown! Tragic train wreck in Mexico! Death! Death! The Telegram has the latest!"

"Deadly train crash in Cualta, Mexico! And Senator's dead son! Read about it in the morning Bullet."

On the ground, an image that might be Tommy on mud-trampled newsprint looks up at Lindy Sue, and below it, she glimpses another portrait, unable to grasp details before Varla pulls her onward. If they found Tommy, they'll be looking for her.

She stumbles up the wooden steps to the street to keep pace with Varla and the tight grip on her wrist. Two blocks away from the river Varla drags her into a recessed doorway and pushes her, face first, into the corner.

"That thing comes out of your mouth, now," Varla

mumbles. With a jerk, the strap is loosened. She pulls the device off of Lindy Sue's face and tucks it into the pocket of her apron.

The inside of Lindy Sue's cheeks and her jaw muscles still ache from the strain, her eyes in tears, but shot with anger. Rubbing the sides of her jaw, she spins to face Varla. "Why'd you do that?"

"Stop crying like a spoiled little bitch."

"That was...you humiliated me."

"Why should you feel humiliated? No one knows you." Varla pulls out a scrap of cloth. "Now wipe away the tears."

"You treat me like dirt. Why don't you take me to East Portland?" Anger wells up as Lindy Sue thinks about her home, her father, her friends...even her stepsisters and stepmother. Knowing Tommy is dead, they'd be worried sick about her. Upriver a couple miles away is the Jefferson Street Ferry that goes across the river to the East Portland dock at V Street, a fifteen-minute walk to her home.

Varla's face softens a bit. "Listen, Goldie. I had to do it. I couldn't trust you not to say anything on the boat."

"Something matter with your son, ma'am?"

Two men are ten feet away, in badly fitting black suits and cheap fedoras.

"You've a fine-looking lad, there," the smaller man says, revealing missing front teeth as he speaks. "If you need money?" Licking his lips, the plumper man stares at Lindy Sue. In a rush of fear, Lindy Sue realizes she's in the dreaded North End.

Though only a few miles from home, Lindy Sue has never been to this part of town, beyond seeing the docks from the safety of a vessel. She remembers her father and stepmother talking in hushed tones, and later, her friends making jokes about it. The North End, also known as White Chapel, is a crime-ridden hell hole, a den of vilest iniquity, a place to avoid, to shun, to fear, where farm boys are shanghaied, and every vice known to man is practiced openly and without repentance. Saloons, dope dens, brothels, and theaters of ill-repute appeal to the gangs of sailors, trappers, loggers, and other men who descend on the North End from the world beyond.

Lindy Sue glances past the two men. On the corner of the street, a few glassy-eyed prostitutes in scanty attire ply their trade. Across the street a man kneels at the gutter that runs along the curbside, vomiting loudly. A shirtless man stands in a doorway, picking his teeth with a knife. Everywhere she looks, shifty eyes, burning eyes of destitute men. Even a hobo has a sneer on his face as he ogles the cooing prostitutes. The air is coarse with obscenities yelled or whispered, and this blends with an eerie hymnal drone from a temperance choir farther down First Street, like a far-off haunting. Tugged by a change of the breeze, the urine-and-excrement stench from an open sewer wafts past to drown out the sour smell of human sweat and lust.

The two men in black suits and cheap fedoras, sidle closer. Their faces remind Lindy Sue of the old lecher in the wheelchair who grabbed at her thigh, the same leering half-open mouths and wolfish eyes.

"You coming or not?" Varla ambles away with her luggage case. In a panic at being left alone in the North End, Lindy Sue scrambles past the men to Varla's side. "Smart move, Cupcake. You wouldn't last a minute alone on these streets."

Lindy Sue clutches Varla's hand. The fear diminishes with Varla beside her, Varla's nonchalance as they walk rapidly up F Street, away from the river and deeper into the North End. Lindy Sue thinks she'll go with Varla now, and wait later for a chance to escape if Varla refuses to take her home.

They step past heaps of horse dung and over sewer gutters and past a bunch of men yelling encouragement to two men in a knife fight. They pass Chinese men with food carts and more prostitutes in further states of undress and a soapbox preacher yelling about salvation and damnation and dozens of ill-shaven faces, hungry eyes of sailors and laborers and farm workers, one man after another, mostly in pairs or small groups. Several inebriated men stumble and swerve, and others mutter to themselves while others prowl with hungry wolfish expressions.

Varla ignores the stares and whistles and catcalls, deflecting several propositions with a curt “No!” A couple times she pushes men out of her way with the deftly wielded cabin trunk, and slams it hard into the stomach of one unrelenting individual, to leave him on the ground, moaning painfully. On the next block, a man urinates into the gutter, fully exposed, while others, red from sun and drink, lie sprawled on the walk, a few are even naked, robbed of the clothes on their backs, singing loudly and hoarsely off-key with nasty lyrics to the songs of the temperance group a street up.

Eyes wide, Lindy Sue takes it in with a mix of curiosity and revulsion and even pity. Many of the men, rather than threatening, look sad and lost.

“Not so bad, is it?” Varla says. “And this is still morning. You should see it at nightfall.”

Chapter 86

Lindy Sue and Varla reach Seventh Street, where a three-floor wood house sits on the corner, the front door half-open. Lindy Sue follows Varla inside, to a dimly lit lobby and beyond, a double-doorway that looks into a parlor, with couches, padded armchairs, and velvet-covered walls. A young woman rises from the chair in the parlor, wearing a frilly negligee and smiles at Lindy Sue before sashaying out of view.

"Varla?" Lindy Sue whispers. "This is a house of prostitution."

"What of it? You want to turn tricks?"

"No! What are we doing here?"

"Staying a day or two while I take care of business."

"You said you'd take me home."

"In a day or two."

At the back wall of the lobby, a plump woman with a round face and a large nest of curly brown hair sits at a large oak desk. She remains impassive as they approach, and when Varla pulls off the gray wig, the woman's face brightens. "Varla, you're back!" She leans over the counter to kiss Varla on the lips. "And what are you doing with this..." She peers down at Lindy Sue and laughs. "I thought you were a boy for a moment." Brows furrow in puzzlement, she looks back at Varla. "What happened to Rosa and Blondie?"

"Bad story. They're gone." Varla sighs.

"No!"

"Later, Nancy." Varla drops a bundle of greenbacks on the counter. The woman pockets them without counting them.

Nancy looks Lindy Sue up and down, her face sharpening to a narrow focus. "And this one? Not your type,

Varla, this frail doll. But she has a young, innocent face. Some pay more for those sorts of girls, good ones that haven't been worked too much in the trade."

Lindy Sue glares at the woman. I'll show you how frail I am, clenching her hands into fists. Was this Varla's plan? To sell her to a madame to be made a whore?

"She's not yours, Nancy," Varla says.

Lindy Sue sighs with relief.

Nancy smiles. "What chicanery you have up your sleeve, Varla? Saving runaway youth?"

Varla shrugs this off.

Nancy takes a key from the mahogany rack behind her. As she places the key on the desk, she catches Lindy Sue's eye. "And you, young girl. What's your name?"

"Her name is Goldie. Isn't that right, Goldie?"

Lindy Sue glances from Varla to the woman, and for one moment, she wants to stammer out her real name, but the woman is Varla's friend, and they are in a house of prostitution. *Maybe later*, Lindy Sue thinks... *Find a way to flee Varla.*

Varla grabs the keys off the countertop.

The woman, Nancy, smiles at Lindy Sue. "Nice to meet you, Goldie. I hope Varla doesn't get you in harum-scarum with her schemes."

"Get her in harum scarum?" Varla laughs. "I'm keeping her out of it."

Chapter 87

Derry Flanders takes a deep breath, inhaling the multitudinous aromas from the farm, the faint tang of animal manure offset by the sweetness of blossoms and the earthy smell of decay. He's in front of a large barn at New Era Valley and facing him are two men.

"You're hard to track down, Flanders." George Emmett offers his hand and a boyish grin. "And we're good at tracking down people."

Derry Flanders gazes at the hand for a moment before accepting it. He shoots a look at Crawford while mostly focusing on Emmett.

"You say you're friends of Willard?" Derry says.

"That's right. I reckon he told you of us?"

"He did. And I told him I wanted nothing to do with this side job. And then he got himself shot."

"Pretty amazing, the fat boy shot him. Unless it's one of them girls. I could see one of them girls shooting Stark and seducing that fat slob to fess to it."

"I really don't know," Derry says. "I wasn't there. By the time I ran down from the room, it had already eventuated."

"Was it the big one with black hair that done it? Did she shoot Willard?"

"I don't know."

"But she might've?" Emmett insists. "Don't you think?"

Derry shakes his head. "I don't even remember if she was in the room."

"It's just her and the kidnapped girl. Only ones that survived. How much you know about this woman since the people at the Outpost saw you cavort with the other two?"

"Varla Vixen?"

"That's who." Emmett nods enthusiastically. "What you know of her?"

"It's her stage name...not her real name." Derry shakes his head. He can't remember being with her, except that she kissed opium into him and stared at him, her eyes like magnets that pulled him in.

"Want to help us catch her?" Emmett asks.

"Help you?" Derry turns from him to Althea, a dozen steps away. She has a concerned look on her face, as she watches them.

"It pays more than this sharecropping. Heap of cabbage you help us catch her?"

Derry shakes his head. "Good luck with that. I can't help. Need to get back to work." He begins to walk toward Althea. He senses their eyes on his back, but they are unwilling to do anything else. He has nothing to offer to them. Soon, the footsteps of their horses fade down the road.

These men, so like Willard Stark. Derry wants nothing to do with them, and their trek. Too many dead already, including Blondie, his first great love. News of the massacre at the Pitts ranch has carried to New Era Valley. As Derry joins the others in the field, pulling weeds and singing, he almost forgets Emmett and Crawford.

Chapter 88

Emmett and Crawford on their steeds trot away from New Era Valley, beyond the farmland to where the road passes sagebrush and tumbleweed.

"A most useless conversation," Emmett says. "That kid, Derry Flanders, no help at all. We could use a third man, to catch this Varla Vixen, or whatever her name is."

Crawford jerks his thumb back toward the farm. "That guy worked with Stark? How could Stark stand him?"

"The young today. Not the same as when we were growing up, Crawford." Emmett sighs. "We could use another war to drum them into real men."

"So what now?"

Emmett pulls on his goatee. "I reckon we'll head west, to Portland. The kidnapped girl's house. Sooner or later Varla will contact the father for a ransom. We keep watch on the Tremain house. She shows up to negotiate, and we get her. We get the reward for the missing girl, and we torture Varla to reveal where she's hidden the money stolen from Pitts."

"What if Varla already returned the girl?"

"We'll track her down. Big Amazon woman like that. Can't be too many places she can hide in Portland, least not from a bounty hunter."

Chapter 89

Varla thinks, *This is the life* while lying in bed with Goldie in the mid-afternoon. It's the third day staying in the small room above the brothel, and earlier, instead of tying Goldie to the bed and gagging her when leaving, Varla took Goldie out to a bar to get a drink that resulted in Varla getting into a brawl while Goldie looked on. Then they went back to the room to make love.

"You feel better?" Varla asks.

Goldie nods, lying on top of Varla, her body relaxed in the same post-orgasmic bliss as Varla.

"Sometimes you make me forget where I am and who I am," Goldie says, snuggling into Varla, her fingers in Varla's dark hair, her cheek rubbing against Varla's.

A knock on the door; their bodies tense up.

"Who?" Goldie says quietly.

Varla puts a finger to Goldie's lips. Goldie nods.

Varla rolls Goldie off her, pulls out of the bed, grabs a revolver off the dresser, then strides quietly to the door. "Who is it?"

"Nancy. Need to talk to you."

Varla opens the door carefully. Nancy Boggs has a worried look on her face, but she's alone. She glances past Varla at the younger woman, lying on the bed, before fixing her eyes on Varla. "I brought you today's paper."

Varla takes the paper from her hand. "And there's something else."

Nancy speaks quietly, out of earshot of Lindy Sue. "I got word from Eliza this morning." Eliza, Nancy's daughter ran the mobile wagon bordello they'd named "Nancy's Nunnery."

"Uh-huh," Varla says.

"Two men yesterday. Bounty hunters. Former graybacks, like the big Pinkerton."

"Go on," Varla says, keeping her voice low too.

"Looking for two women. One woman, bigger and stronger than a man, and the other, a young spoiled society girl, abducted by the other. At least that's what the girls got out of them."

Varla nods.

"You don't seem worried."

"Just a bit." Varla shrugs and smiles.

"You be careful. Bounty hunters..." Nancy cringes. "I reckoned you should know."

"Thank you, Nancy. And don't worry none about me." Varla glances over her shoulder, back at Goldie, on the bed, her hands covering her nakedness, staring at Varla and Nancy.

Chapter 90

Mid-afternoon, their third day in the room above the brothel in the North End, Lindy Sue sits on the bed, still in a slight daze after making love, while Varla talks to Nancy Boggs at the doorway. The room isn't much, small, with the water closet and bathing room down the hall, but with the windows open, cool air comes in at night, even if it does bring in drunken yells and laughter from the street below.

Even the rope burns on her wrists and ankles don't feel as bad, the dull ache and the chafed skin, now that Lindy Sue is not tied up. Her eyes are fixed on the newspaper Varla holds against her hip. Lindy Sue can make out part of the headlines.

The funeral. Tommy's funeral. She grabs the paper eagerly when Varla hands it to her.

"Tommy's dead."

"That's right. But you already knew that." Varla stands by the curtains and looks at the street below.

There, beneath the announcement of Tommy's funeral and an illustration of Tommy in his football jersey, a smaller picture startles Lindy Sue for a moment. The caption under it says: "Still missing, Lindy Sue Hawthorne, daughter of Dr. J.C. Hawthorne, director of the Oregon Hospital for the Insane." A weird feeling sinks into Lindy Sue as if she's looking at a picture of a stranger. But even with her hair cut off, someone will recognize her, won't they?

Varla turns and walks over to Lindy Sue. "Tommy's funeral is happening tomorrow, isn't it?" Varla says casually.

"That's right," Lindy Sue says.

"You remember what happened, Goldie?"

She shakes her head. "No... I can't remember."

"But you knew he was dead."

Yes, she thinks, *I know he was dead. But why can't I remember?*

"Look at me, Goldie. Try to remember."

"We were at that abandoned ranch. Tommy's father got it from a foreclosure. Forced the owners to the poor farm."

Varla is above her, looking down at her with an intent gaze. "Look at me. You must try to remember."

Tommy is dead. An image comes into Lindy Sue's mind. Tommy lying on the ground near the abandoned ranch house. "They broke his neck. They killed him. Broke his neck and left him to die."

"Who did?" Varla smiles. "You do remember, don't you? The old man? His son, the monster?"

"Yes." The old man in the wheelchair, a lecher who kept trying to get her alone. His breath smelled like booze when he grabbed her thigh. And he had a son, a huge brute of a man named Butch who could barely articulate words. Butch's arms and legs were almost twice as thick as Varla's, but he was as mentally incapacitated as the patients in her father's hospital.

"You've tried to erase it from your mind, Goldie. The horror. The loss. But the big one, Butch Pitts, he killed Tommy. The old man, Gus Pitts, told him to do it because you reminded the old man of a girl he once saved from the train accident where he lost his legs. He wanted you because that girl ditched him and took the next train out of town. He had his son Butch kill Tommy to kidnap you."

She can't remember, it's all a blur. Tommy with a broken neck lying in the dirt. The old lecher. The son. The violence at the ranch. Those other two women...Blondie and Rosa.

"Yes. Rosa and Blondie. I lost both of them. We were rescuing you, and they both were killed."

"Rescuing me?"

"Yes. From the old cripple and his sons."

Lindy Sue can barely remember any of it. She looks back down at the paper. "The funeral is tomorrow." She looks up at Varla with pleading eyes, trying to read Varla's expression, unsure Varla will let her go.

"That's right. Your fiancé's funeral." Varla's voice is calm.

"Can I..." *Why ask?* she thinks. Varla never lets her out of her sight in public, and when leaving the room, Varla ties Lindy Sue to the bed with a thick piece of rope and sticks the Whitehead device back over her mouth so that she can not cry out, even though Varla must know Lindy Sue wouldn't dare walk out alone into the streets of the North End.

"You want to go to the funeral, Goldie?"

"You mean... Yes." She stares at Varla. "I must. You have to let me."

"I won't stop you." Varla brushes her hand across the fuzz of Lindy Sue's head. "What kind of horrible person do you take me for? You should go to Tommy's funeral tomorrow." Varla slaps her lightly on the butt. "Now get up. We cross the river tonight."

As Varla wraps the girl's torso in a thick leather strap to disguise her breasts, Lindy Sue's mind leaps and swoons from an overload of thoughts. Tommy's funeral. Her dad. Will Varla really let her go? Why would Varla do that? Perhaps Varla has already collected ransom money or decided she isn't worth a decent ransom. The newspaper didn't mention a reward for her return. She can imagine her stepmother telling her dad that they can't afford to pay much, and she's not a part of the family, just the leftovers from a previous family that never happened.

She compares herself to Cinderella, with a stepmother and two stepsisters, though she can't say that her stepmother is as evil as the hideous creature in the fairy tale. No, her stepmother EC mostly ignores her and gets angry easily with her while doting excessively on her own two younger girls.

And her stepsisters Louise and Catharine are a pair of obnoxious little kids, ten and eleven. And she had once thought that Tommy, the son of a United States Senator and thus the American equivalent of a prince, would take her away to a fairy tale ending, but he was a selfish man-boy, his refusal to commit to marriage, the way he took her for granted. At one time she'd loved him, at the same time, it was always in the back of her mind, wondering if she'd ever feel comfortable with him. Hardly the fairy tale prince.

Does Varla want to get rid of her? If Varla shows up to the funeral with her, they'll arrest Varla for kidnapping her. Maybe Varla is tired of her and doesn't want her around. Perhaps she's become a burden to Varla, in the same way she felt she was a burden to her father and the family, as the odd one who does not belong.

And poor Tommy. He's dead, and she's not even a widow, but she can still feel something of the pain of widowhood. There will be questions, and many of them she will not be able to answer, questions about events that are not clear in her head. When she tries to concentrate on what happened to Tommy, a pang of panic fills her, and the memories are dreamlike, where one knows something happened but does not know how one piece fits with another. Questions from her father, questions from the police, and those will be nothing compared to the questions from Maggie Mitchell, who is both her best friend and Tommy's sister.

Maggie will be wracked with grief. The same grief Lindy Sue now feels, or more grief, because Lindy Sue's grief is tempered with guilt. The guilt at how she behaved, with Tommy not yet buried, at how she behaved at night when lying next to Varla in bed. There'll be no way to explain it even to Maggie her best friend. She'll have secrets even Maggie can't know.

Near the docks, it's big news. Tommy's funeral the next day. Lindy Sue still missing, believed kidnapped. It feels odd to see her face on dozens of papers in people's hands and on the ground, one with a mustached mud print and another of her in profile folded over to vanish most of her face.

Over and over, the thoughts circulate in her head. Once more they are back on the ferry, headed to Albina. Done up with a gray wig, some padding on her belly, and makeup on her face to look older, Varla chats gaily with passengers in a fake chirpy singsong while Lindy Sue, mouth gaped open from the Whitehead gag like some dim halfwit who can only grunt monosyllables, must bear the looks of pity from the others aboard.

Dusk has fallen across Albina, the sun nearly at the Western Hills. They are in a darkened doorway near the edge of the docks. The Whitehead is removed and Lindy Sue gasps for breath. Varla has removed the dress, padding, and wig.

"Let's get that other thing off your body so you can breathe easier," Varla says. "Got a walk ahead of us."

Lindy Sue lets Varla pull the cotton shirt above Lindy Sue's head where it confines her arms while Varla spins her around, tugging and pulling to unravel the thick black leather strap around her torso. "There. Take some deep breaths, then we move." She hands Lindy Sue the strap, which Lindy Sue wraps twice around her waist as a belt. They have no baggage this time, except for a large cheap leather purse Varla carries on a shoulder strap.

"This way." Varla grabs her hand and pulls her along. Soon Lindy Sue recognizes Fourth Street ahead of them, parallel to the river, over Sullivan's Gulch, and through a forest into East Portland. They are halfway across the wood trestle bridge, the stream at the bottom of the gulch fifty feet below, when two horsemen appear ahead, beyond the bridge where the trail cuts through the dense woods that dominate Sullivan's Gulch.

"Keep your head down," Varla hisses.

Lindy Sue stares at the river, the horsemen in the corner of her eye, the clatter of hooves on dirt suddenly getting louder against the wood of the bridge. She recognizes them, now much closer than at the far end of a spyglass, the one gaunt and bent over his saddle, sunken eyes and a dark beard, and the other, riding reclined back in the saddle, with curly blond hair falling out from the sides of his hat.

The two riders pass by. Lindy Sue overhears one speak to the other:

"Maybe we just got lucky. You see those two?"

The hooves stop. A horse whinnies and with a scuffle the horses begin to return. The whish of two guns leaving their holsters.

"Drop the gun." The voice is soft and calm. The men are directly behind them. Varla lets her revolver clatter to the ground. "Now kick it off the side and up with your hands. Raise them higher, both of you."

"This a hold up? We got nothing to steal. You criminals ought to be hanged," Varla growls.

"We're not the criminals, Varla Vixen."

"That's not my name."

"You kidnapped that girl, and we're bringing her back to her folks."

"No one's kidnapped anyone," Varla says. "Isn't that right, Goldie?"

Before Lindy Sue can answer, the man chuckles. "Goldie? That what you call her? Turn around, Goldie, so we can see your face."

Lindy Sue turns to face the men, still on their horses with guns pointed at Varla. The one with the van dyke beard and curly blond hair almost seems handsome, with his smile and twinkling eyes, in contrast with the tall gaunt one and his surly looks.

"You really going to take me home?" Lindy Sue asks.

"Don't trust them," Varla snaps.

"Your family misses you," the blond says. "Your

daddy's giving us five thousand to bring you home. Your family misses you."

"Five thousand dollars?" Lindy Sue gasps.

"A lot of spondoolicks," the man says. "That's how much they miss you."

Lindy Sue glances at Varla, who has her back to the men, and back up at the men. "You'll take me there tonight?"

He grins. "Sooner we do, sooner we get paid."

"Whole lot of flamdoodle, Goldie," Varla says. "Don't trust them."

"Now, help us out, Goldie," the man says. With his free hand, he tosses down some metal handcuffs. "Cuff Varla's hands behind her back."

Lindy Sue glances down at the cuffs. "I-I don't know how they work."

"You put them around her wrists and clasp them."

"No. I can't do it." Lindy Sue looks at the man with tears. She's afraid to get near Varla, afraid of Varla's anger, scared of the guns pointed at Varla.

"Sheesh." The man shakes his head, rubbing at his van dyke. "Crawford, you'll have to get down and do it."

"Why don't we just shoot her?" The other man grunts.

"Not until we know where the money is."

Muttering, Crawford leaps down from his horse. Gun pointed at Varla, he steps closer to Lindy Sue. His eyes dart from Varla to her, his eyes lingering on Lindy Sue's breasts, which she realizes are visible beneath the thin cotton of the shirt.

"Pick up those bracelets, girl, and hand them to me." He reaches out a hand.

"How can I with my hands up?" she asks.

"Just do it, girl. No more clowning." He scowls at her.

Lindy Sue crouches to pick up the shackles and hands them to him. Sneer on his lips, he stares intently at her chest and back at her face. "You're cute, even with your hair cut off. Picture don't give you justice. I see why your dad and mom'd give anything to have you back."

"Stop ogling her and cuff the other one, Crawford," the man on the horse demands.

"She's not my mom," Lindy Sue says. "I don't have a mom."

"Knock it off, Bethany," the man on the horse says. "We met your mom and dad yesterday."

"My name's not Bethany. It's Lindy Sue."

"Knock off the bullshit. Goldie. Lindy Sue, whatever you call yourself."

"You have the wrong people," Varla says, hands still raised, her back to the men. "I'm not Varla. She's not Bethany. Let us go on our way."

"My name is Lindy Sue Hawthorne."

"We got your picture right here." The man on the horse, gun still aimed at Varla, grabs a piece of paper from his vest pocket with his free hand, waves it open, and holds it toward her.

"You know, Emmett, I don't think it's her," the gaunt man says as he glances from the drawing to Lindy Sue's face.

"What do you mean not her?" Emmett, the man on the horse, loses his smug grin and drops the drawing, the paper slicing the air back and forth to land on the bridge decking.

"I don't think it is." Crawford leans forward, two feet from Lindy Sue, his eyes narrow slits on his sun-burned face, his breath hot and stinking of meat and beans.

"Never mind that. Put the bracelets on the other one."

Crawford licks his cracked sneering lips, giving Lindy Sue the up and down. "If you ain't Bethany Tremain, we'll have fun with you later." He plods toward Varla. "You, Varla—"

"I'm not Varla. How many times—"

"Bring your hands down slowly," he demands. "Behind your back."

"We're not who you want," Lindy Sue says. "Let us

go!"

"Maybe you are who we want." Emmett flicks a glance at her, gun still trained on Varla. "Maybe not."

Varla lowers her hands. Crawford reaches out with the handcuffs. "You're going to wear these 'til we know for sure."

Varla moves quickly. Her hand grabs Crawford's wrist, pulls him to her as she spins around. A gun goes off and another echoes back. Varla has the man in front of her, between her and the other on the horse. Emmett falls from the horse, a bloody hole in his shirt. Crawford struggles to escape Varla until a knife appears in her hand. One slash opens his throat to a gusher of spurting blood.

"Drop the weapon," Emmett hisses, prone beneath the steed, gun still aimed at Varla and his partner. He fires and the pistol flies out of Crawford's hand, skittering across the bridge planking followed by a couple of Crawford's fingers. Emmett slowly rises to get a bead on Varla behind his dead friend.

"No!" Lindy Sue rushes toward him, whipping off the black strap around her waist and swinging it at the hand that holds the gun. The strap snaps against his hand and the gun explodes.

"Damn you!" Emmett yells. A flash of movement. A swoosh of flight, a glint of light in the waning rays of the sun, a thunk as the knife hits Emmett in the throat. He thumps loudly on the bridge, gargling an attempt at a scream.

Lindy Sue stares at the body in front of her. "Is he dead?"

Varla saunters over to pull out her knife. "Help me push these two off the bridge. Then we can ride their horses and dump them near Betsy's farm to get our own."

Like that, it's over. More dead bodies... Lindy Sue fights a wave of nausea, touching the first one. They push it across the planking and watch it fall to the gulch below, hitting with a splash. The smell of blood, dripping out of the other man's throat... It makes Lindy Sue think of the other dead, at the Pitts Ranch, and somehow she's more used to it, but will never be completely used to it. At least she no longer feels panic.

Lindy Sue follows Varla up the hill toward the farm where Annabelle awaits.

Chapter 91

Night sets in when Varla and Lindy Sue reach Betsy's farm, on a hillside near the Sullivan Gulch forest overlooking downtown East Portland. Betsy, her long gray hair flowing from a straw brimmed hat, heads to the stable with Varla and Lindy Sue. She unlocks a large cabinet at the corner of the stable where several saddles are hung. Varla and Lindy Sue grab theirs. Varla pulls some bills and gold coins from hers to hand to Betsy.

On their horses, by starlight, they head toward the river. As they approach Fourth Street, Varla turns right and halts.

"My dad's house is the other way," Lindy Sue says.

"Too late tonight," Varla says. "Tomorrow."

"Tomorrow. Always tomorrow," Lindy Sue mutters, but she follows Varla, back toward the bridge across Sullivan Gulch into Albina. Closer and closer to home, but never quite getting there. If she turned and galloped the other way? Varla's steed could quickly overtake Annabelle, and Lindy Sue thinks about the two bounty hunters, lying in the gulch below.

Half-hour ride north of Albina, they reach a small shack of weathered wood on stilts at the edge of the Columbia slough. The interior is a single room that smells of mildew, a mattress on the floor and shelves along one wall. The flame of a candle, lit by Varla, throws bits of illumination off the walls of the room. The room is warm and Varla sits naked on the bed. Lindy Sue strips off her clothes.

Varla pulls out a pipe and a small vial, tapping what is in the vial to the pipe. She flicks a match to get it lit and sucks on the pipe.

"What is that?" Lindy Sue asks.

Varla beckons her with a finger. Lindy Sue steps

toward her, leans down to put her lips to Varla's, and sucks the smoke out of Varla lungs.

Slightly dazed, Lindy Sue blows out the smoke. Varla pulls her onto her lap, and this time Lindy Sue takes a hit off the pipe, and breaths it into Varla's mouth while their tongues entwine in a kiss. The drugs have begun to twitch at the edges of Lindy Sue's vision.

Varla hugs her. "Our last night together, Goldie. Let's make it one to remember."

Chapter 92

A cool, overcast morning. Lindy Sue awakes in the small cabin, lying naked on the mattress, her head a fever-haze from the drugs and sex. For a minute she lies there and remembers the pleasure, wave after wave, until her body was empty and sated. She realizes she's cold and naked, and she remembers it's the day of Tommy's funeral.

Varla is awake and dressed. Lindy Sue's still uncertain Varla will let her walk away. She watches Varla stuff fistfuls of bills and gold pieces into Lindy Sue's saddle bag.

An hour later they are outside the shack. The horses are tied up a dozen feet away, saddled and ready to go. Varla stands in front of her, legs apart, hands on hips, observing her with a contemplative sigh.

"This is where we part ways, Goldie. You need to go back to your family."

Lindy Sue nods and swallows. She glances over her shoulder at the trail and back at Varla. "I'll miss you, Varla," she chokes.

"Miss you too, Cupcake."

"Will I see you again?"

"Listen, kid. I like you. I like you more than I should, but we're from different worlds. I have to keep moving. You'll only get hurt if you stick around me too long. And you're a danger to me. Sooner or later someone'll recognize you."

I don't want to leave, Lindy Sue thinks in panic, but if she tells Varla that, Varla will laugh at her sarcastically. Varla draws her to kiss her full on the lips.

"You mustn't say anything to any of them about you and me. If they found out, it would be terrible for you. Lock you in your father's crazy house and throw away the key.

You mustn't say anything at all."

"No. Nothing at all." Lindy Sue nods. She realizes Varla finally trusts her and that is why Varla's letting her go.

"Our secret." Varla reaches into her vest pocket and pulls out a shiny object. "I have a gift for you."

"Tommy's pocket watch," Lindy Sue exclaims.

"Kept it safe for you. I don't care what time it is. Some people must care to have such an expensive timepiece."

Lindy Sue holds the watch in her hand. The one Tommy owned, the expensive Swiss model his father gave him.

Varla pushes her away and pulls out a box of matches. She takes one out, strikes it against a gold cap on her tooth, and the match flares up. She holds it between them. The flame sparkles in Varla's eyes. Varla stares at her intently. "Love is a flame. But sometimes it keeps burning, whereas a flame leaves nothing but ash and smoke." As she gazes into Varla's eyes, Lindy Sue feels the pull of something in her mind, Varla in her head, her voice and her eyes as she towers over Lindy Sue. Varla tosses the match over her shoulder toward the shack.

"Will I ever see you again?" Lindy Sue asks again.

"I can't read the future, Goldie." Varla kisses her again, this time tenderly, and she brings Lindy Sue's hand up to her mouth, licks the fingers, and places the box of matches in Lindy Sue's hand. "But I think we'll meet again."

"I'll miss you." Absentmindedly Lindy Sue pockets the matchbox in her shirt.

"Past ten days, you hated me. All you thought about was escape."

"I know," Lindy Sue says quietly, holding back her tears.

"It's okay. I'll miss you too. I thought you were some spoiled little brat, but against my will, I've grown affectionate to you. But, you have a funeral to attend, and I must move on."

They kiss again. Varla helps her on the horse. Behind Varla, smoke rises from the front of the shack where Varla tossed the match. Halfway up to the trail, Lindy Sue glances back at Varla, a dark silhouette against the streams of smoke and belching flames that consume the shack. Varla climbs on her horse and vanishes beyond the trees.

A part of Lindy Sue is in disbelief that she's free and going home, like a strange dream. The trail in front of her blurred from the tears that flow from her eyes, from the wind. Near the bustling Albina Docks, where the sails of a couple of freighters poke above the wharf buildings, she catches the road that runs south along the river. Another twenty minutes, she approaches the wooden bridge across Sullivan's Gulch. She slows the pace to a slow trot, the hooves clattering hollowly on the planking, over the gulch and swampy land beyond and soon into downtown East Portland.

I can not tell them, she thinks.

Tell them you can't remember, Varla whispers in her head. "I can't remember." You don't know. "I don't know." Don't let them inside. She can't remember Tommy's murder, only that he's on the ground dead, and she flailed at those around her, anger and fear, but she can't remember faces. An old man lies dead at the bottom of his porch next to his wheelchair. A woman has an ax in her back. A nightmare tableau of murder and blood flashes into her head.

She can't tell them about the nights in the cave or in the room in the North End. She can't tell them she let Varla kiss opium smoke into her lungs and the pleasure of what Varla did to her, so intense her body trembles even as she thinks of it, making love while the faces of devils danced in the campfire a few feet away.

You mustn't tell them. Our secret.

Chapter 93

Ten-year-old Catharine Hawthorne rushes into the house with her sister Louise. "Mommy! Mommy! There's a man on a horse at the front walk."

"It's not a man, mother, it's a girl, and the horse looks like Annabelle." Her sister Louise, one year older, never misses an opportunity to correct her sister and thus prove her own superiority. "Cooter is talking to her now."

EC Hawthorne pulls on her feather hat, looks at herself in the mirror, then follows the girls to the front door. The stranger has climbed off the horse and is tying it to the hitching rail while Cooter stands nearby, calling, "Miss? Can I help you, miss?"

The stranger, a young woman, walks toward EC who tries to recall where she's seen her before.

"Hi, EC."

"Lindy Sue?" EC blinks in disbelief. "Lindy Sue, you poor thing." EC can't conceal how appalled she is.

"That's Lindy Sue?" little Catharine asks.

"I knew it all the time," her sister says.

"Did not!"

"What did you do to your hair, Lindy Sue?" EC is aghast as she holds Lindy Sue at arm's length. "And those clothes! Don't you know Tommy's service is less than an hour from now? You need to get inside and—"

"I want to see dad." Lindy Sue steps around her and enters the house.

"What are we going to do about your hair? You can't be seen in church like that. Gretta!" EC calls to one of the maids as she scrambles inside after Lindy Sue.

Chapter 94

Lindy Sue steps into the library where her father is smoking a pipe and talking to two other doctors from the asylum. JC Hawthorne looks up. “Who are you?” he says, before he drops his pipe, spilling tobacco on his black tailored pants. “Lindy Sue? Is that you?” He stumbles out of his chair.

“Yes.” She rushes into his arms.

“Oh, my god, child. If this is not a miracle. You won’t believe how much I worried.” He wraps her in a hug, clutching her to him, even as his body trembles and shakes with emotion.

“Daddy!” she cries.

“You poor child. You must have been through hell. But at least now you’re home.”

“Yes, home.” Yet the room seems different; her father not quite the same, the house unfamiliar. The other two doctors peer at her as if she is a specimen for their erudite theories. How much she wanted to be here the last ten days, all she could think about was to again set foot in this house, but now that she’s here, everything is different, not in any way she can identify, but in her head she’s changed. The Lindy Sue who had left here with Tommy no longer seems to fit in her father’s affluent world.

Finally home, *but am I really*?

The adventures of Varla and Lindy Sue continue in VIXEN OUTLAWS: ASYLUM STREET

For 15 years, **Rolf Semprebon** wrote scripts for a monthly radio theater show, Ubu Hour, on KBOO Community Radio. He's published music reviews in several publications. He's also had short stories published in Unnamed Journal in 2024 and Northwest Independent Writers Association anthology Journey in 2025. In July, 2025, Rolf self-published his first book, Triangles: a novella and two short stories. His novel Asylum Street was a finalist for Pacific Northwest Writer's Association's 2025 unpublished novel contest. Rolf grew up in New Hampshire, graduated from Oberlin College, and lives in Portland Oregon.

www.ingramcontent.com/pod-product-compliance
Lightning Source LLC
LaVergne TN
LVHW010641110826
845149LV00014B/2911